Born in 1893, **Anthony B‌** ‌s a
novelist. A founding m‌ ‌s
one of crime fiction's g‌ ‌e
first to predict the devel‌
novel. He sometimes wro‌ ‌ncis
Iles. He wrote twenty-fc‌ ‌which feature
his amateur detective, Ro‌ ‌ngham. His best-known
Roger Sheringham mystery is *The Poisoned Chocolates Case*. Anthony Berkeley died in 1971.

THE
PICCADILLY
MURDER

ANTHONY
BERKELEY

HOUSE OF
STRATUS

This edition published in 2001 by House of Stratus, an imprint of
House of Stratus Ltd, Thirsk Industrial Park, York Road, Thirsk,
North Yorkshire, YO7 3BX, UK.
Also at: House of Stratus Inc., 2 Neptune Road, Poughkeepsie, NY 12601, USA.

www.houseofstratus.com

Typeset, printed and bound by House of Stratus.

A catalogue record for this book is available from the British Library
and the Library of Congress.

ISBN 0-7551-0217-7

contents

chapter one

Mr Chitterwick Sees Red

The Piccadilly Palace Hotel is, to the Londoner, a hotel only by the way. From its noble imitation-marble vestibule he sees, tucked unobtrusively away in a corner, the coil of a staircase surreptitiously ascending round a corner, and lifts are at work all day long whisking strange country cousins up into mysterious regions which must, by inference, exist; but play the psychoanalytical game with the Londoner and give him the words 'Piccadilly Palace' and he will reply, without a split second's hesitation, 'lounge.' For him the Piccadilly Palace exists only in its lounge.

To us who frequent it the lounge of the Piccadilly Palace is what Monte Carlo is to Europe's new rich, our pride, our Mecca and our rendezvous. The vastness of its gilt and synthetic-marble interior, the multitude of its chairs and little tables, the agility of its bustling waitresses, who are always far too busy running the liquid errands of one's immediate neighbours to be able to attend to the thirst of oneself, the hum and buzz and heat and smoke of its almost palpable atmosphere – on all these we look round with sober pride and reflect that now at last we are seeing life. Here we sit and sip our so-called Martini, till our thoughts turn longingly upon sole and whitebait, and poulet rôti salade; and we join the queue (by now stretching halfway across the lounge) at the entrance to the three-and-sixpenny table d'hôte dining room. A devil of a fellow.

But that is not the only function of the Piccadilly Palace lounge – to exhilarate the simple pleasure seeker. Its real importance as a social phenomenon is the way in which it brings together, in surprising contact, the most diverse representatives of every class or calling with an income of between, roughly, a hundred and fifty and a thousand pounds a year.

To those who have eyes to see, the kaleidoscopic juxtapositions to be found only on this unique spot are a continual delight. Here a couple of public-school boys, out for a cheap dinner and show and sipping their mixed vermouths with conscious man-of-the-worldliness, are rubbing quite unwitting shoulders with a pair of vermilion-lipped ladies of the night (or, *pace* the shrinking censor, as it is not yet night, of the pavements), who have dropped in to restore themselves with a short drink and a rest; at the next table one of that peculiarly detestable brand of young rounder which seems to be attracted to the Piccadilly Palace lounge like flies to sugar, smarmed and stinking of cheap scent, is backing his chair into that of the highly respectable widow of a retired butcher from Peckham; over there a chorus girl, with the matinée paint scarcely removed from her cheeks, is cocking an impudently amused eye at the glass of lemonade in front of her neighbour (though an empty chair prudently separates them), the white-haired and rather wondering vicar of an obviously country parish. As a benefit performance for those interested in social niceties, a hundred such unconscious little comedies are enacted daily between the hours of five o'clock and half-past seven.

Mr Ambrose Chitterwick, who liked to consider himself a modest student of the human animal, was in the habit of visiting occasionally the lounge of the Piccadilly Palace Hotel to escape from his aunt.

On the afternoon in question Mr Chitterwick had arrived there unusually early. It was barely half-past two, and the after-luncheon coffee drinking was in full swing. Mr Chitterwick found an unoccupied table with extreme difficulty (was, indeed, piloted to one by a lordly but benevolent head waiter after he had wandered helplessly three times round the whole place and assured himself that not a single seat was vacant) and dropped with relief into the chair that was edged against the back of his knees. He had lunched unhappily at a large store, surrounded entirely by women, and not for the first time he had wished very earnestly that his aunt did not disapprove quite so strongly of clubs. But disapprove she did, and where Mr Chitterwick's aunt disapproved...

Unfortunately she did approve of lunching in large stores, and Mr Chitterwick, having several commissions to execute for her, including the obtaining of patterns for new drawing-room curtains, had been bidden not to return to Chiswick for lunch but to have it, so to speak, among the curtains; and Mr Chitterwick, who had somehow got into the habit of taking the line of least resistance where his aunt was concerned, had done so. Now he commanded some black coffee from the waitress, miraculously produced by the same lordly head waiter, with which to restore himself, and wickedly added a glass of benedictine to his order. But for all that, he knew that his aunt did not disapprove of benedictine so strongly as she did of clubs.

Nevertheless, it was with a sense of being his own man again that he set down his glass after the first sip and, mildly beaming, surveyed the accustomed landscape. The scene was particularly interesting to him today, as he had not before had an opportunity of examining the after-luncheon gathering as distinct from the pre-dinner one. His eyes roamed deliberately over his immediate neighbourhood. Then his face fell. This was a very different affair. Here were no piquant contrasts at all. The entire collection was dull, sombre, and ultra-respectable. No impudently amused eyes, no vermilion lips; only the young rounders, the widows of retired solicitors, and a leavening of quite uninteresting middle-aged men. Suburban London, mostly female, held the Piccadilly Palace lounge in flabby thrall.

Some distance away from where he was sitting, alone and at a small table against the wall, was a girl whose appearance arrested Mr Chitterwick's wandering eye for a few moments. She was quite a pretty girl in rather a severe way, but that was not the reason why his glance lingered on her; Mr Chitterwick, it is to be regretted, had not much of an eye for a pretty girl. The point about her that arrested his attention was that she was not the kind of girl one sees alone in the Piccadilly Palace. Her blue coat and skirt were plainer and quieter than most of the coats and skirts to be seen there, the small hat that allowed only a glimpse of black hair more severe, her whole appearance more restrained and not at all expectant. Must be waiting for someone, decided Mr Chitterwick, regarding her with interest. Otherwise –

At this point Mr Chitterwick's eye caught that of the girl, and the latter was distinctly cold. Mr Chitterwick looked hastily away.

Only one other person could Mr Chitterwick see who interested him at all. A few tables away, with a clear field of view between, her back to one of the noble pseudo-marble pillars, sat an elderly woman to whom Mr Chitterwick's

4

heart went out at once. Mr Chitterwick was very fond of elderly ladies, provided that they did not look too much like aunts. This one did not look like an aunt at all. She was alone, for one thing, and she wore no air of authority. The air she did wear was one of complete bewilderment, as if she wondered how on earth she had ever got in here and why, and how on earth she was ever going to get out again. It was quite plain that she was not of the kind that does patronize the Piccadilly Palace, either after lunch or before dinner.

Mr Chitterwick, finding nothing else worthy of his attention, began to play one of his favourite games with her – detectives. From her appearance alone, just her appearance, and perhaps her way of speaking (if she did speak), and her mannerisms (if she displayed any), and any other clue she offered (if she did offer any), he would deduce every single thing about her – her habits, both of mind and body, her character, whether she liked dogs better than cats or vice versa, what sort of meal she would order if she found herself alone in a good restaurant, married, single, or widow, Conservative or Liberal, everything, in fact, excepting possibly, in the case of a married woman, her maiden name. Mr Chitterwick invariably played this game on his way home in the Underground to Chiswick, to the considerable discomfort of the objects of his researches, the unconscious and fixed beam which Mr Chitterwick kept turned on his victims making them uneasily scrutinize themselves in a surreptitious way from head to foot to find out exactly what *was* wrong with their appearance.

While Mr Chitterwick is preparing to exercise his powers of scientific deduction once again, let us turn the tables on him by studying his own appearance for a moment and applying his same methods to the result.

At a glance, then, Mr Ambrose Chitterwick is seen to be a red-faced, somewhat globular, early middle-aged gentleman of independent means, with gold-rimmed pince-nez on a very short nose, less hair than he used to have, and an extremely ancient aunt at Chiswick. From the remarkable mildness which is so obvious a feature of Mr Chitterwick's nature, it is easy to deduce that Mr Chitterwick not only lives with his aunt at Chiswick, but to most purposes for his aunt at Chiswick too. From the same clue the deduction also follows that Mr Chitterwick's aunt at Chiswick rules Mr Chitterwick with a rod of something stronger than iron, for no female could live in the same house with such mild masculinity and not do so; moreover, by the law of averages, as applied to the houses of aunts in Chiswick, it must be clear that Mr Chitterwick's aunt must be an old lady of quite exceptional forcefulness and will.

So far as Mr Chitterwick is concerned, there is another law to be taken into account, the law of compensation. The deducer will therefore at once reach the conclusion that Mr Chitterwick must have some counterbalance in his make-up to this excess of mildness, and this is probably to be found in his hobby; as there is nothing Mr Chitterwick resembles in appearance so little as a murderer, it will readily be gathered that Mr Chitterwick's hobby must be criminology – as indeed it is. From the confidence that he exhibits in every line of him as he sets about making his own deductions, the conclusion is irresistible that Mr Chitterwick once solved, entirely off his own bat, a peculiarly difficult case of murder, and that after it had been given up by the police and all the best amateur criminological brains in the country. And that again is the case.[1]

So much for Mr Chitterwick.

1 As set forth in *The Poisoned Chocolates Case.*

On this occasion Mr Chitterwick was not to get very far with his own game. He had swiftly reached certain obvious conclusions. The lady was between sixty and sixty-five; her face, distinctly weather-beaten and with a pronouncedly aquiline nose and fine eyes, not only proclaimed her a dweller in the country, but unmistakably stamped her as of good family; Mr Chitterwick decided that she might not unreasonably be expected to have a handle to her name. The ring on her left hand made it clear that she was either a wife or a widow, and from a certain air of poise and authority about her underlying her present bewilderment, Mr Chitterwick plumped for the latter alternative.

Her clothes were more than illuminating. They were not fashionable – far from it; but neither were they dowdy; they were simple, straightforward, and eminently suited to their purpose, which was that of covering her body with decency and comfort. It was her clothes, in fact, that inclined Mr Chitterwick toward the theory of a handle to her name; they were the clothes of a woman important enough to wear exactly what she liked and not what some twopenny-halfpenny French tradesman told her she should.

A nice old lady, Mr Chitterwick began to sum up, but with a terribly strong will of her own. Probably she –

At this point Mr Chitterwick's meditations were interrupted. There was a vacant chair beside the old lady, on which her bag had been lying. A man, quite a large man with red, curly hair, had approached the chair, picked up her bag and handed it to her, and dropped into the chair with a word of greeting. The old lady turned to him with obvious relief, and they began to talk.

Mr Chitterwick watched them with interest. So that's what she was waiting for, he thought. Now, I wonder who the man is. Some relation to her, without a doubt. Her son?

They don't look at all like mother and son. Dear me, the poor lady is very short-sighted. Fancy my not noticing that before. She's positively peering at him. Lost her glasses, no doubt. Does that argue something a little slipshod in her character that I hadn't quite remarked? Just a trifle slipshod? But, dear me, she doesn't look a slipshod kind of person at all. Not in the least. Just the reverse, I should have said. Ah, I have it. She has always been proud of her sight, keen rider to hounds, see the fox farther than anyone else, that sort of thing; and she won't acknowledge that her sight is failing her at last. That would be quite in keeping. Dear me, she is talking very animatedly. I wonder whether –

Mr Chitterwick became abruptly conscious of the large, red-haired man's gaze. It was fixed on himself in a positive glare.

Mr Chitterwick started. He knew that when engaged in his game he was apt to forget the rule about staring at strangers. He coloured to the roots of his hair and transferred his regard very hastily to a gilt wreath ornamented with emerald-green leaves, halfway up a purple marble pillar. Really, he must have been staring quite unpardonably rudely to make the red-haired man return his gaze with something that positively approached malignity. In his agitation Mr Chitterwick gulped down three parts of his benedictine, while only opening his throat to sufficient capacity for a quarter of the amount. During the disastrous coughing fit which followed he found time to hope spasmodically that his distress would be accepted by the red-haired man as both an apology and a penance.

The hope was apparently not to be substantiated. Glancing guiltily out of the corner of a streaming eye, when vision at last returned to him, Mr Chitterwick perceived the red-haired man's gaze still fixed on him with the same malignant intensity. Again he sought refuge in the gilt and emerald wreath. But even while endeavouring to admire its striking colour scheme he was conscious of the red-haired man's eyes boring a neat little fiery hole in the centre of his forehead.

If there is one impulse more powerful than any other it is the intense longing to turn one's eyes in a forbidden direction. Mr Chitterwick fought it manfully for more than a minute, and a whole minute, when spent in fighting an impulse, is a very long time indeed. Then he succumbed. Trembling with agitation, he flashed a swift glance toward the red-haired man and away again.

If Mr Chitterwick had been a hen, he would have clucked. For the red-haired man's gaze was still fixed on him, if possible even more malignantly than before.

Mr Chitterwick stifled a foolish desire to squeak. The thing was becoming absurd. It might have been rude of him to stare in the first place, but surely an innocent stare did not deserve such concentrated hatred as the red-haired man was despatching in almost tangible waves through the ether. But nevertheless, reassure himself thus as he might, the more absurd Mr Chitterwick felt it to be, the more his agitation increased.

During the next few minutes, Mr Chitterwick found his eyes engaged, willy-nilly, in a ridiculous cat-and-mouse game with those of the red-haired man. Every few seconds he was compelled, quite impossibly against his will, to pop forth a glance at the red-haired man to see if he was still gazing at him; and every time he was. Mr Chitterwick would have given quite a considerable sum of money to have been able to plunge out of the place, but he had not yet paid for his coffee and benedictine, and of course there was no waitress to respond to the frenzied appeals he was throwing out all round. There was no waitress, no lordly head waiter, no other coffee drinker in the whole crowded place; nobody at all but Mr Chitterwick and the red-haired man.

Mr Chitterwick swore an awful oath to himself. By his aunt's nightcap he swore that he would not glance in the red-haired man's direction again. He began to recite 'The Wreck of the *Hesperus*' to himself in a feverish undertone. He had learned it at the age of four, at the first school he ever went to, and had never been able to forget it; he found it a great stand-by on occasions like this.

'*It was the schooner* Hesperus, *that sailed the...*' Eighteen whole seconds passed. '*The skipper, he blew a whiff from his pipe...*' Another six. '*"Come hither, come hither, my little daught*ER..."' Gradually Mr Chitterwick slackened his pace. The soothing words were exercising their usual effect on him. The ache to glance across that burning space was not quite so intolerable. '*A frozen corpse was he. Lashed to the helm, all stiff and stark...*'

Mr Chitterwick had almost regained control of himself. His agitation was beginning at last to give way to a modest pride in the tempered steel of his will, coupled with gratitude to the late Mr Longfellow. '*A whooping billow swept the crew like icicles from her deck...*' In utter bravado slackening the tempo as stanza rolled smoothly after stanza, Mr Chitterwick swung to the end of the poem, his eyes riveted to the symbolic wreath in front of him, his lips moving devoutly as if in inaudible prayer.

'*A death like this, on the reef of Norman's Woe!*' concluded Mr Chitterwick raptly. And then, because he had so successfully and so long resisted temptation, he felt himself entitled to the reward of one flickering glimpse of his right front.

Mr Longfellow had won again. The red-haired man was listening politely to his companion's words. His face was innocent of all malignity. Mr Chitterwick was not only forgiven but, apparently, forgotten.

That miscreant celebrated his relief by prolonging his flickering glimpse into something not at all unlike his recent steady stare. But really when a man has been registering malignity at you for something like ten solid minutes, the least one can do for one's self-respect is something he doesn't like. Not that Mr Chitterwick put it that way to himself, or any other way; it was simply that his interest in the couple had been rather stimulated than crushed by the resentment of the old lady's companion.

Guardedly Mr Chitterwick studied him, ready to look innocently away in a flash should the red-haired man's head turn ever so slightly in his direction. Obviously his first assumption had been right: the man must be some relation to the old lady. And quite a close one too; for the latter's most striking feature, her nose, aquiline to the verge of beakiness, was reproduced no less strikingly in her companion. It was evidently a family feature, decided Mr Chitterwick; and he set them down tentatively as aunt and nephew. It was a pity, but she must be an aunt after all.

She was behaving too in a more aunt-like manner now. Not only was she doing all the talking, but she was doing it angrily, almost furiously. The young man too, instead of listening with the correct deference of a nephew towards an aunt from whom he has expectations, was answering her just as irately. Evidently the makings of a very pretty little quarrel were brewing up.

But why were they meeting in the Piccadilly Palace? That was the really curious thing. Neither of them was of the type or class that does so. Not in order to quarrel in public, surely.

Mr Chitterwick found this one of the most interesting problems they presented, and it left him at a complete loss.

'Dear me,' he thought, 'this is getting quite serious. I do believe he's being positively rude to her. The poor old lady's quite white with rage. What can it be about? And yet they manage to talk only in undertones. Dear me, dear me.'

He started slightly. The red-haired man had moved his head. But it was not in Mr Chitterwick's direction. He was calling his aunt's attention, more amicably, to something on the other side of the room. She had to turn completely away from the little table in front of them, on which was the coffee tray that the man had ordered on his first entrance, in order to see whatever it might be. As she did so Mr Chitterwick noticed that her companion's hand hovered for a moment over her cup, but the incident was only vaguely recorded in his mind. Then the two turned back again, and Mr Chitterwick received the red-haired man's glare full in the eyes. If it had been malignant before, there is no word to express what it was now. Evidently the red-haired man was quite overwhelmingly angry with Mr Chitterwick.

Startled, Mr Chitterwick looked away with guilty haste, and became aware of a waitress approaching him. 'Excuse me, sir,' said the waitress, 'you're wanted on the telephone.'

'Oh, thank you, thank you,' said Mr Chitterwick gratefully, and made a relieved escape. It was not until he was outside the lounge that it occurred to him to be surprised that anyone should know that he was in the Piccadilly Palace at all. Certainly his aunt did not, and there was, practically speaking, no one else. With some trepidation he began his quest for the telephone.

The telephone room at the Piccadilly Palace is not easy for a stranger to come upon. It is tucked away at the end of a short passage, on a floor that is neither ground nor first but some hybrid between the two, bearing a strange name. It took Mr Chitterwick some minutes to discover it, and then the young woman behind the counter did not seem to know anything about a call for him. She advised him to try the bureau.

The bureau had no telephone call awaiting Mr Chitterwick. The young woman there suggested that it might be a message, and advised him to try the message department. He tried the message department, without result. He also tried the hall porter, and several other equally unhelpful functionaries. Just as he was turning back to the lounge in despair he became aware of the waitress in question about to cross his path.

'Get your call?' asked the waitress pleasantly, evidently recognizing him.

'They can't even trace it,' Mr Chitterwick told her.

'Aren't you number 473?' asked the waitress without emotion.

Mr Chitterwick assured her that he was not Number 473.

'Well, there now,' said the waitress. 'I made sure you were. As like him as two peas, you are.'

Mr Chitterwick accepted this apology in place of a better one and turned toward the cloakroom.

'Excuse me, have you paid for what you had?' inquired the waitress tartly.

Mr Chitterwick blushed warmly and asked what he owed.

'I couldn't tell you, I'm sure,' said the waitress. 'You must ask your waitress.'

Wrapped in confusion, Mr, Chitterwick slunk back to his table. His own waitress, needless to say, was nowhere in sight.

Mr Chitterwick was so overcome for the moment that he scarcely noticed that the red-haired man had gone during his absence – which, glancing at the clock, he was surprised to see had lasted not much short of a quarter of an hour. The place had thinned out considerably by now, and there was actually nobody at all at any of the two or three tables which separated Mr Chitterwick from the old lady, who still remained. When the fact of the red-haired man's absence finally sunk into his mind, he ventured to look at her more closely.

She was leaning back in her chair, her head against the pillar behind it, apparently asleep. Her mouth was slightly open, and she looked as if at any moment she might be expected to snore.

Mr Chitterwick was both distressed and disappointed. The sight of another person asleep in a public place is always vaguely disquieting, but this lady should have been the last person one would expect to be guilty of such a social misdemeanour. And she *was* snoring! No doubt of it. Across the twenty-five feet that separated them Mr Chitterwick could hear her snores coming now in raucous waves. It was all most disturbing.

What was really worrying Mr Chitterwick was the thought of the shame and distress which the old lady herself would feel if she realized what she was doing. It would be most awkward. Already the few heads left in the immediate neighbourhood were beginning to turn her way. Titterings and sniggers reached Mr Chitterwick's ears, and he wriggled uncomfortably. It was quite absurd, of course, but in some way he felt responsible for the old lady. Somebody certainly ought to wake her up and stop her from making any further exhibition of herself. But who? It seemed there was nobody but Mr Chitterwick himself.

He spent a few minutes trying to nerve himself to action and doing his utmost to find a reasonable excuse. Of course there was no waitress in sight to help him out. Finally he decided to tap the old lady lightly on the shoulder and offer her her bag, saying that it had dropped onto the floor. That would be a hint of reproof, and not too strong. Disliking his self-imposed task extremely he rose to perform it.

It seemed to Mr Chitterwick as he did so that the old lady's snores had quietened a little. As he made his reluctant way toward her, he was sure of it. By the time he reached her side she was not snoring at all. But from her attitude it was plain that she was profoundly sunk in sleep. She was lolling in her chair – simply lolling; there was no other word for it.

Conscious of a score of eyes upon him, Mr Chitterwick nervously tapped her shoulder. Nothing happened. He tapped again. No response. And then Mr Chitterwick, writhing under the amused glances he could feel on him from all directions, lost his nerve. He laid rude hands on the old lady and shook her.

The result was unexpected. Her head sagged over onto her shoulder at an unnatural angle, her hands fell from her lap to her sides, she seemed to sink in on herself in the chair. Forgetting all about the eyes on him, Mr Chitterwick, thoroughly alarmed now, bent over her and gently lifted her head.

One glance at her not quite closed eyes was enough for him; that, and the strong smell of almonds which arose from her. The old lady was dead – had died under his very eyes.

chapter two

Direct Evidence

Afterward Mr Chitterwick was always inclined to congratulate himself modestly on the course he pursued immediately following upon his tragic discovery. Instead of rushing off in a panic to give the alarm to all within hearing, he simply seated himself with outward calmness beside the body (though his heart was thumping like a steam engine and he felt decidedly sick), and beat with a spoon on the one empty coffee cup that still stood on the table in front of the old lady. The only coherent thoughts in his mind were that there must be no fuss and that the body must not be touched till the police had seen it.

The unprecedented noise Mr Chitterwick was making brought a waitress at once, haughty and outraged. Mr Chitterwick, however, had no time to consider her feelings. 'Will you ask the manager to come to me for a moment, please?' he said, before she could voice her displeasure.

'If you'd *asked* me for your bill,' said the waitress, taken aback, 'I'm sure I – '

'It's nothing to do with my bill,' interrupted Mr Chitterwick quite brusquely. 'Go and get the manager, please.'

The waitress withdrew. In her place arrived the head waiter.

'I'm afraid,' he began suavely, 'that the manager can hardly – '

'The manager must come here,' broke in Mr Chitterwick with agitation. 'This minute!'

The head waiter was unperturbed. 'If you would be good enough to let me deal with your complaint, sir, I can assure you – '

'Go and get the manager,' squeaked Mr Chitterwick.

The head waiter withdrew. After a very long time there came an exquisite young man, who looked disapprovingly upon Mr Chitterwick.

'Are you the manager?' Mr Chitterwick fumed, with the anger of sheer nerves.

'The manager is engaged,' said the exquisite young man coldly. 'If you will kindly state your business – '

'State my business? Good heavens, this is a matter of life and death.'

'If the lady has been taken ill…' said the young man with indifference. 'There is a doctor resident in the hotel,' he added by way of an afterthought.

Mr Chitterwick rose and faced him. 'Then get the doctor as well as the manager,' he said very quickly. 'This lady is dead.'

The young man went quickly.

This time the manager did come.

He was an intelligent man and grasped the situation at once. Mr Chitterwick briefly explained to him and the doctor that he had seen the old lady apparently snoring, gone over to wake her up, and discovered that she was dead. The manager nodded, waved his hand to somebody in the distance, and as if by magic a barricade of screens sprang up round the spot. Under their cover the doctor made a hasty examination, but without touching the body more than was absolutely necessary.

'Yes, she's dead,' he confirmed. 'And I'd almost swear she's taken prussic acid, or something very like it. Yes – look! Isn't that a phial in her hand?'

In one of the dead woman's hands the top of a small bottle was visible. The doctor bent over the coffee cup on the table and sniffed at it.

'Prussic acid, right enough,' he pronounced. 'She took it in her coffee.'

'Suicide?' asked the manager laconically.

'Looks like it,' agreed the doctor.

Mr Chitterwick put in a word. 'But you'll send for the police, of course?'

The manager, a small, stout Frenchman, who spoke English almost without an accent, informed him that he had given orders for this to be done before he left his office.

'Oh, yes,' said Mr Chitterwick. 'Still, I think, if you don't mind – '

'Yes?' said the manager.

'Chief Inspector Moresby, of Scotland Yard. I know him slightly. I think I'll give him a ring.'

'Oh, the divisional police will do,' said the doctor. 'Scotland Yard won't want to be bothered with a suicide.'

'No, of course,' Mr Chitterwick agreed. 'But then, you see, *is* it suicide?' And he went.

Fortunately Chief Inspector Moresby was in his room when Mr Chitterwick got through to Scotland Yard.

'Mr Chitterwick?' he said, in his jovial voice. 'Yes, of course I remember you. Friend of Mr Sheringham's, aren't you?'

'I'm speaking from the Piccadilly Palace Hotel,' twittered Mr Chitterwick. 'A terrible thing has happened here. Terrible! Actually before my very eyes.' Somewhat incoherently Mr Chitterwick repeated his account of the unknown lady's death and added the doctor's conclusion. 'So I thought that perhaps if you'd care to come along, Chief Inspector... Quite informally, even, if it was outside your routine...'

Chief Inspector Moresby hedged. 'Oh, I think you'll find the divisional inspector will be able to do everything necessary, Mr Chitterwick, sir.'

'Yes, but I thought...that is to say, I don't wish to make a personal matter of it, of course, but I *am* in a terribly responsible position and what I really meant...' When Mr Chitterwick was agitated, he had a habit of leaving his sentences unfinished, but his meaning was usually clear enough.

'Very upsetting for you, of course, sir,' agreed the chief inspector, with genial sympathy. 'But you mustn't exaggerate the responsibility, you know. Bless you, sir, people are killing 'emselves off by dozens every day. These things happen more often than you think. Course, it isn't often that someone actually sees 'em do it, as I gather you did, but – '

'No, I didn't! I didn't!' squeaked Mr Chitterwick. 'That's just the point. I saw her – must have seen her die, poor woman, but not... You see, I'm not at all sure that she really did... Dear me, this is a terrible responsibility, Chief Inspector.'

Chief Inspector Moresby became suddenly very official. From the change in his voice one would have said that a different person had taken his place at the other end of the wire. 'One moment, sir. Let me get this clear. Do you wish me to understand that you have certain evidence which you wish to put before me personally? To consult me privately as to its importance, so to speak?'

'Oh, thank you, Chief Inspector, yes,' said Mr Chitterwick with much gratitude. 'But not exactly evidence. Just something I saw. At least, I'm not quite sure whether I really... Still, I suppose, yes, you might call it... That is, if I really did see what I...'

'I'll be round in fifteen minutes, sir.' Moresby put a brisk end to Mr Chitterwick's agitated babble. 'Please meet me in the main entrance. No need to inform anyone I'm coming.' He rang off.

It is difficult to say at what precise moment since the old lady's death there had presented itself in Mr Chitterwick's consciousness the vague picture of that hand hovering over her coffee cup. At first, not questioning that she had taken poison of her own accord, it had conveyed nothing to him. Then, as the first shock of the death wore away, it was allied with the red-haired man's general air of malignancy as an unimportant part of a sinister whole. Finally it stood out alone in all its horrid suggestiveness. All that can be said definitely is that the possibility of vital importance had occurred to Mr Chitterwick at any rate some minutes before the arrival of the manager and the doctor, and it was this realization which had made him so anxious that the body should not be disturbed before the police had seen it. The same anxiety now drove him back to the lounge instead of waiting for Moresby in the vestibule. His fears were groundless. The body still lay as he had left it.

Only the doctor was with it now, awaiting the police. Such a minor matter as the suicide of a lounge patron could not be allowed to keep the great M. Jacquinot from more important affairs. He would not even return when the police arrived. The police, if they wished to see him, would do so in his own office. M. Jacquinot was not only a great man, but he knew it.

Only two further facts had emerged during Mr Chitterwick's absence: it had been definitely ascertained that the dead woman was not staying in the hotel, and that she was not a regular client of the lounge. The man whose business it was to remember every face that passed through the swing doors of the latter had never seen her before that afternoon.

Mr Chitterwick hovered a few minutes in disjointed conversation with the doctor. Then he glanced at his watch. Moresby was not due for nearly ten minutes, but Mr Chitterwick wanted to be out of the way when the divisional police arrived; otherwise, he suspected, he might be detained and have some difficulty in getting away. He made a vague excuse to the doctor and escaped.

Moresby was exactly punctual. Mr Chitterwick, emerging into the vestibule from an aimless tour of the under regions of the hotel, was in time to see him coming through the big swing doors at the entrance. They shook hands.

'Now, Mr Chitterwick, sir,' said Moresby, 'let's find a quiet corner somewhere and hear all about it.'

Mr Chitterwick led him to the under regions, and they ensconced themselves in an enormous reading and writing room, 'for residents only.' Apparently the residents of the Piccadilly Palace Hotel did little reading or writing, for the room was empty.

'Now, sir,' said Moresby, settling himself to listen. 'Let me have the whole story again, please.'

'You don't think...? I was very careful to ensure that the body should not be disturbed.'

'Quite right, sir,' said the chief inspector with much heartiness. 'Very proper. But we can leave all those details for the time being to the divisional inspector. What I want to hear about is this bit of evidence of yours. Something you saw, eh? Well, let's have the whole thing, and put it in its proper place, please, sir.'

Once again Mr Chitterwick embarked on his story.

He told it haltingly, for he was a kind-hearted man as well as a just one, and he neither wanted to make things awkward for the red-haired man if (as most probably was the case) he really was quite innocent, nor wished to lay undue stress on the quite excusable malignity with which that individual had favoured himself.

Moresby, however, seized on this point at once. 'You say he seemed to resent your looking at him?'

'Well, in a way,' said Mr Chitterwick, desperately anxious to be fair. 'Or one might say, watching him. Because I really had been gazing at him quite intently. Unconsciously, of course, but positively staring. He was quite justified in resenting it. I should have resented it myself. It was most rude of me. I really don't think one should attach *too* much importance to that, Chief Inspector.'

'Very well, sir,' promised the chief inspector. 'But I'll bear it in mind.'

'Besides,' pointed out Mr Chitterwick for the defence, 'he stopped looking at me like that after quite a short while. Stopped looking at me altogether, in fact.'

'After he thought he'd choked you off from looking at *him*,' agreed Moresby. 'Quite so, sir. Well?'

'Well,' said Mr Chitterwick, rather uncomfortably, 'I don't know if you've ever noticed the same thing, Chief Inspector, but if ever there's one thing around me which I know I ought not to look at, I find my eyes irresistibly drawn toward it. Invariably!' Mr Chitterwick's tone apologized for this awkward habit on the part of his eyes, but at the same time indicated that extenuating circumstances were to be found for it.

'Same with most of us, I think, sir,' Moresby reassured him. 'Anyhow, it's lucky in this case. Because as soon as you thought he'd forgotten all about you, you started watching him again?'

'Well, yes,' assented Mr Chitterwick deprecatingly. 'I'm afraid that is so.'

'And what did you see then, sir?'

Mr Chitterwick told how the two seemed to be engaged in a violent quarrel, and then went on to recount the episode of the Hovering Hand. He did so not very willingly, because he was acutely conscious of the possibility that he was turning not merely a holehill but a mere worm-cast into a very formidable mountain; but he knew it was his duty. And by parting with the information he at any rate at the same time parted with his responsibility in the matter. The differentiation of worm-casts from mountains could be left now to the police.

Moresby questioned him closely on the incident. Both men realized that upon it a man's life might ultimately depend, and both were anxious to pin it down, while memory was fresh, exactly as it had happened, no more and no less, before the caterpillar could blossom out into a butterfly or shrink again into a quite insignificant grub.

In the end it was decided that the action had certainly taken place, because Mr Chitterwick could not possibly have imagined it; that the red-haired man's hand had been not in the position of a hand holding a lump of sugar, but in that of a hand holding something surreptitiously concealed in the palm; and that without doubt the red-haired man had distracted the old lady's attention first, causing her to look over her shoulder in a direction pointing right away from the table, and that she could not have seen anything the red-haired man might have done just then to her cup. Put in this way, the affair sounded even more ominous than Mr Chitterwick had cared to think before; but he could not dispute the conclusions.

He told Moresby how the mistaken summons to the telephone had put an end to his observations.

The chief inspector seemed thoughtful. He rubbed his large square chin with a hand like a ham and pulled at his heavy moustache. 'Um! Suppose this does turn out as we fear, Mr Chitterwick, sir. You realize your position?'

'Only too well,' sighed the reluctant Mr Chitterwick.

'You'll be in the situation of having actually seen the murder committed. As a criminologist yourself, sir, I needn't tell you how extraordinary that is.'

'In a poison case,' murmured Mr Chitterwick, 'I should think almost unique.'

'Pretty well so. Direct evidence! That's what we're going to get from you, Mr Chitterwick.'

'Yes,' said Mr Chitterwick unhappily

Moresby seemed to be positively gloating over what he was going to get from Mr Chitterwick. 'Lord, sir, what a lot of trouble you're going to save us. No messing about with all the circumstantial stuff, proving this little thing and that little thing and all the other little things. Here you come into the box and say you saw the blessed murder actually being committed. And that'll be that.'

'We don't know at all that it is murder yet, though, do we?' Mr Chitterwick felt constrained to point out.

Moresby ignored the suggestion. Obviously he felt it to be unworthy of the occasion. 'Won't the prosecution fall on your neck? Why, sir, you'll *be* the prosecution, that's what you'll be.'

'Shall I?' said Mr Chitterwick.

'Well,' said Moresby, 'suppose we go along and have a look at the old girl?'

No doubt, ruminated Mr Chitterwick, as he trotted along in the chief inspector's masterful wake like a dinghy behind a battleship, no doubt familiarity with corpses may be expected to breed a certain *friendliness*, but really –

The lounge, Mr Chitterwick was astonished to see, was still pursuing its normal function of slaking London's thirst. The tea contingent was beginning to arrive, and the place was filling up with its usual rapidity. Not one of the lipsticked young women, dowdy matrons from Surbiton, or glistening rounders had the faintest inkling that behind those decorative screens in the middle was a recently and very horribly dead body; and not knowing, they cared less. Shrill laughter and the clashing of china sounded on all sides just as usual; the incomers ordered their teas, and the outgoers paid for what they had had. Like its manager, more than a mere corpse was needed to upset the routine of the Piccadilly Palace lounge. After all, dividends must be paid.

Scarcely an eye followed Moresby and Mr Chitterwick as they disappeared into the screened space spared to death.

It appeared that the divisional inspector had become perturbed about Mr Chitterwick's absence. He greeted him, on the doctor's introduction, with relief more than tinged with exasperation. He was going on to be somewhat professional when Moresby cut him short.

'That's all right, Parker. Mr Chitterwick's been talking to me.'

The divisional inspector, whose feelings about Mr Chitterwick had blinded him to the identity of that gentleman's companion, swung round in surprise. 'Mr Moresby! Why, I didn't expect to see you, sir.'

'Mr Chitterwick gave me a ring,' Moresby explained easily. 'So I came along to help him out, as you might say.' Which was nothing less than the truth but by no means the whole truth. Chief inspectors do not necessarily tell the whole truth to divisional inspectors any more than Sherlock Holmeses do to Watsons.

'Oh!' The divisional inspector turned back to Mr Chitterwick, but this time with respect. 'You know Mr Moresby, then, sir?'

'Well, yes,' Mr Chitterwick beamed, noting the respect with relief. 'As it happens, I do.'

'Then that's all right. Beginning to think you'd given us the slip, I was. You'd be surprised how often witnesses do that before we can get their names and addresses. Seem to think there's something to be ashamed of, being mixed up with a case, they do.'

'You won't find Mr Chitterwick that sort of gentleman,' said Moresby briskly. 'Well, Parker, what do you make of it, eh?'

Parker looked surprised. 'Make of it, Mr Moresby? Well, it's plain enough, isn't it?'

'What's plain enough?'

Parker looked still more surprised. 'Why, suicide.'

'Um!' Moresby stroked his chin and contemplated the body. 'Haven't moved the body yet, have you?'

'No, sir. I've been taking the doctor's statement – and waiting to take this gentleman's,' he added, with a last reproachful glance in the direction of Mr Chitterwick.

Moresby turned to the doctor. 'And what's your verdict, sir?'

'Why, plain as a pikestaff. There's the phial still in her hand. Suicide!'

'That's a matter for us to decide,' Moresby retorted, but with a geniality which almost took the rebuke from his words. 'I meant, your verdict as to the cause of death?'

'Equally obvious,' replied the doctor, unabashed. He was a very young doctor and not at all in the habit of being abashed. 'Prussic acid. You can smell it from here.'

'Um!' said Moresby unhelpfully, but this time he implied no disagreement. 'I want that phial,' he added softly.

'I'll get it for you,' said the doctor. '*Rigor* hasn't set in yet.'

Moresby stepped forward hastily. 'Thank you, sir, I think I'd rather get it myself.' He stood for a moment intently examining the dead hand, but made no effort to unclasp the fingers. 'On second thoughts, I'll have a photograph of it first. Got a man with you, Parker?'

Parker nodded. 'He's in the office.' It was understood that policemen in uniform could not be left about the public parts of the Piccadilly Palace. Policemen are very bad for dividends.

'Tell him to telephone to the Yard and ask them to send Grey along at once, with his camera. Oh, and I think we'd better have Matthews too.'

Mr Chitterwick watched the divisional inspector's eyebrows with interest. They rose until they almost disappeared into his hair. 'Good Lord, sir, you don't think there – there's any hanky-panky here, do you?' Matthews was the fingerprint expert, in charge of that department at Scotland Yard, though Mr Chitterwick did not know that.

Moresby eyed his subordinate. 'Well – take a look at that hand before you go, Parker.'

Parker took a long look. 'Whew!' he said.

'Those fingers were never conscious when they took hold of that phial,' said Moresby. 'Or, rather, when they didn't take hold of it.'

'That's a fact,' said Parker, and went soberly.

Left alone with Moresby, Mr Chitterwick ventured to take a long look at the hand too.

The fingers were curled only loosely about the shape of the phial, which rested on them but was not clasped by them. 'Dear me, dear me!' said Mr Chitterwick, much distressed.

The doctor took a long look too. 'That's right enough, Chief Inspector,' he confirmed. 'I ought to have spotted it. I'd lay any odds that she was already unconscious when that phial was put into her hand. I say, this is a bit thick. Murder, eh? Rigged to look like suicide?'

'That'll be for the coroner's jury to say, sir,' Moresby genially rebuked him again. 'In the meantime it's our business to collect all the evidence available. The inspector's got your statement, sir, hasn't he? I take it we can get hold of you here whenever we happen to want you?'

'In other words, you don't want me now,' laughed the doctor. 'Yes, that's so. All right; I'll go. I suppose you'll want an autopsy, as it's a poison case?'

'And that's for the coroner to say, too,' said Moresby. 'But no doubt you're right, sir. If you want to attend we'll raise no objection.'

'Yes, I'd like to. This is the first case of murder I've come across. By the way, my room number is 724 if you want me at any time. I've got a telephone in it, of course.'

He went.

Mr Chitterwick, who strongly disliked things having to be hinted to him, prepared to follow him.

'No need for you to go, Mr Chitterwick,' said Moresby. 'That is, unless you want to.'

'I should like to stay very much,' said Mr Chitterwick with gratitude. 'I find this all remarkably interesting.' He looked somewhat apologetically toward the dead woman, as if to excuse himself for finding interest in the mere circumstances of her death. 'That is, if I shan't be in the way?'

'That's all right, sir; if you'll just keep out of our path while the photographs and so on are being taken. To tell you the truth, we owe you something for coming forward so promptly with that bit of evidence of yours.'

'You're quite sure it is murder, then?' said Mr Chitterwick, not quite certain what he was hoping himself.

'It's beginning to look uncommonly like it,' Moresby said guardedly.

'And if I hadn't voiced my suspicions, the – the murderer would have escaped?'

'Well, sir, I don't know that I'd say that. Parker's no fool or he wouldn't be where he is; and he'd have been bound to spot one thing sooner or later, even if he missed the point about the phial for the time being. They say every murderer makes some bad mistake. Can you see what your red-haired friend's is?'

Mr Chitterwick looked at the body, the table, the floor, and the chairs, and shook his head. 'No, I must confess I can't.'

'Why,' said Moresby with much satisfaction, 'look at her left hand. Not the one holding the phial – the other. She's got her glove on, hasn't she? But not on the other hand. Now look at her handbag and the other glove. Not on the table, you see, nor in her lap; on the floor. Don't you see what that means?'

'Oh!' Mr Chitterwick looked intelligent. 'Yes, I think I do. You mean, she was getting ready to go?'

'That's it, sir. Getting ready to go, she was. Well, one doesn't begin getting ready to go before swallowing a quick-acting poison like prussic acid, does one? Not if one's committing suicide, one doesn't. I think, sir, that about clinches it, eh?'

'What do you deduce then, Chief Inspector?' nodded Mr Chitterwick solemnly.

'Well, it looks to me as if your red-haired friend was getting a bit impatient. He'd salted the coffee, and the old lady wouldn't drink it. And he was anxious to make his getaway. So like most murderers, sir, he overreaches himself a bit. "Come on," he says. "Time we were going. Drink up your coffee." But instead of drinking up her coffee she starts putting her things on first. Eh? How's that?'

'Admirable,' said Mr Chitterwick. 'That is no doubt just what happened. And then, of course, he would wait for the requisite minute or less after she had drunk, and then hurry away as soon as the signs of coma set in.'

'You can depend on it, sir,' said the chief inspector with confidence, 'that that's exactly what did happen.'

They stood for a moment in silence, reconstructing those last few moments.

'There's just one thing that rather puzzles me,' said Mr Chitterwick timidly. 'Why is there only one coffee cup? What has become of his?'

'You're sure he had some, sir, are you?'

Mr Chitterwick was quite sure.

'Then I expect he got rid of it. Told the waitress to clear it. After all, sir, that'd be obvious, wouldn't it? Two coffee cups mean two people, and the police would be wondering who the second person was. Why, he'd have to get rid of his own cup if no awkward questions were to be asked.'

'Of course he would. How very stupid of me.' Mr Chitterwick was evidently ashamed of his own obtuseness. 'I ought to have realized that.'

Moresby tactfully passed over his companion's foolishness. After all, amateurs were amateurs, and what could you expect? 'Still, that's a point we can settle easily enough, and perhaps the sooner the better. Will you wait here, sir, and not let any unauthorized person inside? I'm going to get hold of the waitress who served them while she'll still remember.'

Mr Chitterwick was left in sole, and rather tremulous, charge.

Moresby was not away long. He nodded with a good deal of satisfaction as he reappeared.

'That's quite correct, sir. The girl remembers distinctly. They had two cups of coffee, as you said, and not long after your red-haired friend beckoned her over and gave her his own empty cup. Sort of absent-mindedly, she said. The old lady's cup wasn't empty.'

'Exactly as you foretold,' beamed Mr Chitterwick in congratulation.

The chief inspector accepted Mr Chitterwick's congratulation with proper modesty but at the same time managed to convey the idea that, after all, professionals were professionals, so what would you expect? 'I thought that was about how it'd turn out, sir. Sensible girl, luckily. Seems to have got her wits about her. By the way, she'll be able to confirm your identification of the man, of course.'

'You – you think you'll be able to arrest him, then?'

The chief inspector laughed heartily, and the look of satisfaction on his face seemed to deepen. 'Put my hand on him, you mean? Lord, sir, I don't expect much difficulty there. In fact, I shouldn't be surprised if I could put my hand on him this very minute.'

'Eh?' said Mr Chitterwick, startled.

The chief inspector regarded him genially. 'Well, sir, just you take a walk outside these screens for a minute. Bear round to the left, and have a look at the fourth table past the second pillar.'

Mr Chitterwick looked at him for a moment and then went. He was back in a couple of minutes.

'God bless my soul!' he ejaculated in stifled tones.

'See anyone you know?' queried Moresby.

Mr Chitterwick could only nod.

'Funny blokes, these murderers,' commented the chief inspector tolerantly.

chapter three

Observations of a Criminologist

The next half hour passed to Mr Chitterwick in a species of daze, occupied chiefly in getting out of other people's way. The little space inside the screens seemed to be crowded with men.

There was a police photographer, taking pictures of the body; there was the fingerprint expert examining everything, including the phial, within reach of the old lady, and packing various articles away with infinite care for closer scrutiny at Scotland Yard – taking the fingerprints too of the old lady herself in a perfectly efficient and cold-blooded way, which Mr Chitterwick thought a particularly gruesome proceeding; there was Moresby, going through the contents of her handbag and issuing orders from time to time, such as that a plain-clothes officer should put the red-haired man in the lounge under close observation and follow him if he left; there were Detective Inspector Parker and one or two of his subordinates, busy under Moresby's direction with the usual routine work; and finally there was Mr Chitterwick himself, bumped and jostled and eternally, it appeared, in the way of people who had real work to do and very conscious that nobody loved him. But he stayed on, intensely interested if bewildered, knowing very well that this was the chance of a lifetime for a hitherto academic criminologist, and that never again would he be likely to see Scotland Yard actually at work on a murder case.

During this half hour certain facts impressed themselves, in a disjointed way, on Mr Chitterwick's mind. Moresby, he knew, had found a minute to go to the telephone and make a hasty preliminary report to the assistant commissioner at Scotland Yard, with the result that he was put in official charge of the case. Then there was a letter in the dead woman's handbag which seemed to interest Moresby more than a little, causing him to rub his chin with satisfaction, and Mr Chitterwick caught glimpses, through the bustling hurly-burly, of extracts from it being copied into the chief inspector's big black notebook. The fingerprint man, too, had seemed to regard the phial, after Moresby had helped him extract it with infinite care from the dead woman's loose clasp, with a sober pleasure which he shared in a short undertone or two with the chief inspector; something clearly looked hopeful.

It was not until the full half hour had elapsed that anyone took notice of Mr Chitterwick beyond Moresby's occasional preoccupied nods, and then it was the district inspector. Mr Chitterwick, bursting with questions welcomed him eagerly.

Parker was a tall, spare man with a clipped moustache and looked exactly like an ex-sergeant of a line regiment. He accosted Mr Chitterwick with the conscious kindliness of the expert toward the visiting ignoramus. 'Well, sir, I daresay this all seems very strange to you?'

This was hardly less than the truth, but Mr Chitterwick had other aspects of the affair to discuss than its strangeness. 'Tell me,' he asked artlessly, 'has any further evidence come to light?'

'Oh, I daresay we'll find something or other,' Parker answered guardedly. 'Mr Moresby, he's a rare hand at that.'

'Is there anything of importance connected with the phial?' pursued Mr Chitterwick.

But Parker was evidently a reticent man concerning phials. Concerning everything else in the way of discoveries, too, Mr Chitterwick soon realized, even letters in handbags. In fact, it very quickly became evident that Parker's object in seeking him out was not to impart information but to speak an encouraging word or two to an insignificant object who had been elevated by circumstances into a position of considerable importance; much as a perfectly ordinary black kitten, at which no one would look twice, is able to fill half the picture pages and three quarters of the news columns of our obliging popular press if it happens to have had a blue ribbon tied round its neck and been worn in the Magnifico restaurant on her left shoulder instead of a fur by a pretty young actress hopeful of a little free publicity. In fact, Mr Chitterwick gathered that he was now regarded by the police rather as a prize pet who would stand up in the witness box for them and perform his tricks in an altogether charming and gratifying manner.

'In fact, sir,' handsomely concluded Parker his kind word or two, 'We Owe a Great Deal to you, I'm sure.'

Mr Chitterwick hesitated. To say, 'Oh, that's all right,' would strike quite the wrong note; to say, 'I only did my duty,' would be undeniably pompous. He evaded the problem by smiling in the gratified way of a prize pet that has been duly patted.

'You've no doubt about that being the party in question, I suppose?' pursued Parker, testing the pet's capabilities, and jerked a thumb over his shoulder roughly in the direction of the second pillar to the left.

The pet had no doubts.

'That's good, that's good.' Parker administered two more pats.

'Why – why do you imagine he's there?' Mr Chitterwick ventured to ask. 'I should have thought – '

'We've got a pretty good idea why he's there,' said Parker darkly, but did not explain the pretty good idea.

Moresby, who strolled up at that moment, was more communicative. 'If he's the person we think he is, there's a letter from him in the lady's handbag acknowledging an appointment with her here at half-past three,' he explained. 'He knew that letter'd turn up, so along he comes at half-past three, as innocent as you like.'

'Oh, I see,' said Mr Chitterwick, grateful for the information. 'And of course nobody was to know that – that – '

'That he turned up at half-past two first,' Parker amplified kindly, seeing that information was in order. 'You've got it, sir.' He registered gentle approval of the pet's intelligence.

'He must be a wonderful actor, to trust himself to such a situation,' said Mr Chitterwick, more than doubtful whether any acting could rise to such an occasion.

'Well, we're going to give him a chance of showing what his acting's like,' said Moresby, with the utmost cheerfulness. Mr Chitterwick gathered that the situation rather appealed to Moresby, as indeed it did.

'You're – you're going to arrest him at once?'

'Good gracious me, no, sir,' the chief inspector exclaimed, and Parker looked pained at his pet's foolishness. 'Why, we don't even know who he is yet.'

'No, of course; of course,' muttered Mr Chitterwick, confused, and made a mental memorandum that you must always know who a person is before arresting him. 'Then how – ?'

'Why, the name of the man making the appointment – or agreeing to the appointment, more correctly (he's the old lady's nephew, it seems), is Lynn. His Christian name, that is. At least, that's all the letter's signed: "Yours affectionately, Lynn." What his surname may be we can't say for certain. But the old lady's name is Sinclair – Miss Sinclair. So we can back an even chance and plumb for "Lynn Sinclair." Anyhow, that's the name one of those page boys is crying round this place at this very minute. Hear him?'

Mr Chitterwick listened. Faintly above the hum and clatter rose a shrill, moaning yowl, the cry of a page boy in search of a client. 'Mist' Lynn *Sinc*ler, pleece! *Mist'* Lynn *Sincl'*, pleece!'

'You're going to – to question him, Chief Inspector?' Mr Chitterwick was correctly impressed.

'We're going to break the sad news to him,' amended the chief inspector, with a quite uncalled-for wink. 'So I'm afraid I must ask you to go out of here now, sir. You'll have to pick him out of the identification parade later on, you see, and it'd look bad if it came out that you'd been present when we were interviewing him here. His solicitor could make a lot of trouble over that.'

'Yes, of course; I quite see that.' But Mr Chitterwick was disappointed, all the same. He swept a wistful eye over the little enclosure. The various experts had now departed, and their underlings. Only Moresby, Parker, and himself remained. And he *would* have liked to hear the interview in progress.

'But, of course, sir,' twinkled Moresby, 'if you took a chair into that space we've had cleared round the screens and sat with your ear right up against them, as you might say, or even found a little chink to look through and told anyone who tried to stop you that you're with Chief Inspector Moresby – why, I don't see that anyone could very well say you're not, could they?'

'Couldn't they?' beamed Mr Chitterwick. 'Really, Chief Inspector, that's very... I shall take advantage of your... Indeed, thank you very much.' And Mr Chitterwick, twittering gratitude, bustled himself out of the little enclosure and boldly sat down inside the roped-off space round it. It is perhaps worth remarking that though this space was guarded by no less than four of the Piccadilly Palace's staff, besides a plain-clothes man, with the strictest injunctions to let nobody inside, and of these only the last knew that Mr Chitterwick was there under Moresby's wing or had seen him come out of the enclosure, yet such was the air of confidence with which Mr Chitterwick stepped over the ropes that none of the four thought of remonstrating with him. Which points so many morals, and might be the source of so many aphorisms, that the reader may here save three or four pages by taking them all as pointed and as coined.

The enclosure backed upon the pillar in front of which the old lady had been seated (and for that matter, still was). Mr Chitterwick was therefore able, by ensconcing himself in its lee, to remain sheltered from most of the lounge's clientèle while conducting his eavesdropping experiment, and those who could have seen him had they wished, very properly took no notice of him at all. He applied his ear as close as he decently could to the small gap between two screens and waited.

Mr Chitterwick's feelings at this stage might repay a cursory scrutiny. He was still horrified, of course, by the terrible and lonely death, and still more at the thought of having himself witnessed its actual occurrence, and yet more still at the idea that he had witnessed also that death being dealt out and the very hand as it dealt it; and this three-fold horror was quite enough to swamp his normal pity for a criminal with the law's noose poised ready for his neck; as a cold-blooded, utterly heartless murderer he felt that the red-haired man deserved nothing less than hanging, and was perfectly ready (at least, whenever he thought of that pathetic figure lolling so unnaturally in her green wicker chair) to do his own share toward bringing about that conclusion. But over and above everything else – his horror, his pity for the victim, the shock to himself – was a great excitement.

Mr Chitterwick, to put it frankly, was beside himself with excitement as he had not been since the day when, at the age of seven, his parents had taken him to his first circus. Not since then had he experienced this breathless, sick emptiness that felt as if it might turn at any moment into sheer nervous nausea, this wild drumming of the heart, this inability to hold his hands in any other way except with fingertips pressed tightly into hot, moist palms.

He, Ambrose Chitterwick, whose devotion to criminology had been his ruling hobby ever since his first visit to the Chamber of Horrors (just two years after the circus); who knew the names, dates, stories, psychology, and almost the number of their teeth, certainly the colour of their eyes, of every murderer of even minor importance since Alice Arden of Faversham in 1551; to whom murderers were as pearls to women and women to men; who collected murderers as lesser souls collect moths, sticking his psychological pins through their inmost recesses and spreading them out in all their black beauty on card indexes and cross files – he, Ambrose Chitterwick, no less, was actually himself concerned – concerned? the very pit and pivot! – of as bizarre and absorbing a murder as any he had ever pored over in academic seclusion.

No wonder Mr Chitterwick was excited.

Fortunately for his nervous system he had not long to wait. The sound of muffled voices reached his ears within a few minutes, among which he could distinguish the hearty tones of Moresby but not his words. Desperate with fear that he might miss something vital Mr Chitterwick shamelessly edged the two screens still farther apart, so that he could both hear and see.

In the opening to the enclosure Moresby was standing, faced by a superior member of the hotel staff, and even over the former's burly height Mr Chitterwick could see the top of a red head; a little extra thrill went through him at the sight. Then Moresby shifted his position slightly to address the red head, and Mr Chitterwick could hear what he said.

'You are Mr Lynn Sinclair, sir?'

'That is my name.'

Mr Chitterwick could not see the red-haired man's face, but his somewhat stiff tones expressed nothing but a normal surprise.

'You came here to meet your aunt, Miss Sinclair, of Earlshaze, Dorset?' Mr Chitterwick was not so absorbed that a little flutter of congratulation did not shake him for a moment for having diagnosed so correctly the relations of the pair as they sat over their coffee.

'I did, yes.' Again the red-haired man's voice indicated only surprise, mingled perhaps with a little impatient resentment. Evidently he was not accustomed to have his comings and goings questioned by anyone.

Moresby spoke with quite unctuous sympathy. 'Then I'm afraid I have some very bad news for you, sir.' Mr

Chitterwick reflected that if the red-haired man could act, so certainly could Moresby.

And there was no doubt that the red-haired man could act. Moresby had stepped back a little, to shield the body from the other's gaze, so that Mr Chitterwick was now looking once more directly at the red-haired man's face; and of apprehension, or anything like that, he could not see the faintest sign, however hard he looked.

'Bad news?' he repeated, in tones of nothing but bewilderment. 'I don't understand. Who are you?'

'I'm a police officer, sir,' Moresby said glibly, 'and I regret to have to tell you that you must prepare yourself for a shock. A very great shock. Your aunt passed away suddenly, in here, not an hour ago.'

'You mean – she's *dead?*'

Mr Chitterwick sighed with admiration. Sinclair, the red-haired man, might be an abominable villain, but so far as acting went he was superb, and Mr Chitterwick could recognize artistry when he saw it. Not a hint of a tone was wrong, not a hundredth of an inch of expression. Sinclair presented a perfect picture, of a large man learning of the death of a favourite aunt.

'I'm sorry to say she is, sir.'

Moresby moved aside with a sudden movement, so that Sinclair was confronted, with brutal unexpectedness, with the spectacle of the old lady. He started slightly, and Mr Chitterwick nodded breathless approval; an innocent man *would* start; only a guilty one, with knowledge of what Moresby had been shielding, would have received no shock. The man must have studied every tiny detail in advance.

'Good Lord!' he ejaculated now. 'How awful! Was it – very sudden?'

'Very sudden, sir,' Moresby agreed drily.

41

Sinclair remained silent for a moment, gazing at the body. 'Then she must have had a dicky heart after all,' he muttered, almost to himself. 'Well, I suppose we'd better –' He broke off and looked hard at Moresby. 'You said you were a police officer. Do you mean attached for duty at the hotel?'

'No, sir,' Moresby answered benevolently. 'I'm from the Criminal Investigation Department, at Scotland Yard.' In spite of his benevolence Moresby spoke with what seemed to Mr Chitterwick a world of meaning.

But the red-haired man did not appear in the least taken aback, only annoyed. He spoke curtly. 'Then may I ask what you are doing here? What has my aunt's death got to do with Scotland Yard?'

Moresby resumed his unctuous tone. 'I told you to prepare yourself for a shock, sir. The manager here reported your aunt's death to us following the doctor's examination. I'm sorry to have to tell you, sir, that it seems as if your aunt had done away with herself.'

Sinclair's reaction to this piece of artfulness was, to Mr Chitterwick, at any rate, unexpected. 'Killed herself?' he positively snorted. 'Nonsense! Last person in the world to do such a thing.'

From his expression one gathered that Moresby's confidence in the suicide theory had been severely shaken by the red-haired man's words. 'Is that so, sir!' he said, rubbing his chin. 'Well, but things certainly look that way.'

'How do you mean?'

'You see, she died of poisoning. Prussic acid poisoning, to be exact.'

This time Sinclair gave full rein to his powers. In fact Mr Chitterwick even thought he overdid it a trifle. Amazement, incredulity, horror, anger, a dozen emotions chased each other across his face. 'P-prussic acid?' he stammered at last. 'Good heavens, you can't mean – '

'The doctor found prussic acid in the dregs of her coffee,' Moresby said in an expressionless voice, 'and there was a phial in her hand.'

There was silence for an instant. A silence, Mr Chitterwick felt, that marked a more pregnant moment than any yet; a silence bursting with caution and cunning on one side and stern determination on the other. Mr Chitterwick could hardly breathe, and he felt his nausea rising in him like a spring tide.

The two protagonists faced each other. Then the red-haired man spoke. 'Good Lord!' he said in a low voice. 'Then it looks as if she *must* have done it.'

Mr Chitterwick was faintly disappointed. He thought that a trifle obvious.

The two went on to discuss arrangements. Sinclair wished to have the body removed at once to his flat in Queen Anne's Gate; Moresby pointed out that an inquest would have to be held and suggested the mortuary. Sinclair was strongly opposed to the mortuary; Moresby genially but officially insisted. The discussion proceeded in the most ordinary way.

Mr Chitterwick let out a deep breath and found himself at leisure, yet without missing a word of the conversation, to summarize his impressions. First with regard to the murderer's physical appearance. Now that he was seeing him so much closer Mr Chitterwick had to modify a few of his earlier ideas. For instance the man was not nearly so young as he had thought. More like thirty-five than twenty-five, he fancied; there was a suspicion of gray in the close-cropped red curls above the temples. The likeness to his aunt was just as strong as he had gathered, and the closer view brought out other points of resemblance besides the firm, aquiline nose. His largeness was no less than Mr Chitterwick's impression had been; more, if anything. Lastly, he seemed now to be bearing himself with more dignity (Looks more like a gentleman, in fact, thought Mr Chitterwick, apologizing to himself for the phrase) than on the former occasion; his manner then toward his aunt had been casual and offhand, that toward Mr Chitterwick downright rude. But at that time (meditated Mr Chitterwick) he would have been feeling acutely nervous; now every atom of his being is concentrated on playing his part.

And as for the way in which he was continuing to play his part Mr Chitterwick, properly detest the fellow as he might, could feel nothing but admiration. Except perhaps for that one rather unsubtle remark he had not made a single false step; given nothing away at all. Mr Chitterwick could not but realize, in spite of his appreciation of Scotland Yard, that but for his own evidence the police would have had an almost impossible task to bring the murder home to its executant. And that such evidence existed Sinclair of course had no idea.

In the meantime, under cover of making the necessary arrangements, Moresby (as Mr Chitterwick realized with interest) had been delicately pumping his man. One or two quite interesting facts had been dredged to the surface. The dead woman was evidently a person of some consequence. Sinclair spoke of Earlshaze as if it were a considerable property. He himself was her nearest relative and also, he believed (he mentioned it quite casually in answer to a direct question from Moresby, but not casually enough to prevent Mr Chitterwick from jumping a little), his aunt's sole heir.

She had been staying, as she always did in London, at Aldridge's, with her companion. Mr Chitterwick knew

Aldridge's. Apart from anything else, the fact that Miss Sinclair had been staying there stamped her as a Personage. Nobody but Personages were allowed to stay at Aldridge's, though the proprietor did let in now and then one or two of the more respectable foreign royal families. It was a small, dingy hotel situated just inside the borders of Mayfair and probably the least up to date and the most uncomfortable one within a mile radius. But it was simply terribly exclusive, and the air there cost several pounds an hour to breathe.

Why his aunt had wanted to see him Major Sinclair (it had turned out by now that he had been in a Guards regiment during the war and had stayed on for some years afterward, but sent in his papers on reaching his majority) had not the faintest idea, nor why in the Piccadilly Palace lounge, of all strange places. She had written to him, however, suggesting the appointment, or rather, definitely making it, for she was an autocratic woman, and he had written back his agreement. He professed himself completely puzzled.

'I see, sir,' said Moresby. 'Well, the first thing to do is to arrange for the body to be moved. And then, perhaps, you'd like to come along with me to the Yard and put all this information into an official statement.'

'Want me to make a statement?' said Major Sinclair. 'All right; I don't mind, if it's any use to you. But I thought you only wanted statements from suspected murderers.' Mr Chitterwick caught his breath at such sheer daring.

'Oh, in a difficult case like this it sometimes helps,' said Moresby smoothly.

'Very well. I suppose there must be an inquest, as you say, and a lot of damned publicity. Poor old lady, how she would have hated it. We were never terribly good friends, I'm afraid; both of us got too much of the family temper, as well as the family nose, for that; but I must say I'm deuced sorry to think of her going out like this. Wonder what the devil the poor old thing had on her conscience.' Again Mr Chitterwick caught his breath. ·

'Ah, well, we've all got things on our consciences, no doubt,' said Moresby sententiously. 'Now, sir, if you'll go along to the manager's office and introduce yourself I'll join you there in a minute and we'll see what can be done toward getting her away.'

'She really must go to the mortuary, must she? I don't want to upset your routine, but it does seem a bit tough on her.'

'I'm sorry, sir, but she must,' said Moresby with finality, and ushered the other out of the enclosure. 'Take charge, Parker,' he added, when the Major had disappeared. 'I'll be back soon.'

Parker, who had preserved a masterly taciturnity during the whole interview, kept things up by nodding in silence.

Moresby waited a moment, then strolled out and jerked his head toward Mr Chitterwick. That gentleman bounded up from his seat and almost leapt the rope in his eagerness.

'You heard all that, sir?'

'I did indeed. God bless my soul, Chief Inspector, that man is... I simply could never have imagined that...'

The chief inspector chuckled gently. 'Thought he was going to get the old girl all to himself at his flat, did he? Monkey about with her just as he liked, I suppose? No, I don't trust that gentleman, and that's a fact. The sooner we've got him under lock and key the better.'

'He doesn't – suspect?'

'That we've got a star witness up our sleeves, if you'll pardon my putting it like that, sir? Not he! Just like any other murderer I've ever come across, major or no major. Cocksure. Hasn't a doubt he's got away with it. Well, we'll see.'

'But you've let him go now, haven't you?' Mr Chitterwick was evidently a little dubious.

'With two of my men on his tail,' the chief inspector reassured him. 'But, bless you, sir, he won't go anywhere but to the manager's office. He's too fly for that. Well, I must go along and keep an eye on him. Now, sir, I don't want you to get out of touch with me. You're on the telephone at home, I suppose?'

'Well, no, I'm afraid I'm not,' apologized Mr Chitterwick. He was really apologizing for his aunt, who did not like telephones, but he did not add that.

'Oh, well, then, if you'd go along to your club – '

'I'm afraid I haven't got a club,' apologized Mr Chitterwick, again for his aunt.

'Humph!' Moresby scratched his head. 'Well, I'll tell you what. Come along to Scotland Yard at six-thirty, will you, sir? Ask for me.'

'Very well,' Mr Chitterwick beamed. 'Is that for the – the – ?'

'The identification parade; that's right, sir. And I'll arrest him as soon as you've picked him out. At six-thirty, then. Thank you, sir.' And Moresby was gone.

Mr Chitterwick walked slowly out of the lounge, meditating. The responsibility, the first thought of which had weighed on him so heavily, now sat with conscious dignity on his shoulders. Mr Chitterwick could not but be aware that he was now a very important man indeed. He, and practically speaking he alone, was going to put a rope round the neck of a man who unmistakably and most thoroughly deserved it, and he could not feel sorry that he was. The case, with such a distinguished victim, was bound to attract considerable attention. His words in the witness box would be quoted in every newspaper in the country. Probably a good many would want to publish his photograph as well. There would certainly be reporters... Yes, Mr Chitterwick, in spite of his modesty, could not blink the fact that since half-past two that afternoon he had become – well, really one might say one of the most important men in the country.

He glanced at the clock in the vestibule. The time was twenty minutes past four.

One of the most important men in the country started violently and quickened his pace almost to a run. He had undertaken to be back in Chiswick with the curtain patterns for his aunt by half-past three.

chapter four

Identification Parade

The house of Mr Chitterwick's aunt in Chiswick was an anachronism (for that matter, so was the aunt). It was early Jacobean, red brick, gables, and tiles, and had been built as the dower house of the estate on which it then stood. The estate had been Chitterwick property for a couple of centuries before the dower house was built. In the way of estates it had been gradually whittled down, successive Chitterwicks falling to enticing offers from speculative Jacobean builders onward, until now only the dower house, with its half-dozen acres of grounds, remained. But the grounds were spacious for London and quite big enough to hide from the house the fact that Chitterwick Chiswick, with its single village street, was no more; and its populous, cinema-ridden, villa-infested successor was shut off by an opaque blanket of trees. Even the joyous clanging of trams was not heard. And the Chitterwicks, a prudent race, not having gambled or even frittered away the good gold paid them by the various generations of speculative builders, were still able to maintain what was left to them of their estate in more than decent comfort, even after the LCC and the government had taken what they wanted first.

When one says 'the Chitterwicks' what one means is 'the Chitterwick' – Miss Chitterwick, except for her nephew the last bearer of the name. Miss Chitterwick was now seventy-nine, and there seemed no reason why she should not one day be a hundred. The Chitterwick property was hers solely, and she was in every sense of the word an aunt.

Mr Chitterwick entered the big lounge hall, cool and oak panelled, with the June sun on the lawns outside showing through the diamond-paned windows, conscious of guilt but at the same time of an excuse which even his aunt could not refuse to accept. She would be sitting, he knew, in the little room on the right which she called her study, but which Mr Chitterwick himself preferred to think of as the morning room. Except when she was instructing the gardener how to garden, Miss Chitterwick spent most of her time in this room, surrounded by her collections of dried mosses, minerals and polished stones, beetles and old periodicals, and for company (on the rare occasions when her nephew was absent) a large cage in the window containing four canaries. The keynote of the room was faded chintz, and its prevailing smell dusty and rather damp books.

Miss Chitterwick was arranging a new specimen in her *hortus siccus* which had arrived by the afternoon's post (she exchanged items from her collection with other mossy enthusiasts all over the world) and did not look up as her nephew entered the room. As if still unaware of his presence, she kept her white cap with its mauve satin ribbons bent closely over her work, her spectacles balanced as always on the very end of her nose. Mr Chitterwick knew that she was waiting for him to explain himself.

'I'm afraid I'm rather late, Aunt,' he began, with the extreme brightness of a guilty conscience; 'but really, I've had the most extraordinary adventure.'

Miss Chitterwick affected to start, and glanced first toward the cage of canaries as if, considering that she was alone in the room, it must have been one of them that had addressed her. She then, with another start, showed herself aware of the presence of her nephew.

'Lor', Ambrose,' she grumbled, 'how you made me jump. Creeping in like that without a sound. Enough to give anyone a fit.'

Now Mr Chitterwick knew that his aunt had heard him come in, and he knew that she knew he knew; but he recognized the gambit and dutifully made the move expected of him. 'I'm sorry I made you jump, Aunt,' said that dutiful nephew, offering himself to be snubbed. 'But, I was telling you, I've had the most remarkable adventure.'

'Found it in a swamp in southern Nigeria,' observed Miss Chitterwick darkly, but with incredible scorn. 'So *he* says. I'd have said he found it in a pond on Ealing Common.' For some obscure reason Ealing Common, to most people the most blameless of respectable places, was looked upon by Miss Chitterwick as synonymous with everything that was unmentionably impossible.

Mr Chitterwick coughed. In the normal way he would have gone on with his part of Miss Chitterwick's game, pleading to be allowed to explain and excuse his lateness, while Miss Chitterwick blandly pretended not to know that he was late at all, at the same time starting innumerable hares calculated to defer, head off, or chase away the explanation she was really longing to hear. But the occasion for once was not a normal one, and Mr Chitterwick threw the game to the winds. 'Aunt!' he bubbled over, 'I've actually seen somebody murdered. Poisoned! Right in front of my eyes.'

Miss Chitterwick looked him full in the face. 'What've you done with my spectacle case?'

'Your – your spectacle case, Aunt?' stammered Mr Chitterwick, thrown out of his stride.

'It's lost,' accused Miss Chitterwick. 'Most awkward. I've had to carry my spectacles about all day in my hand.' She regarded her nephew with a gloomy frown. 'Something always gets lost,' she added, 'when you go gallivanting about London.'

Mr Chitterwick forbore to point out that matching curtain patterns at the stores was scarcely gallivanting about London, for the Piccadilly Palace, he knew, would require more than a little explaining. Instead he took a fresh grip on himself. 'I'm sorry, Aunt,' he said, 'but I'm afraid I can't stop to look for them now. I've got to go out again almost at once. I only came back to explain that I probably shan't be in to dinner. I have to go to Scotland Yard.'

'Stuff!' observed Miss Chitterwick briefly, and returned with some ostentation to her moss. 'Be telling me next you've got to go to Ealing Common, I suppose,' she added into her *hortus siccus*.

Mr Chitterwick was a very, very good nephew. He might have walked out of the house there and then, leaving the oldest woman in Chiswick in such a state of raging curiosity that she could have fed her whole *hortus siccus* to the canaries. Instead, he sat down in a chair and told her, quickly but efficiently, the whole story.

Miss Chitterwick of course pretended to take not the faintest interest in it; indeed, it was to be gathered that it was doubtful whether she had even heard it, for no sooner had Mr Chitterwick finished than she reiterated, without comment, her inquiry as to the missing spectacle case; but when Mr Chitterwick took a lingering and somewhat apologetic leave of her ten minutes later it was with the sense of duty well done and a grateful aunt left behind him – though she would rather have been bitten to death by her own white Persian cat than admit it.

The trouble about Mr Chitterwick, so far as his aunt was concerned (and he recognized the justice of it), was that he had not been born a girl. His three sisters, all older than himself, had each in turn acted as unpaid companion, dogs-body, and whipping post to the old lady until their respective marriages, and after the last of these it had been perfectly clear that, as Miss Chitterwick utterly refused either to have a paid companion or to be left alone, Mr Chitterwick must step into the vacant place. So, having been brought up in the last generation's theory of duty toward one's elder relatives, Mr Chitterwick had duly stepped. That had been fourteen years ago, when Mr Chitterwick was a bare thirty years old. It is noteworthy that for thirteen and a half of those fourteen years Mr Chitterwick had made quite the best companion, dogsbody, and whipping post of the four; but because he was debarred from assisting at his aunt's morning and evening toilet, Miss Chitterwick professed to hold that the accident of her nephew's unfortunate sex had destroyed all chance of happiness, or even moderate comfort, for her declining years.

This model man reached Moresby's office at Scotland Yard punctually as Big Ben was striking half-past six.

Moresby rose to greet him with warmth, and pressed him to a chair. 'They'll be ready for us at the station in a few minutes, Mr Chitterwick, sir, but I thought I'd like a quiet word here with you first, now we've had time to sort things out a bit, so to speak.'

'Certainly, certainly, of course,' nodded Mr Chitterwick with great gravity.

Moresby leaned back in his chair and contemplated Mr Chitterwick with the air of a paternal sea lion. 'I needn't say again, sir, what a responsible position you're filling. You know that as well as I do. You realize that all our actions, the actions of the police, the public prosecutor, the attorney general even, all depend entirely on your evidence?'

'I do,' sighed Mr Chitterwick. 'Only too well.'

'So I thought I'd just ask you once more, to be quite on the safe side. There's a lot of talk been going on lately about the police using unfair methods, but you can take it from me, sir, that we never make an arrest in a case of this importance unless we're completely satisfied that we've got the right man. So are you as sure as you've ever been of anything that the man we interviewed, Major Sinclair, is the man you saw with the old lady an hour earlier?'

'Positive,' said Mr Chitterwick very firmly.

'I see,' Moresby nodded. 'Well, that's the first point. The other one we decided before, that you certainly did see him put something in the old lady's coffee cup. I needn't point out to you, sir,' continued Moresby, proceeding to do so, 'the importance of *that*, either. To put it shortly, it'll be the whole of our case. The fact that he met her an hour earlier than the appointment he had with her and concealed it afterward may be suspicious, but it isn't really evidence of guilt. That still left it open for the old lady to commit suicide after he'd left her, if she wanted to.'

'Of course. But I thought,' said Mr Chitterwick timidly, 'that the way the phial was lying in her hand, and the fact that she was clearly getting ready to go, were fairly conclusive evidence against suicide?'

'To us, sir,' agreed the chief inspector, 'yes. But those little points, which more or less clinch a case for us, as you might say, don't carry much weight with a jury. They want something more definite than that. The evidence you can give, for instance.'

'Yes, of course. I quite see that. The normal jury doesn't care to condemn a man on what it considers subtleties.'

'Well, sir, what I mean is, counsel for the defence is going to be on to you about that point like a ton of bricks,' said Moresby genially. 'He'll know that that's his one snag, and if he can't break it his client's going to the bottom; if he can, he's bound to be acquitted. He's going to do his level best to tie you up in knots.'

'I must be prepared for a very unpleasant half-hour of course,' mourned Mr Chitterwick.

'That's it, sir. And what I'm saying is this. If you think, here and now, that there's any possibility of him succeeding, let me know at once; because, if he does, there's an end of our case. Are you still, now you've had time to think it over, just as convinced that you saw that man's hand over the old lady's cup as you were when you rang me up here? I'd much prefer you to tell me if you've any doubt at all, however small.'

'I can't doubt the evidence of my own eyes, Chief Inspector,' replied Mr Chitterwick with dignity. 'I can assure you that it is no pleasure to me to be the instrument of justice. Very much the reverse. But I can assure you equally that I have not the faintest doubt as to what I saw, and I shall not flinch from my plain duty in the matter.'

'Then that's all right, Mr Chitterwick, sir,' said Moresby with great heartiness. 'That's good. After all, you did ring me up on the strength of what you saw, didn't you? – which confirms that you did see it. That's settled, then. Well, we'd better be getting along.'

From the added friendliness, amounting almost to affection, of the chief inspector's manner toward him, Mr

Chitterwick gathered that the police pet had passed now his final private test and at last was adjudged competent to perform his tricks in public.

By way of reward he enjoyed the experience of being conveyed from Scotland Yard to the district station in a real police car, driven by a real plain-clothes man.

Mr Chitterwick was not looking forward to his immediate duty. The result would be so final. Once he had picked out his man the full weight of the law would fall on the wretch, bearing him down until it had finally crushed the life out of him. Mr Chitterwick had to remind himself very hard that nobody deserved more thoroughly to have the life crushed out of him.

Moresby introduced him to the station sergeant, who also regarded him with the eye of benevolent proprietorship. A woman was already waiting, who Mr Chitterwick was given to understand was the waitress from the Piccadilly Palace who had served the fatal coffee. The sergeant informed Moresby that the parade was ready and waiting, and without more ado the two of them passed, with the woman, into an adjoining room. Mr Chitterwick, who was left under the charge of a constable, could not help feeling that for so vital an occasion everything seemed curiously informal. Within two minutes the woman was out again, and Mr Chitterwick in his turn was escorted into the next room, a trifle weak about the knees.

It was a motley crowd that was lined up in front of the farther wall in the bare bleak room. Seediness rubbed shoulders with glossiness, highly polished shoes stood next to others that sadly needed polish. The regulation is laid down that for such affairs the outsiders, roped in as they pass unsuspectingly along the street, shall resemble the suspect in appearance as far as possible, but in practice it is not easy to produce at a few minutes' notice a round dozen people resembling a large, spruce, red-haired ex-major, of distinctly soldierly as well as gentlemanly appearance. Certainly the difficulty had not been overcome on this occasion. Of the other ten only one had the faintest claim to anything approaching red hair, based on a mild ginger-and-peppery mixture. Mr Chitterwick's task was a farce.

The sergeant led him slowly down the line and back again, and Mr Chitterwick, his heart thumping oddly, met in turn a dozen pairs of eyes whose expressions varied from sardonic amusement to intense indignation; and it says something for him that, foregone as the conclusion might be, he was ready to give the red-haired man the benefit of any impossible doubt that he could find and did not shrink from subjecting him to a long, steady look before he announced his decision, searching the face and testing it by his memory.

'Well, sir?' prompted the sergeant, impatient of such niceties. 'Can you identify any of these men as having been seated near you in the Piccadilly Palace Hotel this afternoon between half-past two and three o'clock?'

Mr Chitterwick dismissed his last base hope that any doubt was possible and indicated in a mumbling way the red-haired man. The sergeant, aided by an underling policeman, briskly and efficiently ejected the supers into the street. Moresby strolled, as if casually, toward the red-haired man, whose countenance reflected nothing but indignant amazement in which indignation played very much the larger part; he was evidently waiting only till the room was cleared before he burst forth very volubly indeed. Mr Chitterwick, succumbing to a moment's poltroonery, edged out of the room with the last of the ten. He simply did not wish to witness the arrest, he told himself.

The red-haired man's volubility must have been cut ruthlessly short, for it was barely a couple of minutes before Moresby rejoined Mr Chitterwick in the outer room with the information that the other was safely locked in a cell.

'Ah!' said Mr Chitterwick, and looked as unhappy as he felt. Responsibility sits pleasantly on few of us.

Moresby looked at him and decided that the pet must be rewarded. 'Well, sir, I must get busy now. I shall have to make a search of Major Sinclair's flat, though I hardly expect to find anything there, but first I want to have a look through the old lady's room at Aldridge's. Would you care to come with me?'

Mr Chitterwick brightened immediately. To see the police actually at work... For once in his life he forgot his aunt completely. 'Oh, thank you, Chief Inspector. Really, that's very... I should like to very much.'

They went out to the waiting police car.

At the hotel Moresby, with the appearance of being about to be tactful and yet firm, disappeared into the dim office, leaving Mr Chitterwick in the lounge. When he returned it was with the key of Miss Sinclair's room. A small boy covered with buttons led them to the door. Calmly Moresby unlocked it, and the two of them passed inside.

Moresby did not produce either magnifying glass, fingerprint outfit, or any other of the proper impedimenta of the detective. He simply began, rapidly but methodically, to run through such drawers as there were in the room, paying particular attention to any letters or other documents. Mr Chitterwick, who had expected to be breathlessly thrilled, sat on the edge of the bed and grew more and more bored as the search silently proceeded.

Then came an interruption. A door in one of the side walls opened suddenly, and a tall young woman was visible in the doorway. On seeing the two men she stopped short and stared at them. Mr Chitterwick stared back. She was not a very prepossessing tall young woman. Her black, rather dank unshingled hair was drawn straight back from her forehead into two coils over her ears; she wore very large tortoiseshell spectacles and an exceedingly uninteresting plain brown frock; she radiated competence, and she looked alarmingly efficient. Mr Chitterwick, doing a little private detective work of his own, muttered to himself: 'The companion.'

Evidently taken aback for the moment, this efficient young person recovered herself immediately. Though presumably for all she knew she might have been confronting two desperate burglars (that is, had she not looked too closely at Mr Chitterwick), there was not a tremor in her voice as she observed briskly: 'May I ask what you are doing here? This is a private bedroom, and it is engaged.'

'Ah,' nodded Moresby. 'Miss Goole, isn't it?'

The young woman looked suspicious. She had evidently heard of the confidence trick before now. 'That is my name,' she admitted with some reluctance.

'I'm a police officer,' said Moresby, with his usual smoothness, 'and I'm afraid, miss – '

'May I see your credentials, please?' interrupted the young woman efficiently.

With a humorous grimace in the direction of Mr Chitterwick, the chief inspector established his identity. The young woman at once became competently helpful. Briefly Moresby explained the tragedy to her, though without mentioning the fact of murder or referring to the arrest he had just effected. The young woman listened carefully, gave no sign of being shocked, and when he had finished professed herself entirely at the chief inspector's service.

Moresby thanked her and intimated that he would like to put a few questions to her.

'Perhaps we had better go into the next room,' suggested Miss Goole, and shepherded them through the communicating door into a small sitting room. The two followed her meekly.

Miss Goole seated herself in a chair, waved to the men to do the same, and expressed by her attitude that she was awaiting the chief inspector's questions. Mr Chitterwick, catching her eye, smiled nervously. Miss Goole did not smile back. Mr Chitterwick blushed slightly. To tell the truth, young women like Miss Goole simply terrified Mr Chitterwick.

Miss Goole's story did not add very much of importance to their knowledge. With admirable candour she began, in response to Moresby's hint, by giving a short account of herself and her relations with the dead woman. She was twenty-eight years old, the daughter of a solicitor in a small west-country town. Her career had begun with a couple of years' work in her father's office until he had died and she had been left to her own resources. Her father's practice had not been worth much, and she had sold it for what it was worth and migrated to London. There her knowledge of office routine and her shorthand-typing had at once obtained her a post in the office of another solicitor with whom her father had had business dealings. The post was well paid, but she had not held it long, for a rich American woman, a client of the firm, to whom she had been deputed to act as guide and companion during a brief stay in London, had been so much impressed by her efficient manner of exhibiting the sights of the metropolis that she had made a very handsome bid for a longer tenure of this exceptional capability. (Miss Goole did not put it in quite this way, but it was evident that she had no illusions as to her own worth.) The offer had been accepted, and Miss Goole had returned with her to New York.

There she had remained for five years, supervising her employer's many activities, ensuring that she attended the right committees on the right days, distributing the correct amount of largesse to the right almoners, and generally making the American woman's life a smoother affair than it had ever been before. At the end of two years her employer had died, but Miss Goole had had no difficulty in obtaining another post.

During the next three years she had held two other such positions, and then, disregarding the further offers that had been made to her on all sides, had returned to England. She had intended to come back for a holiday only, but a chance meeting with Miss Sinclair had resulted in a mutual attraction of like to like, and her installation as companion-secretary had followed. That had been eight months ago, and now it seemed that another chapter in Miss Goole's efficient life had come to an end.

'Thank you.' Moresby nodded his gratitude. 'If all witnesses were like you, miss, we'd have a good deal easier time of it at the Yard.'

Miss Goole smiled faintly, a brief, competent smile of acknowledgment.

'So now, perhaps,' said Moresby, 'you'll give me as good an idea of the old lady, will you?'

'Of Miss Sinclair?' corrected Miss Goole. 'As I told you, I have only been with her for eight months, but no doubt I can give you all the information you wish.'

'I'm sure you can, miss,' openly admired the chief inspector.

Miss Goole's account confirmed Mr Chitterwick's idea that the dead woman had been a person of more than ordinary importance. She was not only very rich, it appeared at once, but she was what Miss Goole evidently considered of vastly more importance, a member of a very good old country family, the last survivor of her own generation; and finally she was, as Miss Goole clearly held to be of the greatest importance of all, an old lady of highly forceful character. As the narrative proceeded Mr Chitterwick was reminded more and more strongly of his aunt.

Eight months had evidently not been too short a period for Miss Goole to acquire a working knowledge of her employer's family history as well as her affairs. Earlshaze was one of the oldest country houses in Dorsetshire, and the thirty thousand acres of ground that made up the estate had been in the possession of the Sinclair family or its collaterals since Saxon times. It was not legally entailed, but custom had always dictated the bequeathing of it to the legal heir, except in such circumstances as those in which it had come into Miss Sinclair's possession. The Major's father, Captain Sinclair, had been killed in a frontier campaign while the former was still a small child; his mother had died soon afterward. His grandfather, who had survived the deaths of these two for some years, had left the estate to his only remaining child, Miss Sinclair, absolutely, with a small income to his grandson, but the understanding of course was that it should revert to the latter on her death.

Miss Sinclair, however (so Miss Goole hinted), though possessed of a proper respect for tradition, was not the woman to allow custom to override her own feelings. She had hinted, both to Miss Goole and, more directly, to the Major himself, that she did not consider herself in any way bound to leave him the property, though so long as he behaved himself properly she had no intention of doing anything else. Behaving himself properly, Mr Chitterwick wistfully gathered, was doing what his aunt wanted. Here Miss Goole hesitated for the first time.

'What would she do if he didn't, then?' inquired the chief inspector jocularly. 'Leave it to the Cats' Home?'

Miss Goole paused for a moment, as if not quite sure of her ground here. She had gathered that there *was* another possible heir, a cousin of the Major's, if he were still alive. Miss Sinclair had been reticent, for it was a matter of a Family Disgrace, but there had been another of her generation besides herself and the Major's father, a younger sister. This sister, when quite a girl, had fallen in love with a quite impossible person, a journalist, of all awful things, and had actually wished to marry him. On being sternly forbidden by her father to have anything more to do with such scum, she had promptly run away from home and married the creature at the Marylebone registry office. Naturally that was the end of her so far as her family was concerned. Her father did the least he could and cut her off completely, neither answering her letters nor allowing anyone else to do so. Miss Sinclair herself had had one interview with the disgraced one, in the wretched rooms in Bloomsbury which she occupied with the Impossibility, and had implored her to leave the wretch and return penitent to the Ancestral Home, where, if she kept out of his way as much as possible and dressed herself in nothing but sackcloth trimmed with ashes, her father might possibly be clement enough after several months to forgive her.

Letitia (for such was the fallen one's name) had affronted Miss Sinclair by receiving this suggestion with nothing but mirth, whereupon Respectability, curtly refusing to stay and drink a dish of Bloomsbury tea, had departed and never returned.

Captain Sinclair was in India at the time. None of her family ever saw or heard from Letitia again. By indirect routes they had learned that not long afterward she migrated with the Downfall to the United States, and the same source presented them with the news some years later that both were dead, which of course was the best thing that could have happened to them. But before atoning thus correctly at last for the shame she had brought on the family, Letitia Benson had manufactured a further token of it by giving birth in New York to a son. Miss Sinclair had privily kept herself informed of the progress of this benighted child till his adolescence, when the source of her news dried up in death too, and she heard no more. That had been more than ten years ago, but if the man were still alive undoubtedly he constituted another possible heir.

'Ah!' said Moresby, stroking his walrus moustache. 'And she threw this chap up at the Major, did she? Now, why? What had he been doing against her wishes that made her start talking about leaving her money elsewhere? Been pretty wild, perhaps?'

Miss Goole had not definitely said that the Major had done anything against his aunt's wishes, but she had implied it, and she now tacitly accepted implication. But, no; so far as she knew the Major had not been wild at all. His career had been blameless. It was just a matter of marriage.

'Ah!' said Moresby, and leaned forward.

'Miss Sinclair never made any secret to me of the fact that she had set her heart on Major Sinclair's marrying a Miss Carey, the only child of Sir John and Lady Carey, very old friends and neighbours of Miss Sinclair, whose estates touched hers at one point,' went on Miss Goole succinctly.

'Miss Carey is quite a charming woman, not particularly young and not very good-looking, perhaps, but a typical country sportswoman: a rider to hounds and all that sort of thing. Sir John, her father, is the master of the local hunt. As she is almost certain to be his heiress (in fact, I gathered that Miss Sinclair and Sir John had an understanding about both inheritances) the match would have been ideal from that point of view.'

'But not from the Major's, eh?' queried the chief inspector. 'I know those country ladies. Faces like the horses they ride, most of 'em.'

Miss Goole smiled faintly. 'I don't know that Miss Carey particularly resembles a horse, but I do know that the match did not appeal to the Major at all.'

'So there was friction?' nodded Moresby with satisfaction.

'A little, perhaps,' admitted Miss Goole, not without reluctance. 'Miss Sinclair was not the only independent one, you see. The Major is just as much so. I understand that he told her quite definitely that he had no intention of marrying Miss Carey, and would certainly never do so, not even to please the –' Miss Goole checked herself. 'He's had no intention of doing so,' she concluded.

'So his aunt threatens to cut him out of her will and leave the money to the cousin in America?'

'I can't say that she ever definitely threatened to do so. I think she had hopes of bringing him round in the end. Wearing him down, one might say. That was why she arranged that interview at the Piccadilly Palace. A new point had just occurred to her, and she wished to put it to him at once. She wrote off to him and came up to town at once. Miss Sinclair was like that. Impulsive.'

'But why the Piccadilly Palace?' ventured Mr Chitterwick, opening his mouth for the first time. 'Why not here? Or at Queen Anne's Gate?'

'Miss Sinclair never visited Queen Anne's Gate,' replied Miss Goole drily. 'It was her idea that bachelor establishments should be left entirely to their occupants.'

'Yes, but why the Piccadilly Palace?' persisted Mr Chitterwick. 'I mean, the Piccadilly Palace seems so very – '

'She made the appointment,' said Miss Goole with indifference. The inference was that no one could be expected to account for Miss Sinclair's actions, and, in any case, the point was unimportant.

Mr Chitterwick retired, somewhat crushed.

'I see,' said Moresby. 'Now, had you heard anything about the appointment with Major Sinclair being altered? To half-past two instead of half-past three, for instance?'

No, Miss Goole had not heard anything like that.

When had she seen Miss Sinclair last?

At lunch. Yes, Miss Sinclair had seemed perfectly normal. They had had some coffee afterward in the lounge, and Miss Sinclair had then gone up to her room soon after two o'clock saying that she would not want Miss Goole again until shortly before dinner.

Had she said anything about going out early?

Yes, Miss Goole could not be sure, but she rather fancied that Miss Sinclair had said something about having one or two small things to do. Yes, Miss Goole was sure she had, because she remembered now having offered to do them for her, and Miss Sinclair had replied that it did not matter, she could do them herself on her way to the Piccadilly Palace.

Had she mentioned at all what the jobs were?

No, she had not.

Moresby stroked his moustache and gazed benignly at Miss Goole's feet. They might have been quite nice-looking feet had they not been wearing shoes at least a size and a half too large for them. 'This interview with the Major, now. Was it in any way a climax, as you might say? You mentioned that she'd thought of something to put to him about this marriage and came up to town on purpose to do so. That seems as if it was something pretty important, doesn't it? I mean, too important to write. Well, was it anything like an ultimatum, so far as you know?'

Miss Goole couldn't say, she was sure.

'Put it this way, then. Had the old lady said anything to you that might show she anticipated a stormy meeting? A quarrel, or anything like that?'

For the first time Miss Goole hedged. 'I take it that all these questions are relevant, Chief Inspector? I understand from what you hinted that Miss Sinclair had poisoned herself, though I must say that I find it almost impossible to credit. Are you suggesting that it could have been dis-appointment about Major Sinclair's matrimonial awkward-ness which induced her to go to the length of taking her own life? Because if so I must tell you that – '

'I'm suggesting nothing, miss,' interposed Moresby with the utmost goodwill. 'Nothing. And you can take it that anything I ask you *is* relevant. So suppose you tell me what you'd gathered the old lady was anticipating from this interview?'

A brisk, tight little smile expressed at once Miss Goole's recognition of this subterfuge and acquiescence in the assumption contained in it. 'I'd gathered,' she said shortly, 'that Miss Sinclair *was* expecting – shall we say, difficulties; and that in such an event she might issue something approaching an ultimatum.'

'I see,' said Moresby thoughtfully. 'In a way, then, you might say the interview was to be the crux of all the discussions about this Miss Carey?'

Miss Goole thought you could say that.

'That on the result of it everything depended, both for the old lady's matchmaking plans and the Major's prospects?'

'I see. She was expecting him to put forward some other matrimonial ideas of his own, perhaps?'

No, Miss Goole did not think that.

'But he had some, of course; a man of his age?'

No, Miss Goole did not think he had.

'What would his aunt have said about them if he had?'

One gathered that Miss Sinclair's attitude would have been by no means unworthy of her late father.

'You're quite sure the Major never said anything to her about his marrying anyone else, not Miss Carey?' persisted the chief inspector.

Miss Goole, who appeared to think that the point was being laboured, said so once more, curtly.

'Then what would you say,' observed Moresby with pleasure, 'if I were to tell you that Major Sinclair's got a wife of his own at Queen Anne's Gate and has had for the last two years?'

chapter five

Mr Chitterwick Goes A-visiting

And there for a time, so far as Mr Chitterwick was concerned, the matter rested.

A newspaper sensation was created, of course. Photographs of the Piccadilly Palace lounge, the Fatal Table, the smart waitress, the doorkeeper, and the wife of one of the charwomen's brothers, appeared in every journal worth its circulation. Mr Chitterwick appeared too, decorated with a deprecatory beam. But the caption attached to him was only 'Saw Suspected Man with Aunt'; the vital part of his evidence remained a secret between himself and the police.

Sinclair was brought up before the magistrates the following morning, but only formal evidence of arrest was given, and he was remanded. As they left the police court together Moresby gave Mr Chitterwick to understand that the police would now be concentrating their energies in finding other persons besides himself and the waitress who had seen the two together in the lounge during the crucial period between half-past two and three.

'There should be no difficulty about that,' remarked Mr Chitterwick. 'A large number of people seemed to be watching me when I went over with the intention of stopping her snoring. Some of them must have noticed the two together.'

'That's right, sir; we expect plenty of confirmation on that point. Though, as I mentioned to you yesterday, that fact alone isn't going to hang the Major.'

'Chief Inspector,' observed Mr Chitterwick, rather timidly, 'I noticed yesterday when you and one of your colleagues were examining that phial... You won't tell me, of course, if you think it inadvisable, but – '

'You mean, did we get any evidence from it?' kindly supplemented the chief inspector, who was getting used to Mr Chitterwick's ways. 'Well, I've no objection to telling you, sir, though, of course, you'll keep it to yourself. Yes, we did. Our expert found fingerprints on it. In fact, he managed to get a couple of quite good impressions from it. I've got the photographs in my pocket this minute. Care to see 'em?' He pulled them out and handed them to his companion.

Mr Chitterwick studied them with an air of great wisdom. 'Ah!' he said profoundly. They conveyed nothing to him at all. 'Of course, when these have been identified – '

'Identified?' said the chief inspector happily. 'They've been identified all right. No doubt about that.'

'Good gracious! They're not really – ?'

'Well, here's the Major's prints, taken after he was arrested yesterday; and if you can find any difference between the two lots, you're doing something more than our expert can.' The chief inspector pulled out another envelope and obligingly handed that over as well.

Mr Chitterwick stood in the vestibule and compared them. He had never examined fingerprints before, and they are not easy for the tyro to compare, but he was perfectly ready to accept the chief inspector's word. 'That's really quite conclusive, I take it?' he said with solemnity as he gave them back.

'Well, it's a big point, a very big point; but a clever counsel could get round that alone. What we want to do now is to trace the purchase of the poison to the Major too. That's going to be a bigger step still.'

'And do you expect to be able to do so?'

'Can't hardly say that yet, sir. But it won't be for want of trying,' added Moresby grimly, 'if we don't.'

The case went on to run its usual course.

At the inquest, after a couple of adjournments for the purpose of allowing the autopsy to take place and the analysis of certain organs, death was proved conclusively to have been due to prussic acid poisoning. Curiously enough it was shown that Miss Sinclair suffered from an organic disease of the heart and could in any case have lived not much longer than six months. It was proved, too, that Major Sinclair had no definite knowledge of this.

The police succeeded in finding a dozen or more people who had seen the two together, and the evidence of selected members of this collection and Mr Chitterwick, together with the overwhelming motive, sufficed to produce a verdict of 'Wilful Murder' against Major Sinclair. The latter's efforts to prove an alibi, which he could not substantiate by any independent testimony, fell completely to pieces.

The same ground was gone over again, in more detail, before the magistrates, and though the police had failed so far to connect the Major with the purchase of the prussic acid or even to prove any previous possession of it on his part, his committal for trial at the Old Bailey was a foregone conclusion.

'But, mark you, Mr Chitterwick, sir,' observed Moresby, as they sat over a bun and a cup of coffee in a neighbouring tea shop after the conclusion of the proceedings, 'if it wasn't for your evidence he'd get off, almost for certain.' Mr Chitterwick's story of the Hovering Hand had not been told before the magistrates, but was being reserved for the trial.

'You think so?' said Mr Chitterwick rather doubtfully. 'Even in spite of these fingerprints on the phial?'

'Even in spite of them. They're not conclusive, you see, not when the relationship's so close. What's to prevent him saying, for instance, that the phial *was* his (there's no label or identification mark on it, you see) and he'd left it in the bathroom last time he went to stay with his aunt? There's a dozen different ways of accounting for those fingerprints innocently enough.'

'Oh! I see,' nodded Mr Chitterwick.

'But with your story – ! I can tell you, Mr Chitterwick, sir,' said Moresby unfeelingly, 'it wasn't half a facer for the defence. The Major's solicitor was cocksure of an acquittal, but when he'd heard about the evidence you're going to give for us – well, he began to think a bit, I can tell you.'

'You told him?' said Mr Chitterwick, surprised. 'I had fancied you were going to keep my evidence till the trial.'

'Secret from the public, but not from the defence. We never do that, sir; wouldn't be fair to the prisoner. Always let 'em know in good time before the trial just what they're up against.'

Mr Chitterwick nodded and not for the first time marvelled at the fairness of the English judicial system.

'Yes, Mr Chitterwick, sir,' summed up Moresby, regarding that gentleman with pride, 'without you I'm very much afraid we should be in the soup; with you we're as sure of a verdict as one can be of anything in this world.'

'I see,' said Mr Chitterwick, and wriggled slightly.

They went on to discuss the case and all its various ramifications. Moresby, who exhibited no feelings of any sort where the Major himself was concerned, displayed unexpectedly strong sympathy with that erring gentleman's wife, whom he described as a 'proper lady.' 'And bowled over though you might say in a way she is,' he added, 'she doesn't sit wringing her hands and doing nothing about it. Working like a Trojan, she is, for her husband, and I hadn't the heart to tell her it wasn't no manner of use at all.'

'Poor lady, poor lady,' chuckled Mr Chitterwick, shaking his head. 'Is she very charming?'

'Well, I don't know that I'd say charming was quite the right word,' said the chief inspector doubtfully. 'Handsome she is, but – well, no; I'd say determined more than charming. I remember once I had to see her when I was checking up that secretary, Miss Goole's, account of herself. She kept me – '

'Do you mean the story of her life Miss Goole told us?' interrupted Mr Chitterwick, mildly surprised. 'Surely you didn't bother to check that?'

'Certainly I did, sir. I verified every single thing she told us about herself.'

'Good gracious! But why? Surely it was quite irrelevant to the main issue?'

'It is one of our rules, sir,' said Moresby severely, 'never to accept any statement, however apparently unimportant, without confirmation, whenever such confirmation is possible.'

'Dear me!' said Mr Chitterwick and marvelled again, this time at the painstaking thoroughness of the English police system. In his wonderment unfortunately the chief inspector's anecdote was lost.

'You mentioned,' said Mr Chitterwick a few moments later, 'that you had been seeing Major Sinclair's solicitor. Did he tell you whether he had succeeded in finding the missing heir yet?' It had been considered proper by the Major's legal adviser to get into touch with the only surviving relative on the Sinclair side, that same cousin in America whom Miss Sinclair had been reputed to hold up as a threatened alternative heir, but considerable difficulty had been experienced in doing so. His career had been traced, by the solicitor's American representative, for a couple of years after Miss Sinclair had last heard of him, during which time he had apparently gone on the stage; but his present whereabouts could not be discovered or even the question determined of whether he was alive or dead. Discreetly worded advertisements in selected journals had brought no reply.

It was not a question of any benefits under Miss Sinclair's will, for that document left everything unconditionally to Major Sinclair; but the latter had stated bluntly to his solicitor that, in the impossible event of his being hanged, as he had no children of his own he would like the estate, after proper provision had been made for his own wife, to revert to this cousin, although the fellow bore the name of the unspeakable journalist instead of that of Sinclair. Mr Chitterwick had been following at second-hand the progress of the search, which appealed to him as more than a little romantic, with considerable interest.

Moresby told him that the solicitor had not mentioned the matter.

Shortly afterward, rewarded with buns and coffee, Mr Chitterwick was benevolently dismissed until the trial, which was to take place in seven weeks' time, with instructions not to fall down a precipice or get run over by a bus in the interim.

From the beginning Mr Chitterwick had been observing with no little interest, and some awe, his aunt's reactions to the affair.

At first, for a week or so, she had refused to hear a single word about it, flatly denying the truth of anything that Mr Chitterwick tried to tell her on the subject; her grounds for doing so appeared to be the utter impossibility of any nephew of hers ever entering such a place as the Piccadilly Palace lounge at all, from which it plainly followed that the whole story of Mr Chitterwick's connection with the case must be a complete fabrication.

Having been manoeuvred over this stage (on being discovered avidly reading the latest news of the case in the morning paper), and indeed being unable to maintain such a position any longer when actually confronted in that same paper with Mr Chitterwick's unmistakable portrait as that of a star witness in the affair, she then professed to be overcome with the disgrace of seeing a Chitterwick mixed up in such a vulgar and sordid thing as a murder trial, and proceeded to treat her nephew with as much scorn as if he had been the witless victim of a sort of gigantic confidence trick. This attitude did, however, allow her to listen at last to Mr Chitterwick's story, to make him tell it over and over again, and to cross-question him on the details to her heart's content. At this point the secret that had been shared so closely between Mr Chitterwick and the police alone obtained a third confidant.

This second stage lasted nearly a week, during which Miss Chitterwick on three occasions ordered round the carriage and pair (she not only refused to keep a car, but somehow managed to convey the impression that she actually disbelieved in the existence of such things) for the purpose of driving down to Scotland Yard in order to intercede with the authorities on her nephew's behalf, putting forward her conviction that by some peculiar misfortune it would not be the red-haired man at all who would finally end up on the gallows, but Mr Ambrose Chitterwick.

Mr Chitterwick had the greatest difficulty in dissuading her from this course and only succeeded the third time by voluntarily suggesting that they should go together instead to the butcher's with the monthly collection of newspapers, a task which he was usually ready to perjure his eternal soul to avoid. (It was one of Miss Chitterwick's smaller economies to preserve carefully all her newspapers in order to sell them to the butcher at the rate of a halfpenny a pound, and a solemn progress was made on the last day of each month in the carriage and pair to Chiswick High Street to do so. On the last day of each month Mr Chitterwick generally had either a simply terrible headache or else an appointment elsewhere of quite remarkable importance.)

Finally Miss Chitterwick achieved her last reading of the affair: that her nephew wilfully and for the sake of vulgar notoriety had abandoned his proper job of curtain matching and maliciously entered the Piccadilly Palace lounge for the express purpose of watching a murder being committed, in order to see his photograph in the papers later; though this theme sometimes gave way to the opinion that he had really seen nothing at all and his craving for publicity had driven him to the length of inventing the whole thing, the hanging of the red-haired Major being a minor matter as long as Mr Chitterwick's debased lust after notoriety could be satisfied. Mr Chitterwick had a good deal of trouble with his aunt during these days.

A letter which arrived for him one afternoon at teatime went some way to point his aunt's moral. He read it through with surprise and pleasure and then innocently handed it over to Miss Chitterwick. 'What a remarkable thing, Aunt. Do you remember her at all? I can't say that I do.'

'Don't expect me to be able to read it, do you?' grunted Miss Chitterwick. 'Not without my glasses. If only I had some capable *gairl* to look after me! Someone who wasn't always hiding my things away and then forgetting where she'd put them. What's the good of – '

'I'll read it out to you, Aunt,' interposed Mr Chitterwick hastily, nobly refraining (as he had for years) from pointing out that if his aunt really wanted a capable girl she could have afforded to employ half a dozen; but it was another of Miss Chitterwick's economies, a major one this time, never to employ anyone to do those things for her that someone else would do for nothing.

The letter that Mr Chitterwick proceeded to read aloud in his gentle tenor ran as follows:

'Riversmead Priory,
'Dorsetshire.

'DEAR MR CHITTERWICK:
'I can hardly suppose you will remember me, but I used to know your mother very well at one time. We were in fact at school together, and great friends, though we drifted apart later, as schoolfriends so often do. I have been meaning to write to you for some time, as I should like to renew my friendship with your family. Perhaps you will come down and spend a week here, on Thursday next, the 23rd? We should be delighted to see you, and the fishing here is not at all bad. We shall be only a very small party, just ourselves and one friend of

mine, so everything will be quite informal. There is a good train from Waterloo at three-thirty, and our station is Templecombe, so I shall expect you by that.

'Yours very sincerely,
'AGATHA MILBORNE.'

'Humph!' said Miss Chitterwick.

'Agatha Milborne,' ruminated Mr Chitterwick, helping himself absent-mindedly to another muffin. 'No, I don't remember the name at all. But what a very charming letter. Mrs Milborne. No.'

Miss Chitterwick snorted violently. '*Mrs* Milborne! Didn't you recognize the address, Ambrose, you guffin? *Lady* Milborne, of course. Your letter's from the Countess.'

'The Countess?' repeated Mr Chitterwick, gratified. 'Dear me, how very extraordinary. You know her, then, Aunt?'

'Used to come here before she was married,' rumbled Miss Chitterwick disparagingly. 'Friend of your mother's. Flighty sort of gairl. Never thought much of her.' Miss Chitterwick was the kind of snob who dissembles her love of a lord under an affectation of deep contempt. She really was a terrible snob, but Mr Chitterwick could sympathize with her. In her youth the Chitterwicks had been 'County'; now they were, presumably, suburban.

'Indeed?' said Mr Chitterwick, much interested. 'Then what was her maiden name?'

Miss Chitterwick did not reply. Instead she began to sip her tea, rather noisily. Mr Chitterwick was to gather that his aunt had not heard. His aunt never did hear anything she did not wish to.

Usually Mr Chitterwick tactfully accepted this convenient deafness. Now, however, his interest was stronger than his tact. He repeated his question, so loudly that his aunt could certainly not pretend to have heard nothing this time.

But he got little satisfaction. 'Maiden name?' she echoed gruffly. 'How should I know? Can't be expected to remember the maiden name of every friend of your mother's, can I?'

'But if she stayed here, Aunt,' suggested Mr Chitterwick, though he knew it was an empty hope.

'Lord knows what her maiden name was,' replied Miss Chitterwick bluntly. 'I don't; and don't care either. Something good-for-nothing, I expect.'

'Well, it's remarkably kind of her to ask me to stay,' said Mr Chitterwick, in mild protest against this quite unwarrantable suggestion. 'I shall certainly go.'

'Huh!' sneered his aunt. 'Obvious to *me* why she asks you.'

'Is it, Aunt? Why?'

'Drops your mother as soon as she's got her earl,' observed Miss Chitterwick with intense bitterness. 'Then, forty years afterward, finds she's been waiting all the time to see some of her family again. Huh! Doesn't take *me* in.'

'Why then, Aunt?'

'Why? What do you suppose? You're a notorious person now, aren't you? Just what you've always wanted to be, it seems.' The mauve satin ribbons on Miss Chitterwick's cap positively trembled with sarcasm. 'Photographs in the papers, and the Lord knows what. Chief witness in a murder trial, heaven save us all. No wonder she remembered she once knew your mother.'

'You mean – you mean, she's only asked me to stay because I am – because of my – because she supposes I'm – '

'Because you're one of these noospaper sensations,' supplied Miss Chitterwick. 'Anyone but a downright guffin could see that. Collect notorious people, all these countesses, don't they? Actresses and murderers and authors and Lord knows what. Now you're one of them, and she's collecting you too.'

'God bless my soul!' supplicated Mr Chitterwick, quite perturbed. Really put like that it did seem as if... And everyone knew that countesses *did*...

'Huh!' repeated his aunt, and betook herself again to her tea.

'Then I shall certainly not go,' decided Mr Chitterwick with energy.

His aunt almost dropped her teacup. 'Not go? Fiddle-sticks! More out of your senses than usual, Ambrose, are you?'

'But really, Aunt, if she only asked me because – '

'When I was a gairl,' observed Miss Chitterwick irrelevantly, 'we used to stay every year with the Dook of Dorset. Your grandfather was always asked for the shootin'. Every year. And, of course, I went with him.'

'Yes, Aunt. But if you're quite sure that's all she asked me for, I think it would be *most* undignified to – '

'If I was thought good enough to be asked to stay with the Dook you're good enough to stay with a twopenny-half-penny countess, aren't you?' argued Miss Chitterwick, with remarkable scorn.

'Yes. Oh, yes. No doubt. But what I was meaning is – '

'Fiddlesticks!' snorted Miss Chitterwick.

So Mr Chitterwick went.

He took with him, besides the more conventional part of his outfit, a rubber hot-water bottle (for even in July you never know), a red flannel chest protector (for his dear grandfather was carried off by chest trouble, as he very well knew, and it is tempting providence to be flagrant in one's recklessness), a white cotton nightcap, once the property of his dear grandfather (for if Ambrose's hair went on disappearing at that rate he'd soon be as bald as a coot, and the only way to stop hair disappearing, as anybody but a perfect guffin knew, was to wear a nightcap), and two dead moths (which had got in by mistake). The footman who unpacked for him handled all these things reverently, except the moths.

Of course, once his aunt had taken such a definite line Mr Chitterwick would have gone in any case, as he very well knew; but he was able to find one factor in the situation with which to salve his male independence. Riversmead Priory, he had discovered, lay within a few miles of Earlshaze; and though this undoubtedly gave strong support to Miss Chitterwick's cynical reading of the invitation, it would nevertheless afford the chief witness an opportunity to examine the prize which seemed to have been the mainspring of the crime. He would also, no doubt, be able to gather excellent first-hand information about the accused Major's early youth and general character, which would not only be exceedingly interesting to himself as a criminologist, but might even be the means of enabling him to assist the police still further; one never knew what one might pick up. Thus Mr Chitterwick as he dressed for dinner on the night of his arrival.

So far he had met no one at all. His train had been late, and the drive to the Priory had been at least twenty miles. Mr Chitterwick, arriving with only just comfortable time to dress, had been received by nobody beyond the butler, who had managed to convey a tinge of reproof in his welcome, as if to imply that although he knew Mr Chitterwick could put up a very good defence for being late, yet a real gentleman would surely have done something about it with the train.

Mr Chitterwick was a shy man. The thought of descending those noble stairs to a room full of strangers was an unhappy one. As he plucked for the last time at his tie and applied the final and unnecessary touch of the brush to his thinning hair, he wished violently that he had not come. He was a quiet man, contented enough really with his aunt, his criminology, and his stamp collection, and to go a-visiting did not come naturally to him. Still, come he had, and go down he must. So down he went.

The others were already waiting in the huge hall into which the staircase led, but Mr Chitterwick, descending with immense dignity and secretly wondering if his tie had retained its correct pose for the thirty yards he had already travelled, had no time to admire the groined stone roof, the mullioned windows, or even the suits of armour standing here and there against the grey stone walls; he was far too busy feverishly searching the little group at the far end for a hostess who had been at school with his mother; it is an awkward thing for a guest to select the wrong hostess at the first contact.

Fortunately his problem was solved for him. A woman in a pale pink frock, with very wavy fair hair, blue eyes, and a perfectly enchanting smile, detached herself and came across the hall to meet him, arriving with nicety as Mr Chitterwick reached the bottom step. 'Good-evening, Mr Chitterwick,' she said pleasantly, turning the smile on him to the full, so that Mr Chitterwick had a momentary illusion that this was the one moment in her life for which the lady had been waiting and that it came even beyond her expectation. 'So sorry I wasn't here when you arrived. Awfully sporting of you to come and risk a lot of strangers. Strangers are such a toss-up, aren't they? Come along and have a cocktail.'

Mr Chitterwick, beaming vaguely, went along to have a cocktail, filled with a great wonder. This woman had been at school with his mother, so that putting it at its lowest she must have been sixty if a day; and yet she did not look a minute over thirty-two, and not really that. Marvellous are the ways of the English judicial systems, and marvellous are the ways of the British police force, but far, far more marvellous still are the ways of women.

And then Mr Chitterwick saw the foolish mistake he had been making. Obviously this was not, could not possibly be Lady Milborne. It was her daughter. Dear, dear.

'It was very kind,' murmured Mr Chitterwick politely, 'of your mother to ask me, Lady – Lady – er – Lady...' His politeness trailed off into deprecatory blushes as he realized that he did not know the daughter's name.

The daughter paused in her progress across the hall to glance back at Mr Chitterwick in some bewilderment, causing his blush to deepen. Then an unmistakable giggle escaped from her, she whisked round again, and continued her path rather more quickly than before. Wondering fearfully what horrible solecism he must have committed, Mr Chitterwick ambled unhappily after her.

The small group gathered about a little table by a large leather settee consisted of a tall man aged somewhere between forty-five and fifty, with a greying moustache and very piercing grey eyes which looked at Mr Chitterwick from under shaggy grey brows; a young man, not much more than five-and-twenty, short but sturdily built, with the same blue eyes as those of the woman in the pink frock, and the same rather mischievous twinkle in them, too; an elderly lady, tall and erect, with white hair and rather a sad expression, and lastly a still taller girl, about twenty-eight years old (whose appearance seemed vaguely familiar to him, though he could not quite place it), with black hair, an oval face very delicately featured, quite huge brown eyes, and an air of dignified aloofness which at once struck alarm into Mr Chitterwick's soul. Mr Chitterwick, not really at his ease with anything feminine, was particularly alarmed by tall young women with airs of dignified aloofness. He began to wish quite intensely that he had not come.

'This is Mr Chitterwick, everybody,' announced the pink lady (? daughter) cheerfully. 'So now,' she added without truth, 'you all know each other.'

A subdued murmur from four throats acknowledged acquaintanceship with Mr Chitterwick.

It must not be supposed that Mr Chitterwick had thus examined, with the cool unemotionalism of the professional detective, the characteristics of the five persons with whom he now found himself in contact, even to noting the colours of their eyes. To him they were merely five blurs. Short pink blur, (?) daughter of house; tall grey and black blur, (?) host; tall black and silver elderly feminine blur, no doubt hostess; still taller flame-coloured blur, unknown and unco-ordinated female of terrifying aspect, and so on. By and by, no doubt, when Mr Chitterwick's initial alarm had worn off, their outlines would become clearer; in the meantime he accepted with gratitude an amber-coloured cocktail from the hand of the pink blur and hastily drowned his lack of ease in its depths. Almost immediately afterward, to his relief, dinner was announced. No one took anybody in; they trooped up four steps at the end of the hall into a large panelled dining room, and Mr Chitterwick was bidden by the pink blur into a seat. To his secret sorrow he found himself sitting next to the flame-coloured blur.

During the pause while table napkins were unfolded Mr Chitterwick had to readjust his ideas. The tall grey-and-black male must be Lord Milborne because he was seated at the head of the table, but the white-haired black-and-silver feminine blur could not after all be Lady Milborne because she was not at the foot; on Mr Chitterwick's left there sat instead the welcoming pink blur. It was all very confusing.

Then Lord Milborne addressed the pink blur down the table as 'Agatha,' and to prove he had made no mistake the young male blur sitting opposite Mr Chitterwick on her left did so too. This then must beyond doubt be Lady Milborne, who had been at school with his mother. Well, all Mr Chitterwick could say was that she did not look her sixty years.

To the polite queries she put to him about his journey down Mr Chitterwick's replies were a little jerky.

By degrees, as the excellent sherry (a wine to which Mr Chitterwick was particularly drawn) aided the cocktail in getting to work, Mr Chitterwick found himself able to reduce the blurs to firmer outlines, and even to fit names to the results. Lord Milborne, for instance, was George; the young male blur was Mouse; Mr Chitterwick's flame-coloured neighbour was Judy, and the black-and-silver lady was Mrs Relph to all the rest of the party and Aunt Mary to the flame-coloured young woman (another aunt, thought Mr Chitterwick feelingly; really, the world seems full of aunts). But of other surnames there was no sign.

To his relief, as dinner proceeded, the flame-coloured girl showed no sign of anxiety to engage Mr Chitterwick in conversation; in point of fact, she preserved her aloofness in his respect very nearly to the verge of discourtesy, though Mr Chitterwick was far too grateful to recognize any such possibility. To a few tentative observations, forced out of him by mere politeness, she replied kindly but briefly, and without in so many words informing Mr Chitterwick that she considered him as rather less than a worm under her feet, she nevertheless quite competently conveyed that impression. To Mr Chitterwick's diffident suggestion that they had met somewhere before she was uninterestedly certain that they had not. Conventional requirements satisfied, Mr Chitterwick was able to turn to his vivacious and astonishingly youthful hostess.

'It was a great surprise to me, Lady Milborne,' he observed, thinking to be delicately complimentary, 'to learn that you were at school with my mother.'

'Was it, Mr Chitterwick?' she said, with what struck Mr Chitterwick as a slightly cautious air, though her blue eyes continued to twinkle. 'Why? After all, your mother must have been at school with quite a number of people.'

'Oh, yes,' agreed Mr Chitterwick, a little disconcerted. 'Quite. Of course. Let me see now, which school was it? She was at two or three if I remember rightly.'

The lady opened her mouth to reply and then turned suddenly to her other neighbour. 'What did you say, Mouse?'

'Nothing. I was listening, that's all.'

'Oh. I thought you said something.'

'No, it was Mr Chitterwick who spoke. He asked you which school you met his mother at.'

'I know that. I was just going to – '

'Mr Chitterwick!'

To his surprise Mr Chitterwick found it was his flame-coloured neighbour who had addressed him, in a not unperemptory tone. He hastily slewed himself about to attend to this phenomenon.

'Was it raining when you left London?'

Mr Chitterwick assured her that it was not raining. She seemed relieved.

Mr Chitterwick turned back to his hostess. 'My aunt remembers you quite well. You remember her, of course?'

'Oh, yes,' agreed Lady Milborne with enthusiasm. 'Of course I do. A dear old lady.'

'Well, she wouldn't have been so very old *then*, would she?' suggested Mr Chitterwick dubiously, thinking that it must have been at least five-and-forty years since the two had met.

'Oh, not so old as she is now, of course. But – well, getting on, you know. I mean, she seemed old to me, even then. But of course – '

'Mr Chitterwick!'

Once again it was the flame-coloured girl, and she spoke even more urgently than before. Mr Chitterwick welcomed these signs of friendliness in one so apparently so inhuman. 'Yes?' he beamed.

'Did you go to the Chelsea flower show this year?'

As a keen member of the Royal Horticultural Society Mr Chitterwick most certainly had been to the Chelsea flower show. He said so, with emphasis. The flame-coloured girl had not been, and it seemed that she too was an enthusiastic horticulturist. She was perhaps a little vague as to what branch of the art interested her particularly, but Mr Chitterwick gathered that she was catholic in her horticultural tastes. Moreover, he found himself required to describe this year's show to her, not merely tent by tent or stand by stand, but almost flower by flower. The flame-coloured girl without a doubt must be one of the world's most enthusiastic gardeners. Delighted to have found this common ground on which he could meet this alarming young woman with practically no fear at all, Mr Chitterwick embarked on a one-man dissertation with all the zest of a hobbyist whose hobbies are his life. Whenever he showed signs of flagging his fellow enthusiast would revive him again with some such remark as 'But what about the cinerarias?' or 'You haven't told me about the *coboea scandens* yet.' The dissertation, in consequence, was still in progress when Lady Milborne rose at the end of dinner.

For twenty minutes Mr Chitterwick sipped his port and listened to a desultory conversation between the other two men about how many eggs old Tom had put down last year, and how many brace old Bob had bagged when he went over to old Bill's, and other such abstruse mysteries. It was good port, very good port ('87, fancied Mr Chitterwick, who imagined himself able to tell one port from another), but he had remembered that he had completely forgotten to tell the flame-coloured girl about the *crapula bulbosa* in Messrs Watnot's display, and even the port could not allay his anxiety to retrieve this omission. When at last his host led the way to the drawing room Mr Chitterwick followed with an eager alacrity that he had never before experienced at this difficult stage of the evening's proceedings.

The flame-coloured girl was sitting alone on a settee close to a big open French window leading onto a stone-flagged terrace outside, and it seemed to Mr Chitterwick that she had been awaiting him. He plumped down beside her and continued the dissertation exactly where it had been broken off.

'Perfectly im-*mense* blooms,' he twittered happily. 'Bright scarlet, with a – '

'Let's go out in the garden,' remarked the flame-coloured girl abruptly, and promptly rose. Mr Chitterwick rose too, somewhat surprised. 'There are some very fine *crapula* in one of the hothouses here,' the girl threw back over her shoulders, as if by way of an afterthought. 'You'd like to see them.' She led the way with decision out onto the terrace.

Mr Chitterwick followed her, his alarm, temporarily allayed, sweeping back over him in waves. He felt like a small child being taken out for an airing by his nurse.

Not even bothering to let Mr Chitterwick get level with her the girl led him down the terrace, across a lawn, through a shrubbery, and finally, not into a hothouse at all, but into a small pseudo-Greek stone temple overlooking a wooded lake. It was a charming scene, with the setting July sun reddening the water to a dull glow, but Mr Chitterwick was far too perturbed to pay attention to it. Why had this masterful young woman, who had seemed at one moment to despise him as something a little worse than dirt and at another to tolerate him for his interest in a common hobby, brought him to this deserted spot? It was hardly necessary to sit in a pseudo-Greek temple overlooking a lake nearly half a mile from the house to discuss adequately the merits of *crapula bulbosa.* Why? The obvious suggestion which would have occurred to one less modest than Mr Chitterwick he had dismissed before he ever even thought of it at all.

His companion proceeded to explain herself. 'Mr Chitterwick,' she said, standing in the entrance to the temple and looking him full in the face, 'Lady Milborne never introduced us properly. I don't think you know my name, do you?'

'Well, no,' mumbled Mr Chitterwick apologetically. 'That is – well, no I'm afraid... But I did fancy, you know, that we had – '

'It is Sinclair. I am Mrs Sinclair. The Major Sinclair, who was arrested last month for the supposed murder of Miss Sinclair, his aunt, is my husband.'

chapter six

Improper Treatment of a Witness

The pseudo-Greek temple was a hexagonal affair with a wide entrance overlooking the lake; round the inside ran a deep stone seat. Mr Chitterwick moved from the entrance to the seat. He was not sure if his knees would hold him up if he tried to stand any longer.

Wild thoughts chased one another through his mind.

No doubt the lake was very deep; Mrs Sinclair was at least an inch taller than himself; probably, in these days of athletic womanhood, she was considerably stronger; had she brought him here to throw him into the deepest place and so rid her husband of the witness on whom the prosecution's whole case depended? Forcibly Moresby's words recurred to him: without his own evidence the man would almost certainly get off. And Moresby had said too that Mrs Sinclair was a singularly determined woman. Really, if she believed that there was no other way, a singularly determined woman would hardly hesitate...

Mr Chitterwick, meditating panic-stricken flight back to the house and safety, looked at the doorway; but Mrs Sinclair, who was now gazing abstractedly out over the lake, blocked the path.

Mr Chitterwick's alarm deepened. They must all be in the plot! They knew that Mrs Sinclair *was* Mrs Sinclair, and they had inveigled... No wonder that woman looked as if she had never been at school with his mother! And if Mrs Sinclair failed to throw him into the lake, there were those two men... And they would all combine to swear he had never been near the place. No doubt even the servants had been bribed...

Mr Chitterwick forgot his alarm of Mrs Sinclair individually in his alarm of the whole situation. He jumped to his feet. 'This is a conspiracy,' he squeaked. 'I have been inveigled... This is... I am going back to London this minute.'

Mrs Sinclair looked at him calmly. 'Not quite this minute, Mr Chitterwick, please,' she said in even tones. 'I want to have just a little talk with you first.' And she moved, as if unconsciously, into the very centre of the entrance. A tragedy queen.

Mr Chitterwick could not get out without using physical force, and of the outcome of that he felt decidedly dubious. He hesitated.

'You're quite right,' the girl took the opportunity to continue, but still speaking in the same unhurried way. 'It *was* a conspiracy. For the sole purpose of providing an opportunity for this talk. As you must have gathered, Agatha Milborne was never at school with your mother at all. But we felt – I felt, that it would be impossible in any other conditions to induce you to listen to what I want to say; so I persuaded her, and the others, to stage this little deception.'

'It was outrageous!' spluttered Mr Chitterwick, filled now with righteous if nervous anger. 'I cannot listen to you. It was unpardonable.'

'Quite,' agreed the lady, unperturbed. 'But in a matter of life and death one really can't bother too much about the niceties. You're quite justified in being angry, Mr Chitterwick, but please try to realize the position I'm in and forgive my rather drastic methods.' She smiled faintly.

In Mr Chitterwick anger was now slowly giving way to uneasiness. Undoubtedly one must forgive some small subterfuge on Mrs Sinclair's part considering, as she reminded him, that her husband's life might, in her opinion, depend on this interview which she had schemed to get. That, now that one was beginning to see things in perspective, was after all a small matter. It was the interview itself that was making Mr Chitterwick uneasy. She would want to discuss the case with him, and there was nobody with whom Mr Chitterwick wished to discuss the case less than Major Sinclair's wife.

He shuffled his feet and rubbed his small, plump hands unhappily together. 'Quite so,' he mumbled. 'Yes, of course; I quite see that. But really, I am afraid no useful purpose could be served by – '

'Come and sit down, Mr Chitterwick,' ordered Mrs Sinclair calmly, fulfilling that gentleman's forebodings. 'I want to talk things over with you.' As if sure now of her ground she left her post of vantage by the door and seated herself on the stone bench.

Mr Chitterwick, so far as physical force was concerned, was free to go. But to go was the last thing in the world of which he was capable, much as he longed to do so. Judith Sinclair dominated him, and she knew it.

With lingering reluctance he sat down a little way away from her and stared out toward the lake. His instincts of alarm on first viewing this young woman had not been misplaced. In spite of himself he felt like clay for her to mould as she would. If he had been a dog he would have lain abjectly on his back and offered his tummy to her foot, not through affection (not by any means), but in token of sheer submission. Not being a dog, he continued to sit on the stone seat and feign an intense interest in the sunset.

Mrs Sinclair began to address him with an easy assurance that showed, not only that she knew herself quite well to be mistress of the situation, but that she was thoroughly accustomed to that position. Mr Chitterwick gathered that there were few situations encountered by Judith Sinclair which did not at once acknowledge her mastery.

'Mr Chitterwick, you have been making a very terrible mistake.'

Have I? thought Mr Chitterwick mutinously. Rats!

'You don't know my husband, of course, but I do, and I can assure you that he could not possibly be guilty of this awful crime.'

My good madam, thought Mr Chitterwick to the sunset, your husband is a thorough-paced scoundrel, and the sooner you realize the fact the better.

'I know you were quite honest in your identification of him as the man you saw with Miss Sinclair in the Piccadilly Palace – '

Thank you very much, thought Mr Chitterwick without gratitude.

' – but you must believe me that, somehow or other, you were wrong. Terribly wrong!'

Indeed, observed Mr Chitterwick silently to the lake, I shall do nothing of the sort.

'I'm not trying to influence you in any way – '

Ho!

' – or induce you to act against your conscience – '

Ha!

' – but you really must examine the possibility that you have, as I say, been making this dreadful mistake (quite unwittingly, of course) and take some steps to remedy it before it's too late.'

Had the lady been not quite what she was, had she been rather more pathetic than confident, more appealing than alarming, had she even been the pink-frocked little Lady Milborne herself, it is probable that Mr Chitterwick would have recognized that however reprehensible her methods she was at any rate fighting, according to her lights, for her husband's life and deserved at least that amount of consideration. But decidedly she was not pathetic, nor appealing, nor anything remotely resembling Lady Milborne, and the assumption Mr Chitterwick sensed in her that he, Ambrose Chitterwick, was not merely a worm but an idiotic worm, a fatuous worm, an almost completely imbecile worm, and it is an uphill task trying to make a demented worm see plain reason...well, the truth was that Mr Chitterwick was suffering from a bad attack of inferiority complex, and the result was to make him uncomfortable, suspicious, and sullen.

'I'm afraid there is no use in continuing this discussion,' observed Mr Chitterwick sullenly to the doorway.

Mrs Sinclair sighed, almost inaudibly but not quite. Evidently it was proving to be a worse job than she had expected, to make an idiot worm understand simple justice. 'We all make mistakes,' she said kindly, and went on to say a good many more things, all couched in terms to suit a puerile intelligence.

Mr Chitterwick stared with hot eyes over the darkening landscape as the one-sided argument went on. He was embarrassed, he was sulky, he longed for the interview to terminate. Deliberately he shut his ears to what she was saying. It would do no good to listen, it might do harm. If this woman thought that she could argue him out of his bare duty, frighten him with the bogey of responsibility into letting a heartless murderer escape his just deserts – well, she had picked on the wrong man. It was an abominable situation, and though Mr Chitterwick was constrained to lend his bodily presence to it, at any rate, he would lend nothing else.

'There must be a likeness, of course, between my husband and this other man, because I know you're not the only witness to the identification, but with your evidence about this man actually in the act of poisoning Miss Sinclair it's evidently on you that the prosecution will rely. Now, I see you wear glasses, Mr Chitterwick, and you must admit that at a distance of nearly thirty feet it is quite possible that...

It is not easy deliberately to shut one's ears to an earnest voice. Mr Chitterwick had recourse to his old friend.

'*It was the schooner* Hesperus, *that sailed...*'

Slowly Mr Chitterwick's sullenness subsided; slowly his alarm was stilled beneath the soporific beauty of the lines; slowly the skipper's little daughter turned him into his own man again.

'*The lantern gleamed through the gleaming snow on his fixed and glassy eyes...*'

And when he had come to the end he would rise firmly to his feet, terminate the interview, and escort his companion back to the house. He would!

'*Christ save us all from a death like this...*' recited Mr Chitterwick appropriately, and promptly did rise to his feet.

'I'm afraid I cannot listen any longer,' he said, with the utmost firmness. 'It is quite impossible. Shall we go back to the house?'

Mrs Sinclair rose also, somewhat dubiously. 'Well, will you at any rate do that, Mr Chitterwick?'

'I'm sorry,' responded Mr Chitterwick, 'but I regret that I can do nothing at all.'

It was dark now, and Mr Chitterwick was glad of it. The walk back to the house was performed in complete silence, and with every step Mr Chitterwick found the soothing calm induced by Mr Longfellow growing more and more faint. Somehow Judith Sinclair contrived to be far more alarming in her dignified silence of disappointment than in argument. Although Mr Chitterwick was not in the least anxious to renew acquaintance with the other members of the plot, it was with immense relief that he followed his companion in at the drawing-room window.

Only Lady Milborne and the elderly black-and-silver lady were in evidence, and if any sign passed between the former and Judith, Mr Chitterwick did not notice it. No reference was made to the thing which must have been uppermost in the minds of all four, and only a few general remarks passed about the beauty of the evening and the charm of the lake by moonlight. Mrs Sinclair dropped into a chair and picked up a magazine; her aunt continued to sit placidly, Mr Chitterwick hovered in uncertainty.

Lady Milborne jumped up. 'The men are in the library, I think, Mr Chitterwick. You'd like to join them, of course. I'll show you the way.'

Mr Chitterwick gathered that he was being got rid of so that the other two could learn what had happened at the interview, but he was not sorry; the atmosphere in the drawing room, to his sensitive perceptions, was distinctly tense. He hurried to open the door for Lady Milborne, and followed her out of the room.

She led him down a stone passage, across the big hall, down another passage, and into a small room which, whatever it might be, was certainly not the library. As certainly it was a feminine room.

'This is a little den of mine,' she smiled, 'where I do the flowers and make as much mess as I like. You don't mind my bringing you here, do you? I wanted to have a word with you before we went to the library.'

'Oh, yes?' said Mr Chitterwick uncomfortably.

'I wanted to apologize for the way I deceived you, pretending I was at school with your mother. But I was simply desperately anxious to get you down here, and I knew you wouldn't come if you guessed anything. You see, Judy is one of my very closest friends. You do forgive me, don't you?' And she smiled at Mr Chitterwick with her head a little on one side and an air of charming penitence that no male being could possibly have resisted.

'Of course, of course. Quite understandable,' beamed Mr Chitterwick.

'And of course we know Lynn, her husband, simply terribly well. Mr Chitterwick, you can't really think it was him you saw with Miss Sinclair in the Piccadilly Palace? I mean, not *really?*'

'I'm afraid there can be no doubt of it,' said Mr Chitterwick soberly.

'But Lynn couldn't do a thing like that not, even if he wanted to. He's the dearest thing, really. Mr Chitterwick, there's a terrible muddle somewhere in this business. There must be!' And Lady Milborne went on to enlarge on this theme very earnestly indeed, pleading for her friend as whole-heartedly as if for herself.

Mr Chitterwick was touched but, as he asked her, what could he do?

'You must take back that evidence about the identification,' replied Lady Milborne promptly. 'It couldn't have been Lynn you saw, so it must have been someone else, mustn't it? You must see that it would be too awful if Lynn were hanged when really he's as innocent as you or I.'

It was not an easy task to assure her that there could be no mistake, that undoubtedly Lynn was guilty, and that Mr Chitterwick could not retract or alter his evidence by one jot. It was not easy, but Mr Chitterwick got through it somehow, feeling this time every kind of inhuman brute there is; and it was a subdued Lady Milborne who led him a few minutes later down another stone passage to the library, where she left him with a muttered word to her husband.

Lord Milborne was alone. He gave Mr Chitterwick a cigar, offered him a whisky-and-soda, put him into the most comfortable chair in the room, and then began on him.

'Glad that boy's not here for the moment. I wanted a word with you alone, Chitterwick.'

'Oh, yes?' said Mr Chitterwick, still more uncomfortably.

'Judy Sinclair's had a talk with you, hasn't she? You must forgive our deception to get you down here, by the way. All in a good cause, you know.'

'Oh, yes; quite; of course,' muttered Mr Chitterwick.

'Well, all this nonsense about Lynn Sinclair poisoning his aunt, eh?' Lord Milborne pulled at his greying moustache and looked almost as uncomfortable as Mr Chitterwick. 'All rot, of course. Known the feller since he was so high. Wouldn't hurt a fly. Nasty mix-up somewhere.' The imputation that Mr Chitterwick was responsible for the nasty mix-up was obvious.

The culprit moved uneasily in his chair. 'But – I saw him do it, you know.'

'Nonsense! My dear chap, I know you're perfectly sincere and all that, but you're wrong. It's clear enough you saw someone with Miss Sinclair, but it wasn't Lynn. Couldn't have been.'

'I'm afraid there can be no mistake,' muttered Mr Chitterwick miserably. 'I recognized him instantly the next time I saw him.'

'But Sinclair swears he never got to the place till nearly half-past three and never saw his aunt alive at all; and what Lynn Sinclair says is good enough for me.' Lord Milborne implied that what Major Sinclair said should also certainly be good enough for anyone else, especially one who had shamefully confessed at dinner that he neither hunted, shot, nor even fished.

'But his fingerprints were on the phial,' countered Mr Chitterwick desperately. 'One can't get over that.' He did not want to argue the case in the least, but presumably one owes certain duties to one's host.

'Coincidence,' retorted Lord Milborne robustly. 'Lynn's solicitor isn't bothering too much about that. It's your evidence about seeing the feller actually putting the stuff in Miss Sinclair's cup, and this idea you've got that it was Sinclair himself – that's the snag we're up against. I'd hoped Judy might have shown you that you must be wrong.' This time the implication was that anyone with the least pretensions to being a gentleman, even one who neither hunted, shot, nor even fished, would at least remove any snags in the path of a lady.

'I'd much rather not discuss it, really,' almost begged Mr Chitterwick. 'My position is intensely distasteful to me; I would have given anything to avoid it; but as things are I must tell the truth as I believe – as I *know* it to be. I'm sure it would have avoided much embarrassment and unhappiness if I had not been inveig – invited down here at all. I realize, of course, that there was no intention of attempting to tamper with justice, but my position here is quite impossible and, if you will excuse me, I propose to return to London first thing tomorrow morning.' Mr Chitterwick spoke from his heart and therefore a good deal more firmly than he felt.

Lord Milborne eyed him with dubious disappointment, pulling at his moustache and obviously uncertain what to do next. 'Of course, if you feel like that…' He seemed to arrive at a decision. 'Well, we'll say no more about it. Naturally Sinclair doesn't mean as much to you as he does to us. Play billiards?'

'Well, in a way,' said Mr Chitterwick humbly. 'But – '

'My wife's brother thought you might like a game. I believe he's waiting in the billiard room. I'll take you along.'

Once more Mr Chitterwick was shepherded down stone passages and passed from one keeper to another. But this time, as the older shepherd handed him over to the younger, Mr Chitterwick did see a distinct sign pass between the two – a raising of eyebrows from the latter, and a shake of the head and shrug of the shoulders from the former. It is well known that women are more subtle than men.

As the door closed behind Lord Milborne, Mr Chitterwick's heart, which he had already thought to be in his shoes, sank to somewhere below the floor. It was quite obvious what was being done with him; he was being passed from one to another in the hope that where others had failed the next might succeed. After this young man had dealt with him presumably he would be handed on to the black-and-silver lady, and after her – well, there seemed no reason why the dome-like butler should not be called in to have a try. To tell the truth, Mr Chitterwick felt that the butler stood the best chance of the lot; he simply would not have the moral courage to stand out against him for long.

The information that the young man, still known to Mr Chitterwick only as Mouse, was the brother of his hostess and that the last piece of the social jigsaw had been fitted into place did not console him for the forthcoming interview at all.

The preliminaries were settled with great heartiness on the part of the young man and something approaching moroseness on that of Mr Chitterwick, who, in his agitation, miscued his opening and allowed his opponent to run off a break to twenty-six.

'I'm afraid you're too good for me,' said Mr Chitterwick, and missed a simple cannon.

'Not a bit,' said the young man, with obvious untruth, and went on to compile a break of thirty-four.

The game ended a few minutes later. Scores:

Mouse	100
Mr Ambrose Chitterwick	3

'You *were* too good for me,' fluttered Mr Chitterwick, seeking to put off the unwelcome moment and not despising the use of self-evident truths in doing so. 'Er – no doubt you play a lot?'

'Quite a fair amount,' agreed the other, putting the cues back in their rack. 'I say, this is all rot about you making out that Lynn Sinclair, Major Sinclair, poisoned his aunt, isn't it? You're not really serious, surely?'

Mr Chitterwick groaned.

The interview proceeded on the stereotyped lines.

When Mr Chitterwick had at last succeeded in putting an end to it (the young man was more tenacious than any except Mrs Sinclair) he announced his intention of going to bed. It was not yet half-past ten, but only in his bedroom, with the door locked, did Mr Chitterwick feel that he would be safe from the black-and-silver lady; and the thought of another interview made him almost hysterical.

Without going back to the drawing room, or saying goodnight to anyone but the chastened Mouse, he slunk upstairs.

Of one thing Mr Chitterwick was not sorry. His room seemed to be well away from those of the rest of the party. It was down a little corridor all to itself in the east wing, which was otherwise empty; the others, so far as Mr Chitterwick could gather, were all in the main part of the building. If, therefore, his nerves should so far give way in the night as to cause him to scream violently, there was little chance of his being overheard.

It was a nice room, and Mr Chitterwick locked himself into it gratefully. Not being in the main building, it was not so old as the rest, a mere sixteenth-century room instead of thirteenth; but there was a nice open fireplace, plenty of oak beams, and two latticed windows with deep window seats overlooking the grounds. It was a big room, and its low ceiling made it look larger still. In other circumstances Mr Chitterwick could have spent a very pleasant week in it.

He undressed and got into bed.

Of course he could not sleep. Things had been far too agitating. But a copy of the latest psychological novel (after he had read through the first two pages four times in an effort (*a*) to concentrate, (*b*) to make out what it was about, (*c*) and why) worked wonders. By the end of the first chapter he was definitely soothed; by the end of the second things had fallen into their proper perspective; by the end of the third he was really sleepy; at the end of the fourth, at half-past eleven, he put out the reading lamp by his bed. By a quarter to twelve, with the aid of Mr Longfellow to prevent his mind going over and over again the events of the evening, he was sound asleep.

It seemed to Mr Chitterwick when he woke up that he had been asleep a very long time. He did not wake somnolently and lazily as one does in the morning, but suddenly. One moment he was asleep, the next he was awake – and afraid. He did not know what had wakened him, but whatever it was there was an ominous feel about it; and he was almost sure there was someone, or something, in the room. Mr Chitterwick was not a nervous man, or a superstitious; but the house was very old, he knew for certain that he had locked the door, and yet he was convinced...

Mr Chitterwick might not have been morally the bravest of men, but to this occasion he certainly rose, both literally and metaphorically. Without even a moment's cowering under the bedclothes he sat bolt upright and switched on the lamp. He was perfectly right; there *was* someone in the room, and it was Judith Sinclair.

They faced each other; Mr Chitterwick sitting up like an Epstein statue, his face very flushed and his rather scanty hair at all angles (and, shameful disobedience, uncovered by any nightcap); Judith Sinclair, tall and dark and beautiful and slim, in a pale-blue silk wrapper. It was an interesting situation, and Mr Chitterwick's aunt would have been surprised at it. His aunt had a poor opinion of Mr Chitterwick in more ways than one.

Mr Chitterwick's first words were somewhat of an anticlimax. 'How – how d-did you get in?' he gasped.

'There's a door to the next room at the back of that cupboard,' replied Mrs Sinclair in a low, toneless voice. She paused for a moment, then began to speak in hurried, urgent tones, jerking her words out and nervously plucking at the lace on her bosom. 'Mr Chitterwick, they told me you're leaving first thing tomorrow. I couldn't let you go without... I had to see you again. Mr Chitterwick, let me implore you. You hold my husband's life in your hands. I'll do anything to redeem it – anything. Because he's innocent. I know he's innocent. You don't know him. I do. He's the most upright, honourable man I've ever known. He couldn't have done this terrible thing. It's impossible. If you kill him you kill me too. He's everything to me – everything. You can't go into court and swear his life away. I'll do anything in the world to save him. I mean it. Mr Chitterwick!' To Mr Chitterwick's dismay she fell on her knees by his side and seized one of his hands in hers.

For a moment or two Mr Chitterwick was speechless, in sheer, choking consternation. This was a very different Mrs Sinclair from the collected, consciously superior young person of the pseudo-Greek temple, and infinitely more alarming. This was a desperate woman, the mask off, the veil of convention thrown aside; no tragedy queen, but a distracted wife employing in despair the only resources left to her. And Mr Chitterwick had no experience in dealing with desperate women.

They gazed at each other in silence, Mr Chitterwick's eyes round with dismay, Judith Sinclair's swimming with tragic entreaty. Her wrapper had fallen away from one bare shoulder, and through the thin silk of her nightdress her skin showed white; her hands clasped Mr Chitterwick's in a feverish grasp.

When at last Mr Chitterwick did speak he failed lamentably to cope with the situation. 'Mrs Sinclair, isn't – isn't this rather – rather imprudent?' he stammered. 'I – I could see you in the morning before I go. I mean, if – if anyone heard you...'

The lady spoke scornfully. 'Oh, what does anything like that matter? Not that anyone will hear us. But this is a thing of life and death. I'm here to save my husband's life, and I can't help who knows it. Mr Chitterwick, I'm on my knees to you.'

'Please – please get up,' begged Mr Chitterwick, in high embarrassment.

Bed is not a good place from which to conduct an interview, if one happens to be a man. A woman in bed is not only decorative but at home. A man is at a complete disadvantage. He is not decorative, and he knows it, and his morale is at its lowest. If this interview was to be prolonged (and it looked distressingly probable) Mr Chitterwick badly wanted the moral as well as the physical support of his own feet, to say nothing of a dressing gown, to help him with his share of it; but he could see no chance of achieving it.

A certain measure of relief was accorded him, however, for Judith Sinclair did rise from her knees, though only to stand over him and continue her entreaties, her hands clasped tensely.

'I don't want you just to take my word for it that my husband's innocent, Mr Chitterwick. That would be unreasonable, I know. All I want you to do is simply to recognize that you might have been making a mistake and take some steps to prove it. That's all. It isn't much to ask, surely. And you must! In common justice. Mr Chitterwick, there's some devil going about the world who did this thing. Somebody who must be very much like Lynn. And I must find him. I must!'

'But your husband's solicitors – ' mumbled Mr Chitterwick.

'They think he's guilty. I'm sure they do. They don't say so, but I'm sure that's what they think. They say there could be nobody as like Lynn as all that, and it would be a waste of time to look. Mr Chitterwick, you hold my husband's life in your hands. You hear what I tell you about him; you've heard what the others think of him. Isn't that enough to make you doubt that a man like him could be guilty of such a mean murder? I don't want you to be dishonest or to swear to anything you don't believe. All I want is for you to save an innocent man's life by simply admitting that it is possible that you were mistaken in what you thought you saw. That would be honest enough, wouldn't it? It's so easy to make mistakes. And you can't be *quite* certain, in any case. Mr Chitterwick, that's all I want you to do. You will, won't you? And I know you wouldn't want to make a bargain with me, or – or anything like that; but if you'd just let me show my gratitude, and – and – ' She wavered into silence and stood looking at him appealingly, an attempt at a smile on her lips. Her wrapper had slipped almost to the ground by now, but she did not seem to notice.

Sheer nervousness made Mr Chitterwick perhaps brusquer than he intended, or it may be that he judged it kinder to be cruel. 'Really, Mrs Sinclair, I'm afraid I can't… The matter is out of my hands. I appreciate… Believe me, I am exceedingly sorry, but no. It's – it's out of the question.'

There was a moment's pause.

'You mean,' said the girl slowly, 'you won't do just that little thing? Not even if… That's quite final?'

'I can't,' almost bleated Mr Chitterwick. 'My dear young lady, I would if… Yes, quite final.'

There followed quite the most unhappy minute in Mr Chitterwick's life, while the girl looked at him in complete silence, her eyes full of unutterable things. Then her lower lip began to tremble, at first spasmodically and then without control. She buried her face in her hands. 'Oh, God,' she moaned, 'what am I to do? What am I to do?' The next instant she seemed to collapse onto the end of Mr Chitterwick's bed, and her body shook with sobs. She wept quietly but hopelessly, as if, having nerved herself to stake everything on the last throw, she had lost and now had nothing left.

Mr Chitterwick gazed at her in frozen consternation. What on earth was he to do? He had probably never seen a woman weep before except his own relations, and relations don't count. That crumpled body, its weight actually across his own feet, seemed to him quite unbearably pathetic, while the stifled sobs that issued from it distressed him almost to a similar point. There was a large lump in his throat as he crept out of bed and sought distractedly for his dressing gown. Of course, poor woman, really convinced as she was of her husband's innocence... It was too dreadful.

But having found his dressing gown and duly arrayed himself in it, what to do then? It was impossible to stand there and calmly look on. Not that Mr Chitterwick was calm or anything resembling it. As he ran his hand through his already dishevelled hair and wondered desperately what ought to be done he felt like running round the room in aimless and distracted circles. Should he go and rouse Lady Milborne and get her to take the situation in hand? Or the black-and-silver aunt? But that would be to... No. Besides, he didn't know their rooms. Then, what?

Timidly he touched one shaking shoulder. 'Please, Mrs Sinclair, don't – er – don't cry.' His tones were almost as quavery as those of the muffled voice which answered him.

'It's – it's all right. I'm s-sorry. I'll be better in a minute. Just l-leave me alone.'

But she wasn't better in a minute, and to leave her alone seemed to the conscience-stricken Mr Chitterwick just about the most heartless thing in the world. Something had got to be done, and done manfully. The room seemed to swim round him, echoing with those heart-breaking sobs. Mr Chitterwick swam with the room...

How he had managed it Mr Chitterwick never afterward knew, but when he recovered his senses it was to find himself sitting on the end of his bed and rocking the girl in his arms, while she wept on his shoulder and he promised her all sorts of impossible and utterly dishonourable things.

'Yes, my dear,' babbled Mr Chitterwick, 'I'll look into the matter. No doubt I was mistaken after all. We must try to find the man. If your husband is innocent it is bound to be established. There, there.' For the truth was that for the first time in his life Mr Chitterwick had lost his head – and let the man who has never lost his own to feminine tears utter the first snigger at him. And for the first time in his life too he had kissed a woman who was not a relation (most decidedly relations do not count), and that woman another man's wife. Mr Chitterwick's aunt *would* have been surprised.

Moreover, and as if no limit were to be set to his devilry, he went on kissing her. They were only paternal kisses, it is true, and confined to the top of her dark head, as much of one cheek as he could reach, and her right ear; but the lady seemed to find them soothing, and Mr Chitterwick himself found them by no means unpleasant.

Gradually her sobs lessened.

She sat up, rubbed her eyes with the backs of her hands, and retrieved her wrapper from the floor, whither it had finally and modestly retired, to dab her cheeks. 'I'm sorry. It was foolish of me, but for the moment everything seemed so utterly hopeless.'

'I know,' nodded Mr Chitterwick, exuding sympathy in all directions. 'I know. I know.'

'Then, Mr Chitterwick, you will? You really will?'

'I'll look into it for you, yes,' continued to nod Mr Chitterwick, with a perfectly fatuous beam. 'Depend upon it, we'll find some way of saving your husband if he's really innocent. Oh, without a doubt.'

The lady hesitated for a moment. 'Mr Chitterwick,' she said in a low voice, 'it's no good pretending to try to thank you. Perhaps you can imagine what it means to me. And – and – '

'I'll let you out by the other door,' said Mr Chitterwick hastily.

But he kissed her goodnight after helping her on with her wrapper (an avuncular kiss rather than paternal this time, perhaps), and quite right too.

chapter seven

Conversation in a Temple

Worn out with the varied emotions of the night before, Mr Chitterwick slept the next morning till an indecently late hour. To his shame he found himself easily the last down to breakfast. But this shame was rapidly dispelled, for never had Mr Chitterwick received such a welcome

Lady Milborne turned her most delightful smile on him and kept it there. Lord Milborne quite unnecessarily got up to show him which dish contained the porridge, which the kedgeree, which the eggs and bacon, and which the kidneys – a puzzle which Mr Chitterwick could quite easily have solved unaided by the simple ruse of lifting the covers and looking for himself. Mouse (surname still unknown) positively leapt up to pour out his coffee for him. The black-and-silver aunt (now a grey knitted-silk aunt) wished him good-morning in the tone of one welcoming a favourite brother back from Australia. And her niece smiled at him in silence, but such an understanding, grateful, altogether intimate smile that Mr Chitterwick's heart gave quite a little jump.

In fact, it seemed that everyone was delighted to do Mr Chitterwick honour.

Basking in this universal appreciation, and trying not to realize how little he deserved it, Mr Chitterwick made a triumphal breakfast. Nobody referred to such a thing as a train, and plans were openly discussed covering the whole week of Mr Chitterwick's invitation. Behind his beam that gentleman wondered, a little guiltily now in the broad daylight, just what version of the previous night's episode Judith Sinclair had issued for publication. He hoped that it was a prudently expurgated one.

Not until he was smoking his after-breakfast cigarette in that same little pseudo-Greek temple by the lake, whither he had succeeded in retiring alone for the purpose, did Mr Chitterwick make any real effort to estimate the position to which he had committed himself; and when he did so he found himself very uneasy indeed. Not that he actively regretted the promises he had made to Judith Sinclair. It was emotion which had brought them into being, no doubt, but they were grounded on something firmer. One argument that had been used, and one only, had impressed him. Would it be likely that a man who was held in such estimation, not only by his friends but by his own wife (thought Mr Chitterwick with unaccustomed cynicism), as was Major Sinclair should be guilty of such a particularly mean murder? Mr Chitterwick had to admit that it was not likely. For though a man may successfully deceive his friends as to his true character, it is not so easy for him to hoodwink his wife.

No, on psychological probabilities Major Sinclair had a chance.

On the other hand, on straightforward evidence he had none.

As for the extraneous evidence, that, as Moresby had explained with regard to the phial, though awkward was

111

not damning. Mr Chitterwick's evidence, however, was damning, quite damning; and abstractedly smoking his cigarette, that gentleman himself did not at all see how he was going to get round it.

The only possible way of approach to the problem (if as a problem the case was now to be treated) seemed to be temporarily to ignore that evidence altogether, assume the Major's innocence, see what new facts or fancies arose from that assumption, and then endeavour to work the awkward evidence in to corroborate them. It was a difficult way of going to work, and Mr Chitterwick had to admit that the chances of success appeared so remote as to be imperceptible; but his word had been given, and he must offer the thing a trial.

Nevertheless, his position at Riversmead Priory was going to be embarrassing. Though it was no fault of his own, that position seemed to rest at present on quite false pretences. From the way in which he had been treated at breakfast it was clear to Mr Chitterwick that it was understood not merely that he would examine the possibilities of Major Sinclair's innocence, which after all was all he had undertaken to do even at the most emotional moments of the night before, but that he would secure his life and liberty. Even, no doubt, to the extent of perjury.

Mr Chitterwick's regard for truth and honesty was wont to reach at times an almost morbid degree. He felt it would be quite impossible to stay on unless the real state of affairs was made quite clear, that he was willing only to test the case from the angle of the Major's possible innocence and, should he not be able to satisfy himself that there were any grounds to support that theory, he must revert to his previous attitude and give his evidence in the High Court with as much conviction as he had given it before the magistrates. That must be clearly understood.

But how to convey it?

He could put it to Mrs Sinclair; but though of course she would be quite sensible about it he was unwilling to do anything at the moment to dampen the spark of hope which his promises had kindled in her. He could put it to either Lady Milborne or her husband. But the former, he felt sure, would not altogether appreciate the delicacy of the situation; and the idea of making what amounted to conditions with his host for a continuance of his stay seemed tactless, to say the least. Mrs Relph, the aunt? She would understand without a doubt; but...

In the end Mr Chitterwick decided to make use of the young man they called Mouse as the most suitable channel for disseminating his decision.

It is a trite observation that to think of a thing is often to call it into being. Hardly had Mr Chitterwick arrived at this conclusion than the young man himself materialized in the entrance to the temple, a pipe in his mouth and a newspaper in his hand.

'I saw you start off in this direction and guessed you might be here,' he said with a friendly smile. 'Not butting in if I join you, am I?'

'By no means,' beamed Mr Chitterwick. 'I should be very pleased. As it happens I was thinking of coming to look for you. There is something I wanted to say.' And while the matter was fresh and clear in his own mind, he straightway put it forward.

The young man seemed endowed with understanding. 'Oh, that's all right. Of course. Couldn't expect you to do anything else. The great thing is that you'll keep an open mind for a bit, at any rate.'

'Oh, yes,' agreed Mr Chitterwick, much relieved. 'Certainly I will do that.'

'While you investigate,' said the young man called Mouse.

'Eh?' said Mr Chitterwick.

The young man blew a cloud of smoke in the direction of the entrance and watched it as it settled into thick grey folds in the still, sunshine-laden air. 'You did promise Judy to look into matters for her, didn't you?' he asked, with an air of carelessness.

'Did I? I don't... It may be. But if so it was very... Dear me.' Mr Chitterwick had only a very vague idea of what he had promised.

'So she seems to have understood,' observed the young man.

'Oh!' Mr Chitterwick contrived to look both blank and unhappy at the same moment.

Mr Chitterwick was a modest man. It is true that he had, by a simple process of putting two and two together, solved the previous year an exceptionally difficult case; but no publicity had attended that effort, for owing to lack of evidence it had been impossible to bring the criminal to justice. So that, although Mr Chitterwick had received unofficial congratulations from the chiefs of Scotland Yard, his name had not been made known to the public in that connection at all. Indeed, it had been understood that the truth must remain a secret and the case be officially written off as insoluble, so that Mr Chitterwick was even precluded from referring to it had he wished to do so.

But the point was that Mr Chitterwick's modesty prevented him from believing that any great credit was really due to himself. He had done no investigating at all. The idea of active detection, ferreting out things that people were trying to conceal, grimly following up slender clues, making a general nuisance of himself, repelled him completely. He was a quiet man and one who always tried to live at peace with his fellow beings; and no one can do that and be a detective as well. All he had done in that case was to sit tight while other and more adventurous people did the spade work of investigation, and then simply use their results to draw the correct conclusion; a procedure (thought Mr Chitterwick modestly) which might have been followed by really anyone of moderate intelligence. There was therefore no experience behind him of real detection on which to found the fulfilment of this unfortunate promise which he seemed to have made; and, as before, he simply had not the faintest idea of how to go about it.

'Dear me,' said Mr Chitterwick, harassed.

The young man gave further proof of his endowment of understanding. 'As it happens, I'd rather been trying to do something on those lines myself. At least, I went so far as to get all the facts tabulated, and so on. But after that I came to a dead end. Couldn't see how to get any farther. So if you are going to look into things, I wonder if you'd care to take me on as a sort of assistant? Join forces, in fact.'

'That would certainly be a very great help,' warmly agreed Mr Chitterwick, who found himself liking this young man more and more. 'But really… And in any case, isn't this a matter for Major Sinclair's solicitors?'

'No. They didn't tell Judy so, of course, but they gave me quite a definite hint. I'm sure they haven't the least doubt that Lynn's guilty, and they're actually frightened of employing a private detective for fear of what he might find out. They think Lynn has a sporting chance at present, in spite of your evidence, and they don't want any more awkward facts brought to light.'

'I see. And you, of course, are still more sure that Major Sinclair is innocent?'

The young man called Mouse looked a little embarrassed. 'I don't want to buck about him, Chitterwick, but Lynn really is one of the very best. Not too many brains, perhaps; Judy's got them, plenty for both. But I'd as soon believe that he'd done this thing as I would that I'd done it myself.' He went rather red.

'Then what do you believe?' asked Mr Chitterwick, with sympathy but with interest as well.

The other laughed shortly. 'Blessed if I know what to believe. Knowing Miss Sinclair, I can't credit her with suicide at all, let alone in such a place as the lounge of the Piccadilly Palace; and yet... Still, that's what we've got to try to find out, isn't it?'

It was Mr Chitterwick's turn to look embarrassed. 'Yes. Of course. No doubt. Without question I am very willing to do my best. That is, what I can. But the trouble is, you see... Well, really, detection is a specialist's work, and I have no qualifications at all.'

'Is that so?' asked the young man, and his smile was strangely confident. It was as if Mr Chitterwick had made a very subtle joke, the point of which one might well be forgiven for not seeing.

'Quite so,' replied Mr Chitterwick with much earnestness.

'Then,' said the young man, 'what about that Poisoned Chocolates case, as the papers called it?'

'Eh?' said Mr Chitterwick.

'I know all about that.'

'You – you do? Er – how?'

'The son of the assistant commissioner happens to be rather a friend of mine.'

'Oh!' said Mr Chitterwick.

'So I don't think we'll bother about lack of qualifications.'

'No, but really,' said Mr Chitterwick, and tried very hard to explain how he had not solved that case at all but simply allowed it to solve itself.

'Pooh!' said the young man, or made noises to that effect.

Before he realized how it had happened Mr Chitterwick found the partnership fully established, with himself in the rôle of governing director.

'Very well,' sighed Mr Chitterwick, accepting the inevitable. 'You may assure Mrs Sinclair at least that I shall do all I can, little though it may prove to be, Mr — I'm really very sorry, but I haven't discovered your name.'

'Oh, call me Mouse,' said the young man carelessly. 'Everyone does.'

They proceeded to get down to the case.

It was the matter of Major Sinclair's alibi that interested Mr Chitterwick chiefly in the new circumstances. If that could be substantiated to cover the time right up to half-past three, of course the Major was proved innocent, whatever might be the real truth of the mystery. Unfortunately, however, he had been unable to produce a single witness in support of it.

According to his own account the Major had lunched at his club, the Rainbow, in Piccadilly. At about a quarter-past two, when he had finished lunch, he was called to the telephone. So much was not in question. The person at the other end of the line announced himself as one Eccles, a man who had been up at Oxford with him. Major Sinclair was surprised. Although they had gone up to the same college in the same year, he had barely known Eccles. Their interests had been completely different, and St Mary's is well known to be a cliquey college; Major Sinclair had been a member of the Bullingdom, and Eccles had been what members of the Bullingdom would have described as 'a pretty ghastly sort of feller; writes poetry, or some rot like that.'

However, the Major was no longer a member of the Bullingdom, and so was able to feign an interest in Mr Eccles and ask politely after his present circumstances. Eccles told him that it was too long a story to relate over the telephone, but what he wanted was to see the Major in person, adding mysteriously that it was the chance of a lifetime for both of them, and that if the Major missed it he would kick himself forever afterward. He refused to explain any further, saying that he would go into the whole thing when they met. Would the Major come round as soon as possible to his, Eccles' office, where they could talk in privacy?

Naturally Sinclair agreed to do so. Eccles gave him the address, adding that it was the top floor and, as he had only just taken the place, there was no name on the door. He added as if by an afterthought that he had to pop down the road to see a man first, but would almost certainly be back before Sinclair arrived; but should he be detained for a few minutes, would the latter wait. The Major gave him a few minutes to see his man and then, pleasantly curious, left his club at about half-past two.

There was no difficulty in finding the building. It was a small one in an unimportant street in the neighbourhood of Covent Garden. Sinclair climbed three flights of stone steps, which could well have done with a washing, to the top landing. This was even dirtier than the rest and showed no signs of occupation at all. There were cobwebs in the corners, but the Major, not usually a particularly observant man, noticed that the dust had been cleared away round the edges of the door and the door-frame, which pointed to the fact that it was in use. There was no other door on the top landing.

Sinclair gathered that Eccles must still be seeing his man, for there was no answer to his rings. He composed himself to wait and began to read a lunchtime edition of the *Evening Standard*, which he had fortunately bought on the way in case of such a contingency. The place had not impressed him favourably, and he was half suspecting by now that Eccles only wanted him to invest money in some wildcat scheme, or perhaps even to effect a personal loan; but he knew from experience of the offices of certain solicitors that one cannot always judge by appearances and decided to give him the benefit of the doubt and go on waiting.

He continued to give Eccles the benefit of the doubt until twenty-past three when, in view of his appointment with his aunt at the Piccadilly Palace for half-past, he could wait no longer. Asked why he had waited as long as all that, Sinclair replied that he kept thinking that Eccles must be back the next minute, and having waited so long already it seemed a pity to spoil things by not staying for another couple of minutes.

'And I don't know if you've noticed it,' observed Mouse, 'but that's just about what always does happen on those occasions.'

Mr Chitterwick agreed that he had noticed it.

Not another soul had paid a visit to the top landing while Sinclair was waiting there, nor could anyone be found who had seen him either enter the building or even on his way to it. His solicitors, whose fears regarding the employment of a private detective had not extended to an attempt to prove this alibi, had done everything possible to unearth such a person, and none could be found. On the other hand the police had discovered at once that the office in question was empty and had been for months, and that Eccles himself was in the consular service and at present stationed in the Malay States; he would not be in England till his leave became due next year.

'Um!' said Mr Chitterwick thoughtfully. 'Yes. You see, the trouble is that Major Sinclair, by leaving his club at half-past two, as he certainly did, would arrive at the Piccadilly Palace, had he gone straight there and this story were false, at exactly the time when I myself actually saw him – er – actually saw the other man arrive, about twenty minutes to three.'

'Yes, but that's the whole point. That's exactly what was intended. You see, if Lynn really is innocent, this getting him to such a place, where the chances were a million to one against anyone seeing him, was obviously very carefully planned; and the man who rung him up and said he was Eccles was the real murderer.'

'Yes, I quite see that. No doubt that is exactly what did happen. But it hasn't been possible to check that telephone message to his club, or find out where it came from?'

Mouse shook his head glumly. 'No. I thought of that myself, but apparently they keep no record of local calls; and the solicitors found out that none of the operators had listened in to any of that particular conversation. So far as I can see, the only thing we can get from that call is Lynn's description of the man's voice. He says it was low, educated, and quite pleasant, and that he spoke quite like Eccles actually used to, only more so, with a slow drawl; almost an exaggerated version of what they call the Oxford manner.'

Well, it is certainly possible to draw some deductions from that,' agreed Mr Chitterwick. 'But it doesn't lead us very far, does it?'

'Not as far as a horse could canter,' admitted his companion.

'And as a balance against the other side,' ruefully reflected Mr Chitterwick, thinking of what his own eyes had shown him, to say nothing of such other difficult matters to explain as fingerprints on phials and the like. It was not so easy to ignore these things as Mr Chitterwick had hoped.

'Oh, yes, I know what we're up against. But honestly, Chitterwick, we've simply got to do something about it. I've known Lynn for years, but apart from that Judy's one of my sister's oldest friends. Agatha would never forgive me if I didn't raise heaven and earth. I've tried them at Scotland Yard, but of course their hands are tied; it's their simple duty to prosecute. Rather awkward for the assistant commissioner in a way, because, although he didn't know Lynn personally, he knows any amount of people who do. But they've none of them any doubt there about him being guilty. Rather hellish, isn't it? I mean, for Judy. She's so damned loyal. Never doubted him for a second.' He broke off and smoked furiously, frowning out over the lake.

Once again the pendulum of Mr Chitterwick's emotions swung back. 'Hellish' was not by any means too strong a word. Without doubt something must be done for that brave woman.

'You said that Mrs Sinclair was one of your sister's oldest friends,' Mr Chitterwick hesitated.

'And mine. Known her nearly as long as I can remember. Of course, that follows. Agatha's a good bit older than me, you see.'

'Yes, quite. I mean, that being so, perhaps you could tell me something of Mrs Sinclair's marriage. I understand from the police that it is considered the Major's strongest motive for seeking his aunt's death.'

'Oh, that's nonsense. I know the idea. Miss Sinclair wanted him to marry another girl, and threatened to disinherit him and all that if he didn't. Well, she may have wanted, and she may have threatened, but I'm sure she wouldn't have done anything. Anybody round her will tell you that. She could bark like blazes – bay, if you like; but she hadn't got a bite in her. Dear old thing, really.'

'Then in that case why didn't Major Sinclair tell her of his marriage?'

'I don't altogether know. Silly of him, really. He and Judy got married rather suddenly, on the spur of the moment; passing a registry office one day and just popped inside; that sort of thing. And I imagine that he funked telling Miss Sinclair at the time and then, not having told her once, so to speak, went on not doing it. But apart from just not telling her, he made no effort to conceal the marriage from her. She could have found Judy in possession any time she'd cared to call at Queen Anne's Gate. But that was another fad of hers. She would never go even to Lynn's rooms when he was at Oxford, I've heard. Didn't believe in maiden aunts poking their noses in bachelor nephews' affairs. And,' added the young man with some feeling, 'damned sensible too.'

'Extremely sensible,' agreed Mr Chitterwick, with no less feeling.

'Mind you,' the other reverted to the more important point, 'it's only a guess of mine about Lynn funking telling her about his marriage, but I should think that's what happened. You see, Miss Sinclair always had an eye for the main chance, and poor old Judy never had a bean. Not one. And Lynn hadn't got many. So he must have known there'd be bound to be a bit of an uproar when he did break the sad news. Still, I'll ask Judy herself, if you like.'

'Perhaps it would be better. She will understand that it is not an impertinent and idle query?'

'Good heavens, yes. Judy's no fool.'

'Because I really do think,' observed Mr Chitterwick with some gravity, 'that we ought to examine the question of this marriage as closely as possible; for if we could definitely show that Major Sinclair had nothing to fear from its becoming known to his aunt, then we have spiked at all events one of the prosecution's guns.'

'I'll tell you everything I know,' said the young man promptly, 'and Agatha will be able to fill in any gaps...'

Judith Pennington (as she had been born) had had an unhappy childhood. Her father died when she was only eight years old, and her mother, an incompetent manager at the best of times, was left with only a pittance, actually insufficient to support both of them. She tried to find some work suited to her very meagre capabilities, but though she was set up from time to time by more prosperous relations in turn in a dress shop, a manicure parlour, a typewriting office, and other such ventures as her fitful enthusiasms suggested, she failed in all of them. Judith, a lonely little girl, spent most of her time waiting for her mother to come home, when not pressed into service in some business-bringing capacity, if only to look pathetic in the dress shop or carry bowls of soapy water about the manicure parlour. Finally the relations tired of seeing their good money frittered away and combined to raise Mrs Pennington's pittance by a small allowance which just allowed the two to exist in a little Kensington flat (Mrs Pennington held fast throughout her widowhood to only one principle: she could never possibly live anywhere else but in London). Judith was educated as cheaply as possible and grew up as unlike her mother as two human beings could well be.

It was in the dress shop, the first of the ventures, that Mrs Pennington's brilliant idea of utilizing her small daughter to emphasize the pathos of the situation met with its reward. The mother of Agatha and Mouse, who had known Mrs Pennington in her more socially presentable days, called at the shop as in duty bound to help an unfortunate friend, and there saw Judith, a small dark child with an air of aloof misery, sitting on a chair in an obscure corner, and was so touched that she carried her off the next week to her place in the country for a long stay. Actually the stay lengthened into two months, at the end of which Judith admitted gravely to her hostess that she had never been so happy in her life and expressed the candid hope that she might be asked to come again soon.

She was asked again soon, for the experiment had proved a success not only from Judith's point of view but from that of her hostess as well. There was such a disparity of age between her own two children (nearly seven years) that Mouse as a little boy of six was in danger of becoming a lonely child himself, with only a maturing young woman of thirteen to rely on for companionship. Judith bridged the gap. Mouse could usually be found some part in her games with Agatha, and she was quite happy to play with him alone in Agatha's absence. The result was that Judith usually spent most of the holidays with them, and both Mouse and Agatha looked on her more or less as a part-time sister; though as they grew older she gravitated naturally more toward the latter than the former.

This state of affairs pleased Mrs Pennington, who thankfully relinquished this much of her responsibility and found herself for some months of the year without any domestic tie to impede the new activity of the moment; but when she was grown up enough to realize it fully it did not please Judith at all. Having done so, at the age of nineteen, she went out one morning and got a job as mannequin in one of the big (and cheaper) London stores. She explained to her mother that she was tired of being an object of charity all round.

Mrs Pennington was shocked; not so much at the idea of her daughter being a mannequin as that she should be one in such an impossible place. Social niceties appealed very strongly to Mrs Pennington, and she could not but recognize the difference in standing between a mannequin at, say, Reville's and one at Ponsonby & Tompkins'. Judith, however, to whom practical values were more important than social, pointed out with reason that one cannot hope to join the mannequin staff at Reville's without training, whereas one could at Ponsonby & Tompkins', as witness the fact that she had just done so. And the pay was pretty good.

So for three whole years Judith continued to display frocks and coats that did not belong to her for the benefit of fat women who could not possibly wear them. Not all the time at Ponsonby & Tompkins'. Mrs Pennington was spared that enduring humiliation, at least; for although Judith never actually attained to Reville's, she did get into Piccadilly, within a few doors of that sacred temple. And the nearer to it she got, the more money she earned. Then she gave up being a mannequin altogether and went on the stage. Contrary to the usual prophecies, she did very well there.

During this time the visits to Mousc and Agatha, though much curtailed, did not cease altogether. At first Judith often went down for weekends when they were in the country, and she generally spent Christmas and a good part of her annual holiday there. Changes occurred in course of time. When she was twenty-three Agatha married, and three years later Mrs Pennington died. Judith moved from the flat in Kensington to a smaller one in a more expensive neighbourhood and went to stay with Agatha at Riversmead instead of to Agatha's mother in Warwickshire. She now had the hundred a year which had been her mother's own income, and wrote very charmingly to the relations who had made up the balance thanking them for what they had done for her mother and gratefully refusing in advance a similar favour for herself. Independence had become almost a fetish with her. Besides, she was earning better money now on the stage than ever and could afford it.

It was when staying at Riversmead that she met Major Sinclair, who was staying with his aunt at Earlshaze, twenty miles away. They fell in love almost immediately, and after taking a year to make quite certain that Sinclair wanted to marry her because he loved her and not because he was sorry for her, she promised to do so. Whereupon Sinclair, a man of action, who had thoughtfully provided himself some months ago with a licence in view of such a possibility, bundled her then and there into a taxi, drove to the registrar's, and married her out of hand before she could change her mind. That was four years ago...

And that was really all Mouse knew about it.

'I see.' Mr Chitterwick thanked him. 'But even that doesn't throw any further light on their reasons for keeping it from Miss Sinclair, does it? No doubt it is as you imagine, but I think it would be better, if she would really have no objection, for me to ask Mrs Sinclair one or two questions myself.'

'Of course,' said Mouse, relighting his pipe. 'I'll warn her. She'll be only too glad. Show her that you're taking the thing up properly, too.'

'Does she – does she know my connection with – er – that other case?' asked Mr Chitterwick diffidently.

It seemed that she did not; it had been told to Mouse in confidence. 'But of course the police will pay tremendous attention to what you tell them,' said Mouse flatteringly. 'And when I realized it was you who were the chief witness against us...' The inference was that no greater calamity could possibly have befallen the defence.

'Oh, no,' expostulated Mr Chitterwick, with a deprecatory beam. 'Dear me, no. You mustn't think that, Mouse. I assure you, it isn't so at all.' But he was so pleased with the young man's words, and with the sincerity which certainly informed them, and so afraid that his beam might give away the fact that he was so pleased, that he got up and took it right outside the little temple, letting the sunlight play on it in the open air.

A rustling on his left, as of some heavy body ploughing through the undergrowth, caused him to look around. The portly butler, looking like a monstrous black codfish, was progressing with measured paces along the little path through the shrubbery. He approached Mr Chitterwick.

'Excuse me, sir, have you seen His Grace? I understand that he came this way.'

'His Grace?' repeated Mr Chitterwick.

'The Duke, sir,' said the butler patiently, as one explaining the alphabet to a backward child.

'The Duke?' repeated Mr Chitterwick, more backward than ever.

Mouse emerged from the temple. 'Hallo, Wilkinson. Want me?'

Her Grace has just rung through on the telephone. I searched the house but had to inform her that I could not find you. She requested me to ask you if you had forgotten that you are opening the flower show at Netherton-Muchford this afternoon at 3 p.m., Your Grace.'

'Oh, Lord, I'd forgotten all about it. Never mind, I'll send 'em a wire. Terrible regrets and all that, but unavoidably detained on national business. Trust it will be a tremendous success. Love to the Vicar. Got a pencil, Wilkinson? I'll scribble something out, and you can telephone it through for me.'

'I'm sorry, I haven't, Your Grace. But if you care to leave it to me, I will see that a suitable message is despatched.'

'Will you? Stout man. Right-o. Thanks.'

The butler ploughed away again, and the young man knocked out his pipe against the temple.

'God bless my soul,' observed Mr Chitterwick. 'Are you – ?'

'It's a bit of a bore when it comes to local flower shows,' said the young man, almost apologetically, 'but really on the whole I don't find it so bad as you might think. And my mother keeps me up to scratch, you know.'

'I hadn't the faintest idea,' said Mr Chitterwick.

'Agatha always was rotten at introductions,' sympathized the young man.

It is noteworthy that Mr Chitterwick's first reaction was to think how pleased his aunt would be.

chapter eight

Dastardly Assault on a Lady

When Mr Chitterwick returned to the house for lunch it was to find the party diminished by one. The late black-and-silver aunt, and still more late knitted-silk aunt, had unobtrusively disappeared back to the haunts from which she had emerged. Mr Chitterwick gathered that her presence at Riversmead had been to extend to Judith the consolations of kinship, and now that more solid support was forthcoming Judith had need of her no longer. Mr Chitterwick hoped, earnestly but dubiously, that this new support would prove as solid as everyone except himself seemed to imagine.

After the meal he drew her out onto the terrace, under the subtle pretext of examining the gloxinias, and with not a little diffidence set about questioning her regarding the concealment of her marriage from Miss Sinclair.

Judith was quite frank with him. 'I was against it from the beginning. I detest anything savouring of hole-and-corner methods. But though Lynn pretended not to be anything of the kind he really was rather afraid of his aunt.' She smiled, a little sadly, as if at some private reminiscence. 'I think one often is, quite unnecessarily, of people whom one held in awe as a child, don't you?'

Mr Chitterwick did, sincerely.

'Lynn isn't usually the *laissez-faire* type by any means, but in this case he certainly did procrastinate. He knew there would be a terrible row when it came out, and he simply took the line that he wasn't going to precipitate it; he'd just wait till it came. It was an excuse, of course. He had plenty of temper when it was roused, and would stand up to anyone if the other person attacked him. But he hated beginning a quarrel. And of course, with Miss Sinclair...'

'And then, of course,' said Mr Chitterwick cunningly, 'there was the threat of disinheritance.'

'Oh, he never took that seriously. I know the police are trying to make a great point of it, but it was really more of a joke than anything, even between him and Miss Sinclair. She was an autocratic old woman and liked using her power, and naturally to threaten disinheritance was a good way to enforce it. But Lynn knew perfectly well that she would never make anyone her heir but himself, whatever she might say in a temper. And as for a nephew in America whom she had never set eyes on, whose father she had detested, and whose name isn't even Sinclair – ! No, it was simply that Lynn was very fond of his aunt and kept putting off the really serious quarrel that would certainly follow on her discovery of our marriage,' said Judith earnestly. 'But he never tried to stop her finding out or hearing of it elsewhere.'

'Her secretary seemed to think that Miss Sinclair was serious in her threat,' ventured Mr Chitterwick.

'Miss Goole?' observed Judith, not without scorn. 'She couldn't tell whether anyone were serious or not. She couldn't see a joke, even such a bad one as that, if you held it under her nose on a toasting fork.'

Mr Chitterwick, who had no intention of testing the efficient Miss Goole's capabilities in this way, hastily changed the subject. 'I suppose nothing further has come to light about the missing cousin in America?'

Mrs Sinclair looked slightly surprised. 'Yes, as a matter of fact, something has. I had a letter from Lynn's solicitor this morning to say that he has been found and is catching the next boat.'

'He's coming over here?' Mr Chitterwick felt shocked. The vultures should not foregather before the victim is actually condemned.

Mrs Sinclair read his look. 'Oh, it's not so bad as that. He says he's coming over to do what he possibly can for his cousin, which is very kind of him. Apparently he must have imbibed some of the impulsive energy of his adopted country.'

'I see,' said Mr Chitterwick.

And that was about all he did see. As for any channels of further detection, or possibly fruitful avenues to explore, he could spy not a sign of one. Mr Chitterwick, the hope of Riversmead, was ignominiously flummoxed.

It was Mrs Sinclair who suggested a glimpse of one avenue. 'I'm going over to Earlshaze this afternoon. The place is legally my husband's now, of course, and though I couldn't bear to stay there I run over occasionally to keep an eye on things. Mouse is driving me over. Would you care to come too? You might like an opportunity to see Miss Goole again. I'm keeping her on till – till things are more settled.'

It was not Mr Chitterwick's greatest wish ever to set eyes on Miss Goole again; on the other hand, the visit to Earlshaze meant action, and something, at any rate, to pretend to be doing; at least it was better than mooning forlornly about Riversmead, feeling (and no doubt looking) rather less like a detective than anything in this world.

Mr Chitterwick intimated that an opportunity to see Miss Goole again was just the very thing he had been wanting.

Mouse was a vigorous driver for so small a man. They covered the twenty-odd miles between the two houses in twenty-seven minutes.

Miss Goole received them kindly but firmly. To Mr Chitterwick's relief she bore Judith Sinclair away with her immediately to discuss certain accounts. The collaborators were left alone together.

Freed from Miss Goole's intimidating eye, Mr Chitterwick was able to look about him with interest. This, then, was the prize for which the prosecution maintained that murder was not too great a crime, this ripe Georgian mansion of soft red brick and high, airy coolness inside. Mouse, observing his companion's interested gaze, offered to show him round and proved to know almost as much about the place as any professional guide.

It was, apparently, not the original house on the site. An earlier Elizabethan Earlshaze had been burnt down in the reign of George the Second, and the ruling Sinclair of the time had built the present mansion. Mr Chitterwick viewed the pine-panelled walls, the carved mantelpieces, the ballroom, the picture gallery full of previous Sinclairs, the gun room, the grounds, the ornamental water, and sighed. Perhaps after all the prosecution was right. Murder might not be too high a price. Earlshaze was a highly desirable residence.

The tour took them the better part of an hour. When they got back again to the house the business of the two women was finished, and to Mr Chitterwick's dismay Judith seemed to be trying to find an excuse to leave Mr Chitterwick and Miss Goole together for a time. Mr Chitterwick was quite sure that, left alone with this formidable young woman, any question he might have thought of putting to her would go clean out of his head.

Perhaps his dismay was a trifle too plain, perhaps Mouse was giving yet another instance of his remarkable ability in reading Mr Chitterwick's mind; anyhow, he took matters in hand. 'Judy, you're looking rotten. Tired out. Black rings under eyes and all that. Isn't she, Miss Goole?'

Miss Goole agreed that she was with an almost imperceptible degree of the scorn that a healthy young woman feels for her less vigorous sisters.

'I tell you what, then,' cried Mouse happily, with the air of one solving a difficult problem. 'You go and lie down somewhere for a bit, Judy, and Miss Goole, Chitterwick, and I will stroll round the garden till teatime. How's that?' He made a secret sign to Judith.

Taking her cue, Judith fell in at once.

Miss Goole, however, did not. 'I'm afraid I can scarcely spare the time to stroll aimlessly, Your Grace. Being in sole charge here, I find my time very fully occupied.' It was surprising what a number of intimations Miss Goole could manage to convey in a couple of simple sentences. Listening between the words one gathered that Miss Goole did not approve of the sentimentality which prevented the legal mistress of the house from taking up her residence there and directing in person; that, nevertheless, it was just as well that she should keep out of the way and leave such direction to more competent hands; that she had no objection to Mouse being Duke, indeed forgave him for it freely, but with the proviso that he shouldn't expect to be treated by Miss Goole differently from anyone else except, perhaps, a little more strictly; that strolling round gardens for the sake of strolling was the last thing in the world that Miss Goole would care to do, and a duke about the last person one would wish to do it with; and that Mr Chitterwick simply wasn't there at all.

Disregarding these insinuations, Mouse dealt with the situation with an easy competence that aroused Mr Chitterwick's wistful envy. 'Oh, but it won't be aimless. I particularly wanted a chat with you, and this will be a good opportunity. See you at tea then, Judy. Try and get a nap.' And before Mr Chitterwick could realize how it had happened the party had broken up and Miss Goole was strolling down a garden path between them with a long-suffering expression on her face and a rebellious glint behind her huge horn-rimmed spectacles.

'You remember Mr Chitterwick, of course?' Mouse remarked pleasantly by way of opening the important topic.

'Perfectly,' responded Miss Goole, who had hitherto given no sign of recognition at all. 'You came with Chief Inspector Moresby to Aldridge's on the day of Miss Sinclair's death.'

'That is so,' beamed Mr Chitterwick, pleased with this crumb.

'But you are not actually connected with the police, Mr Chitterwick?'

'No, no. Dear me, no. Only in connection with this case. Most distressing, most distressing.'

'And of course I saw you at the inquest and the police court.'

'Yes, yes. That would be so, naturally.' Mr Chitterwick had seen Miss Goole at those places too, but she had not appeared to see him.

'Yours is a very responsible position, Mr Chitterwick.'

Mr Chitterwick agreed that it was.

'It is fortunate that you are so sure of what you saw.'

'Fortunate?'

'Any doubt would be so distressing,' observed Miss Goole drily.

Mouse took a hand. 'Yes, and in view of Mr Chitterwick's position in the case, no doubt you were rather surprised to see him here today, Miss Goole?'

'Very few things surprise me, Your Grace,' replied that young woman cynically.

'Still, I think it would surprise most people,' said Mouse patiently. 'But the fact of the matter is that Mr Chitterwick doesn't feel nearly so sure now as he did, and if you don't mind he would like to put a few questions to you about Major Sinclair.'

'I have already given the police all the information they required,' said Miss Goole, being awkward.

'Oh, this isn't an official interrogation. Just a few quite private questions.'

'I fail to see how any private questions to me concerning Major Sinclair can help Mr Chitterwick make up his mind what he saw in the Piccadilly Palace.'

Mouse sighed inaudibly and handed the ball to Mr Chitterwick. That gentleman, in sheer alarm, plunged straight through these niceties into the heart of the business. 'I remember you telling us next day, and I heard you repeat it in evidence, that you were quite sure that Miss Sinclair had definitely made up her mind to disinherit her nephew if he refused any longer to fall in with her matrimonial plans,' said Mr Chitterwick quickly and all in one breath. 'I take it that you still think that, Miss Goole?'

'I know it.'

'Yes, yes; of course. I mean, you haven't changed your mind?'

'I very rarely change my mind, Mr Chitterwick, and never on questions of fact.'

'You do put it as a fact, then?' persisted Mr Chitterwick.

'Without doubt. Unless she was trying to deceive me. She told me so herself.'

'And yet this matter of disinheritance had actually been for years quite a joke between her and her nephew,' puzzled Mr Chitterwick.

'Who told you that?' asked Miss Goole sharply.

'Mrs Sinclair,' responded Mr Chitterwick with meekness.

Miss Goole raised her thick eyebrows. 'Please don't think I have any prejudices against either Major or Mrs Sinclair. I haven't. Indeed, so far not, that I am extremely sorry for Mrs Sinclair and anxious to help her to the utmost in my power – provided, of course,' added Miss Goole with rectitude, 'that I am asked to condone or shield no crime. But I am not a child. It is obviously to Major Sinclair's interests to minimize the disputes about the inheritance. Naturally Mrs Sinclair would say that he never took his aunt's threats seriously.'

'Then – then you don't agree?' ventured Mr Chitterwick.

'I am not in a position to say how Major Sinclair took them. But I am,' said Miss Goole with finality, 'with regard to Miss Sinclair. And if it is any help to you to know, Mr Chitterwick, I can tell you that she herself took them very seriously indeed.'

'I see,' said Mr Chitterwick, who did not seem to himself to be advancing very much.

There was an uncomfortable silence.

It was broken by a sneeze from Miss Goole. It was a violent sneeze, so violent that it blew her spectacles into a neighbouring rose bush and caused Mouse to scratch himself severely in the retrieving of them. Miss Goole looked properly ashamed of herself, as well she might (a sneeze is perhaps the least efficient exhibition of self-control), and had Mr Chitterwick not held the opinion he did of her he would have said that she actually blushed. In any case, she put the spectacles on again with a nervous haste that spoke many things. Mr Chitterwick was vaguely sorry that she found it necessary to do so. Her features, as revealed in that short couple of seconds, were regular, classical, and by no means ill-pleasing; with a little more attention to appearance and a little less to efficiency Miss Goole might have been a good deal more pleasant to look upon than she was, reflected Mr Chitterwick, who liked pleasant-looking things.

Another impression remained with Mr Chitterwick, too, besides Miss Goole's personal possibilities, and that was that without her spectacles she had seemed for an instant vaguely familiar to him. He could have sworn he had seen her face somewhere before. But it was, of course, impossible that this could be the case.

'There was another thing you wanted to ask Miss Goole about, Chitterwick, wasn't there?' said Mouse, tactfully smoothing over Miss Goole's exhibition of putting on the spectacles.

'Was there?' said Mr Chitterwick vaguely, pondering the matter of this reminiscence. 'Oh, yes. Of course. To be sure. Er – ah, yes; I remember. It was about the behaviour of Major Sinclair to his aunt. Did he seem fond of her? Was he what you might term an affectionate nephew? Did he strike you as – as, in short, an affectionate nephew?'

'Major Sinclair always seemed to me as affectionate as any nephew would be toward an aunt from whom he had such expectations,' replied the cynical Miss Goole, rendered perhaps even more cynical by the accident to her spectacles.

'Apart from the matter of his marriage, they appeared to be on the best of terms?'

'Oh, certainly.'

'I see. You – er – liked Major Sinclair personally?'

'Really, Mr Chitterwick,' observed Miss Goole with some exasperation, 'does the question of whether I personally liked or disliked Major Sinclair help you to make up your mind whether you saw him put poison in his aunt's coffee or not?'

'Er – no,' Mr Chitterwick had to admit. 'That is... You see, the fact of the matter is... Well...' He looked imploringly at Mouse.

'Mr Chitterwick has rather more purpose in his questions that that,' Mouse came to the rescue.

'Of course,' agreed Mr Chitterwick with relief. 'Rather more purpose. Exactly. Quite so. And now,' continued Mr Chitterwick, feeling more like his own man again, 'there is another matter. I ventured to ask you before, if I remember, whether you could explain why Miss Sinclair made the appointment with the Major at the Piccadilly Palace. You replied, I think I am right in saying, that you did not know, at any rate, such was my impression. Can you alter that at all now?'

'Do you mean, do I know now what I did not know then?' A direct young woman, Miss Goole, and an awkward one, too.

'No, no. Oh dear, no. That would be impossible, of course. I meant, could you not cast your mind back and recollect, perhaps, some chance remark of Miss Sinclair's which might throw some light on it. I don't say it is inconceivable that she should not have felt called upon to explain such a strange choice of meeting places, but I do feel that it is extremely likely that she should have done so. Can you remember nothing at all?'

'The point seems to puzzle you very much,' observed Miss Goole, with the first sign of curiosity she had yet shown.

'It does.' Mr Chitterwick shone agreement, glad to have roused even this faint show of interest. 'It is, to my mind, the one quite unexpected (I do not say inexplicable, for an explanation there must be) point in Miss Sinclair's behaviour. After all, the lounge of the Piccadilly Palace is the last place one would look for Miss Sinclair, isn't it?'

'I remember I was surprised myself when she made the appointment,' admitted Miss Goole.

'You are sure,' asked Mr Chitterwick darkly, 'that she did make the appointment?'

'How do you mean?'

'It was not the Major who made the appointment and she who agreed to it?'

'But the police have Major Sinclair's letter to her agreeing to the appointment.'

'Oh, yes. Yes, exactly. But the suggestion might have come from him in the first place.'

'So far as my knowledge goes, it did not. Certainly Miss Sinclair dictated a letter to me, making the appointment. She did not explain it in any way, nor did she make any comment when I brought it, with others, for her to sign.' Miss Goole was evidently tired of the matter. 'In any case, the point seems to me of very small importance. Miss Sinclair might have thought that, having an important question to discuss, one is never so much alone as in a crowd.'

'But why did she not summon him to Aldridge's, where it would have been possible to hold the interview in complete privacy?'

'Really, I'm afraid I can't tell you. But doesn't the point occur to you that if it had been Major Sinclair who made the appointment, with the result we know, that only makes the case against him blacker still?' said Miss Goole tartly.

'Oh, yes; quite so; that might be so, of course,' mumbled Mr Chitterwick in some embarrassment.

Mr Chitterwick knew that very well indeed, but he did not want it pointed out in the presence of such a pro-Sinclair partisan as Mouse. For Mr Chitterwick was determined to be neither pro- nor anti-Sinclair. If he was to be driven to investigate, then his object must be, not to clear Sinclair, but simply to discover the truth, whatever that might be. And this matter of the appointment at the Piccadilly Palace had seemed to him of great importance from the very beginning of the case. It was so utterly improbable from every psychological as well as material standpoint that Miss Sinclair should have made it herself, and Mr Chitterwick had suspected very early that the suggestion had come from the Major; for though the lounge of the Piccadilly Palace is a bad place wherein to threaten a nephew with disinheritance, it is an excellent place to poison an aunt in such a way as to make the result look like suicide. Mr Chitterwick had therefore recognized that if it could be shown that the suggestion had come from the Major, the case against him (as Miss Goole had inconveniently pointed out) became a good deal blacker. Now that he was bound on the quest of the truth it was a point Mr Chitterwick very much wanted to clear up; but apparently it was impossible to do so satisfactorily. However, on balance, Miss Goole's replies favoured the Major.

Mr Chitterwick being unable to think of anything else to ask, they returned to the house and tea.

Whatever may have been Major Sinclair's feelings toward his aunt there was little doubt of the old lady's toward him. The place was plastered with his photographs. In the small, cosy room which had done duty for Miss Sinclair's boudoir there were no less than five of him, including an enlargement in profile which particularly caught Mr Chitterwick's eye. His heart sank as he studied it during tea.

140

The Sinclair profile was more characteristic than its full face. Undoubtedly it was that profile, quite undoubtedly that nose, which he had seen in the Piccadilly Palace.

The journey back to Riversmead Priory was taken more calmly. Mouse sat alone in front; Mr Chitterwick kept Judith company in the back. Their conversation turned on the newly found cousin, and Judith gave further details from the solicitor's letter.

'He seems to have had a most romantic career. His parents left him absolutely nothing, of course, and he had his own living to make from the beginning, but he's comfortably off already, I understand, and only twenty-eight.'

'Dear me,' said Mr Chitterwick, registering admiration.

'He's been simply everything, too. Bellboy in a hotel, waiter, motor mechanic, shop assistant, in the films and on the stage too, even part owner at one time of a travelling circus and his own exhibition rough rider in it! A regular Jack of all trades.'

'One of those fortunate people who can turn their hands to anything,' amplified Mr Chitterwick, thinking with interest that he had never heard of a rough-riding waiter before; the combination must surely be unique. He began to look forward to meeting this accomplished young man.

Judith ceased to make conversation, and Mr Chitterwick retired into a reverie.

He could not disguise that he had made no progress at all. Miss Goole had nothing helpful to offer. She did not seem in the least antagonistic to the Major; but, then, neither did she appear to be prejudiced in his favour; she was simply neutral, as indeed was only correct in her position. Only one point could Mr Chitterwick recall of real interest in the interview, and that was the glimpse he had had of her without her glasses.

Definitely she had reminded him of somebody. Quite definitely. But of whom? Mr Chitterwick could not imagine. Somebody, he was inclined to think, seen fairly recently. At any rate within the last six months; but he could get no nearer than that.

And there was another thing too. She had seemed confused. Surprisingly confused. She had blushed far more than the accident warranted. She could not have blushed more had it been a more vital portion of her attire than her spectacles that she had sneezed off. And with his impression of the lady Mr Chitterwick was convinced that in the ordinary way a mere sneeze would not suffice to confuse her. No, there must be something behind it. But then, what? And then again, her complete ignoring of him at first. Might not that be significant?

'I have it!' cried Mr Chitterwick in sudden triumph. 'They're a disguise!'

'What did you say, Mr Chitterwick?' asked his startled companion.

'We must return at once,' said Mr Chitterwick, in high excitement.

'Return? To Earlshaze?'

'Yes, at once.'

Judith leant over and thumped the driver on the shoulder. 'Mouse, Mr Chitterwick says we must go back to Earlshaze at once.'

'What's that? Go back? Good. Got an idea, Chitterwick?'

'Yes. I feel certain... I want to make sure whether... Please leave everything to me. If Mrs Sinclair can just think of some excuse to explain our return...'

Judith and Mouse were model detective's companions. They asked nothing further. Mouse turned the car with flattering promptitude, while Judith gazed at Mr Chitterwick with still more flattering respect. Mr Chitterwick beamed vaguely back.

The truth was that he was beginning to wonder what on earth he was going to do. The request to be taken back to Earlshaze had been made on the impulse of the moment, in the excitement of his new idea. But how he was going to test that idea he had not an inkling. He had twelve miles in which to find one; and Mouse was driving disturbingly fast.

By the end of the twelve miles no plan had presented itself.

To Judith, however, the making of plans presented apparently no difficulty. 'Oh, Miss Goole,' she said smoothly, 'I'm so sorry to bring you down again, but I left my gloves behind. No, don't bother. I'm sure they must be where I was lying down. I'll run up myself. Besides, I think Mr Chitterwick has remembered something else he wanted to ask you.'

'Yes,' said Mr Chitterwick. 'Er – yes.'

Judith disappeared. Mouse asked delicately with his eyebrows whether Mr Chitterwick wanted him to disappear too. Mr Chitterwick returned a desperate signal with his whole face that he did not.

'Yes, Mr Chitterwick?' prompted Miss Goole, who had been watching Mr Chitterwick's face with efficiently concealed surprise.

'Er – yes,' agreed Mr Chitterwick. 'That is,' he blurted out, unable to uproot his mind from the main point, 'it was about glasses.'

Mr Chitterwick was not so agitated that he was unable to watch Miss Goole for the effect of this observation. Had she started slightly? Had a faint blush stained her sallow cheek? It had not. She remained as imperturbable as before.

'Glasses?' repeated Miss Goole calmly. 'Oh, yes? And what can I tell you about glasses, Mr Chitterwick? Tumblers, do you mean?'

Mr Chitterwick had a better grip on himself by now. 'It's just a small point that occurred to me. Nothing of real importance. But I remembered that Miss Sinclair in the Piccadilly Palace seemed to be peering rather at the Ma – the man who was with her, and it struck me at the time that she must be short-sighted. Can you tell me if that really was the case?'

'It was,' assented Miss Goole, without very much interest. 'She usually wore glasses, but the pair she took to London had got broken that morning, and unfortunately she had left the others behind.'

'I see. That is just what I thought,' said Mr Chitterwick, and gave the impression that he was artlessly pleased with himself. 'Now, what sort of strength were Miss Sinclair's glasses? About the same as yours?'

'About the same,' said Miss Goole indifferently. 'Perhaps a little stronger.'

'Ah, yes. Now I rather wanted to get an idea of the extent of Miss Sinclair's shortness of sight. Perhaps if you would be good enough to let me look through your glasses for the moment,' said the cunning Mr Chitterwick, 'that would give a fair impression.'

'Miss Sinclair's second pair is still upstairs,' returned Miss Goole with equanimity. 'If you really want to know what lenses she used I'll get them for you.'

Mr Chitterwick appeared much distressed at the thought of putting Miss Goole to all that trouble. 'Oh, no. Dear me, no. I wouldn't think of it. There is no need at all. It will serve my purpose quite well enough if you just let me look through yours.' Which, as Mr Chitterwick knew, was no less than the truth; but the best liars, as Mr Chitterwick knew also, always make as much use of the truth as possible.

'I'm afraid it would hardly be the same thing,' said Miss Goole kindly, but evidently determined to stand no nonsense with *her* glasses. 'Mine are quite appreciably weaker than Miss Sinclair's. I remember now that we were unable to exchange them. I offered to lend her mine when she went out that afternoon, but she said they were useless to her.'

'Oh!' Mr Chitterwick looked disappointed.

'But I'll get hers for you with pleasure.'

'Oh, no,' said Mr Chitterwick. 'It's of no consequence, really. None at all. Ah, here comes Mrs Sinclair.' He hurried courteously to meet her across the big hall. 'Did you find your gloves?'

'Yes, thank you. Where I thought I'd left them.'

'Please get me some pepper,' said Mr Chitterwick surprisingly; but he said it in such a hurried undertone that the two at the other end of the hall could not have heard it.

Judith looked momentarily astonished, then nodded slightly. They strolled over toward the other two. 'Oh, by the way, Miss Goole,' she said easily, 'I was nearly forgetting. I want some pepper. Have you any to spare? They've run right out at Riversmead, and its early closing day in the neighbourhood.'

'Pepper?' repeated Miss Goole calmly. 'Yes, I'm sure there's plenty. If you'll wait I'll get you some.' She bustled efficiently away.

This time the situation was too much for Judith. 'Mr Chitterwick, what *do* you want with pepper?'

'Hush!' said Mr Chitterwick, with the uneasiness of a guilty conscience. 'She may be listening. I want you to give it me to hold,' he added in a conspiratorial whisper. 'And if I drop it, or – or anything like that, upbraid me severely.'

ANTHONY BERKELEY

'Very well,' Judith smiled. 'But it's all very mysterious.'

'Shall I upbraid you too, Chitterwick?' Mouse wanted to know.

'Indeed, yes. Er – you see what I want to do, of course?'

'You want to get those glasses off her.'

Mr Chitterwick beamed nervously. 'Yes; I can't help feeling that... You noticed she wouldn't fall in with my suggestion? Dear me, this is very difficult.' Mr Chitterwick felt himself to be appearing like anything rather than a detective; he was grateful to the other two for apparently continuing to look on him as one.

Miss Goole returned, bearing the pepper in a small tin. Judith thanked her graciously, and extended it toward Mr Chitterwick.

'Will you take charge of it for me, Mr Chitterwick? Mouse will be driving.' Anyone, implied Mrs Sinclair with dignity, can see that it is impossible to drive a car and have possession of pepper at one and the same time

'Certainly,' said Mr Chitterwick, and held the tin gingerly. 'I – I remember,' he went on nervously, 'when I was at school attending a lecture on – er – pepper. It was – er – most interesting. There are, if I remember rightly, quite several different kinds of pepper. Quite several.'

'Indeed?' said Miss Goole, in a must-you-be-going kind of tone. A doorstep discourse on pepper was evidently, in Miss Goole's opinion, out of place. The other two members of Mr Chitterwick's audience, however, wore on their faces expressions indicating that all their lives had they wanted to hear an authoritative pronouncement on pepper and never had this simple wish been gratified.

'There are, of course,' continued Mr Chitterwick, as if encouraged by these expressions, 'different colours in pepper, and these indicate to some extent the – the various

146

places of origin. Red pepper for instance, as its name shows, comes from Cayenne, grey pepper from – from somewhere else, and – er – black pepper from – h'm! – from somewhere else still. Red pepper,' went on Mr Chitterwick, rather red himself, 'is of course the strongest. Now it would be interesting to see what sort of pepper this is.' He plucked off the lid of the tin and peered wisely inside. 'This is grey pepper,' he announced, catching his glasses in the nick of time from falling into the tin with the pepper.

But this was apparently one of Mr Chitterwick's unlucky days. In the effort of catching his glasses the tin slid through his hands. He made a desperate effort to seize it, but only succeeded in batting it up in the air. The tin shot straight in the direction of Miss Goole, upside down, distributing the pepper on the atmosphere like a miniature turbillon, and finally came to rest, still upside down, on the top of Miss Goole's head. If Mr Chitterwick's dastardly object had been to introduce pepper to Miss Goole, nothing could have been more successful.

The three then stood round and, in the intervals of sneezing themselves, watched Miss Goole do so. They watched in vain. This time Miss Goole, though sneezing no less explosively, maintained with one hand a firm grasp of her spectacles.

It was Mouse who came to his chief's rescue. While Mr Chitterwick was twittering anxious apologies, Mouse went up to the lady, bodily removed her hand from its grip, and began to dust the pepper from her hair and features. The prize dropped into Mr Chitterwick's outstretched hands.

The experiment so far had been turned firmly into a success, if success meant the divesting of Miss Goole of her spectacles; but at that point success stopped short. In the distorted, ravaged, reddened vision which the unfortunate young woman presented to the world it was impossible to trace resemblance to anyone on earth.

Mr Chitterwick's anxious apologies redoubled themselves. It was evident that Mr Chitterwick knew himself for a bungler. A real detective, intent upon introducing pepper into a young woman's nostrils, would have measured out the requisite dose beforehand and injected just so much; he would not have dusted a good half pound over the victim. Mr Chitterwick clearly felt this very strongly. His embarrassment turned into agitation, and that into downright panic. He lost track of his actions, even. In his confusion, setting Miss Goole's spectacles on his own nose, he tried to press his pince-nez upon her. He even went so far as to endeavour to fix them in position for her as, still half blinded, she fumbled awkwardly with them herself, guiding her hands and pressing her shaking fingers with his to a firmer clasp of the lenses. His shameful confusion when the mistake was discovered was plain to all.

By degrees Miss Goole recovered. It cannot be said that when her eyes ceased to stream and she could see clearly out of them again she looked with any love upon Mr Chitterwick, but she forgave him in words, at any rate. She even, such was her devotion to duty, retired to the kitchen for more pepper, thus unconsciously heaping coals of fire on her torturer's head.

During her absence Mr Chitterwick retired to an open window and stared out over the garden. One gathered that after such a fiasco he was ashamed to face his assistants.

Nor did he speak again, with the exception of further stammering apologies to the outraged victim of his experiment, until the car was right down the drive and out of sight of the house. Then, very carefully, he took off his glasses, drew a clean silk handkerchief from his breast pocket, swaddled them tenderly in it, and laid the result on his knee. 'Most successful,' he beamed at Judith.

'Successful?' Judith repeated, with perhaps more of a query in her tone than was altogether polite.

'Quite,' Mr Chitterwick assured her. 'Perhaps I was a little drastic, but that was better than the reverse. I was not only able to try her glasses on, but to pretend to help her on with mine.'

'But – but what result did you get from that?' Judith asked in bewilderment.

Mr Chitterwick's beam deepened in radiance. 'Her spectacles are a fake. Plain glass! Do you know, I suspected it. She is disguised. I cannot tell you for what purpose; that we must find out. But her pretences are false, and that stamps her as a suspicious person at once.' So there, added Mr Chitterwick's expression, is one suspicious person for us to play with, at any rate.

'Good gracious! But the other thing, Mr Chitterwick. Helping her on with your glasses. What did you get by that?'

Mr Chitterwick's beam almost overspread the confines of his face. 'Perfect impressions on the lenses of the prints of both her fore and middle fingers,' he replied very happily; for that, if you like, *was* real detecting, and no mistake about it.

Judith looked at him with respectful awe.

Mr Chitterwick did not go on to explain why he had wanted Miss Goole's fingerprints, or what he expected from them. Perhaps he did not quite know.

chapter nine

Reconstructing the Crime

It became increasingly obvious to Mr Chitterwick during
the next day or two that his stay at Riversmead was on
increasingly false pretences. There was simply nothing more
for him to detect. He held interminable conversations with
Mouse, and less frequently with Judith, but nothing fresh
seemed to emerge from them by way of either fact or theory.

He had posted his precious pince-nez to Moresby at
Scotland Yard, but with only a very cautious letter to
accompany them. Without giving the name of the owner of
the fingerprints, he apologized in vague terms for the
trouble he was causing in asking the records to be searched
for comparison, and hinted clearly that he hardly expected
any result; but if it would not be asking too much for them to
be photographed and an enlargement sent him…? Why Mr
Chitterwick withheld the name of the owner even he was
not quite sure. Probably the fact was that he was too
diffident about his discovery that Miss Goole was wearing a
disguise (a) to be quite certain that she really was, (b) to give
her away to the police on such slender suspicion before
making perfectly sure that her disguise was directed toward
some criminal end. In any case, he did withhold it.

As to why he wanted an enlargement of the fingerprints there was no doubt at all. This was the first piece of real detecting Mr Chitterwick had ever done (whether it led to anything or, much more probably, not), and he wanted a souvenir of it.

Two days later he received a jocular letter from Moresby, enclosing two sets of the photographs and regretting that there was no counterpart of the prints in the police records. Not knowing what to do with the second set, Mr Chitterwick finally sent it off to the police bureau in America, with a similarly worded letter to that which he had written to Moresby. After all, Miss Goole had spent some time in America, and one never knew.

In the end it was Mouse who suggested to Mr Chitterwick an idea for further researches. 'Well, we talk and talk,' he remarked ruefully, at the end of one of their confabulations, 'and we're sure of this and we're sure of that; but we don't really seem to advance very much, do we?'

'No,' Mr Chitterwick had to agree. 'I'm afraid that is so. You see, the trouble is that there is so little to work on. Some professors of criminology, I understand, can theorize correctly at a distance from the scene of the crime, but unfortunately, so far as I am concerned – '

'The scene of the crime,' Mouse mused. 'Well, after all, we haven't explored that yet, have we?'

Mr Chitterwick clutched at the chance of action, however apparently unprofitable. 'We should leave no stone unturned,' he said, with unwonted energy. 'I must confess I cannot at the moment see what we could hope to gain by it, but the French have a method of reconstructing the crime on the scene of its occurrence, which they invariably pursue; and presumably they must often obtain results from it or they would not do it.'

Mouse too seemed pleased with the idea of action. 'You mean, we might have a cut at it too? By Jove, Chitterwick, that really is a scheme. I agree that one doesn't see at the moment what one could get out of it, but there's no harm in trying, is there?'

'None at all,' said Chitterwick, growing every moment more enthusiastic. 'By no means.'

'Just the two of us, I take it? One impersonating the old lady and the other the unknown man?' Never did Mouse so much as hint at even the possibility of Major Sinclair being guilty. In all their conversations he took the Major's innocence as the one fact in the case which was definitely certain.

Mr Chitterwick could improve on that suggestion. 'I think there should really be three of us. It would be a waste of time for either of us to enact Miss Sinclair, whereas one of us certainly ought to reconstruct my own part in the affair. Indeed it would be better that we should do so in turns, as what one might miss the other might realize.'

'We'd better take one of the girls with us, then.'

'Your sister,' said Mr Chitterwick promptly.

But Mouse shook his head with decision. 'No. If Agatha were more like her name, perhaps. As it is, I don't really think she'd do. She's a dear, but she simply can't help turning everything into fun. We shouldn't get the right atmosphere at all. It must be Judy.'

'Wouldn't it be much too painful for Mrs Sinclair?' suggested Mr Chitterwick dubiously.

'She'd never forgive us if we left her out,' replied Mouse, without any doubt at all.

They arranged it between themselves. Making an early start, they would go up in Mouse's car so as to arrive in town for lunch and go on to the Piccadilly Palace at about two.

The little tragi-comedy could then be staged at exactly the time when the real drama had begun to display itself to Mr Chitterwick's notice.

'And we'd better arrange to stay in town for the night,' Mouse added, 'in case anything crops up to be done on the spot. Unfortunately our place is shut up now it's August, or I could have put you up there. We'd better wire for rooms somewhere.'

'If you would care to come out to Chiswick...' said Mr Chitterwick diffidently. 'My aunt would be exceedingly pleased to put you and Mrs Sinclair up.'

'That's extraordinarily kind of you,' said Mouse. 'We'd love to.'

Mr Chitterwick retired to despatch an agitated telegram.

The journey the next morning was accomplished in what must have been even for Mouse something like record time. The sports Bentley in which it was his pleasure to hurtle along the highway devoured the miles to such purpose that they were able to have not only an unhurried lunch in London but a leisurely cocktail before it.

During the previous evening Mr Chitterwick had spent some considerable time with Mouse in compiling as accurate a timetable of the tragedy as he possibly could. From the moment of his taking his seat in the Piccadilly Palace lounge, the time of which he was luckily able to fix almost to a minute through having glanced at the clock in the vestibule as he came through, to the moment when he had got up to arouse Miss Sinclair from her supposed sleep (rather more difficult to fix, this, though Mr Chitterwick knew the time of his return to the lounge after the abortive visit to the telephone), every incident, however trivial, that he could remember was sorted into its appropriate minute. Judith and Mouse had then been furnished with another copy apiece, and the three had set to work to learn it off by heart. If they were to do the thing at all, at least they should do it thoroughly.

It was their purpose to run through the whole thing twice, on the first occasion keeping the exact times as shown in Mr Chitterwick's timetable, on the second occupying the same period but without regard to the true time. Mr Chitterwick was to play himself at the first performance, changing places with Mouse for the second. In view of the importance of securing the exact tables, they arrived at the Piccadilly Palace some time before the programme was to begin and made sure of them.

As Mr Chitterwick sat alone at his own table he felt curiously excited. Most of us have our own private superstitions and fancies, and by some occult means Mr Chitterwick had arrived at the quite illogical but no less firm conclusion that this was the last throw of the dice to determine Major Sinclair's fate; if he was to be proved innocent then the revelation which was to accomplish this miracle would make itself apparent during the playing of this tragic farce; if nothing emerged, he would hang. There was no reason for this decision of Mr Chitterwick's; he argued against it, telling himself that it was preposterous; and the more he argued the more firmly he found himself believing it.

At the other table Judith was sitting alone, her face showing the anxiety she was feeling. It was perhaps the hesitation she had displayed for a moment when first told of the plan that had first induced this unreasonable conviction in Mr Chitterwick's mind. That something like it was in her own too he felt sure. She caught his eyes and smiled nervously. Mr Chitterwick tried to send a reassuring smile back, but felt that its lines were a little uncertain. The right atmosphere had been caught, without doubt. If Mouse had been certain that Lady Milborne would spoil it, Mr Chitterwick himself was not sure that Judith's presence was not making it almost a little too poignant.

He glanced at his watch and saw that it was almost half-past two. Beckoning to a waitress (for once one happened providentially to be hovering in the neighbourhood), Mr Chitterwick ordered black coffee and a benedictine.

There is no need to detail the events of the next thirty-five minutes. Everything proceeded as had been arranged. For four minutes Mr Chitterwick studied the apparently unconscious Julia, for six he played the cat and mouse game with a ferociously glaring Mouse, even going so far as to con over certain selected passages from 'The Wreck of the *Hesperus*' again – a point about which he had not thought it necessary to enlighten his collaborators. At two forty-seven he pretended to look up at an imaginary waitress and left the lounge.

The following quarter of an hour Mr Chitterwick found uncommonly slow in passing. He wandered about the lower passages as he had done on the day of the tragedy when awaiting Moresby, peering into deserted rooms 'for residents only' where one resident might have killed another resident with the apparent improbability of the body being discovered for several weeks; he sauntered about the vestibule, watching the rounders and their female friends streaming out in the great after-lunch exodus; he even found himself in the telephone room, and fled hastily on being demanded his number by the ear-phoned young woman knitting behind the counter. Finally, at one minute past three, he returned to his table, which a turned-up chair and his unfinished coffee upon it had preserved for him.

The little drama had played itself out.

But Mr Chitterwick was not dissatisfied as he got up and joined Judith at her table, Mouse materializing there too a moment later.

'Well, Mr Chitterwick?' Judith asked, the commonplace words a little unsteadily spoken. Judith was evidently feeling the strain.

Mr Chitterwick nodded sagely. 'One point, at any rate, occurs to me,' he said, trying to speak as matter-of-factly as possible. 'You probably noticed yourself, Mouse, that – '

'No, don't tell me yet,' Mouse interrupted. 'I've got a point too, but I want to see if you discover it independently.'

'So have I!' said Judith.

Mr Chitterwick permitted himself a small beam. 'Come, that really is most encouraging. If none of them overlap, there is three distinct points already. I quite agree that it would be best to test them by independent observation. In that case, perhaps we might...?'

'At once, yes,' Mouse assented, and rose. 'Keep your heart up, Judy, old girl. We really are getting hold of something now.'

'Yes, certainly I do anticipate quite definite results from this experiment,' said Mr Chitterwick, with much earnestness.

Judith smiled at them both.

Really, thought Mr Chitterwick, as he scuttled away to the entrance to the lounge, that is one of the bravest women I have ever heard of. One would do a great deal to reward such courage, a very great deal indeed.

The following thirty-five minutes passed much as before, except that Mr Chitterwick found that glaring was not one of his accomplishments. The three met once more at Judith's table.

Mr Chitterwick was undisguisedly excited. 'I have made another discovery,' he burst out. 'A second one. Dear me, I really wonder if... Well, it must have been that, or that he was a consummate fool. God bless my soul, this may alter everything!'

'What, Mr Chitterwick?' Judith implored. *'What?'*

'Do you see that mirror on the opposite wall?' babbled Mr Chitterwick. 'Well – !'

'Got it in one,' Mouse chimed in, no less excited. 'That was my discovery. You mean, you saw...?'

'Couldn't help seeing!' Mr Chitterwick spluttered. 'Good gracious me, Mouse! I just happened to glance in what I thought the right direction, and I couldn't help seeing.'

'What couldn't you help seeing?' Judith moaned. 'Oh, *please* tell me, one of you.'

Mr Chitterwick was contrite. 'I beg your pardon. I should have explained, but really I was quite carried away for the moment. You see that mirror there? Well, when I was extending my hand over your cup I looked in that direction in which I fancied that man had been looking and it took my eyes directly to the mirror; and in it – in it,' positively squeaked Mr Chitterwick, 'I plainly saw Mouse watching me!'

For a moment Judith turned rather white, and her hand clutched at the lapel of her coat; the next instant she had recovered herself. 'And – and that suggests to you...?'

'For the moment, if you don't mind,' said Mr Chitterwick, rubicund with emotion, 'I should prefer not to say. In point of fact, it suggests such a revolutionary theory to me that I hardly like to commit it to words before I've thought it over carefully. But it may (I only say it *may*, mind you) alter the whole aspect of the case.'

'You mean,' Judith breathed, 'definitely prove Lynn's innocence?'

'I mustn't commit myself.' Mr Chitterwick shook his head, but his beam committed him completely.

'Do you think the same, Mouse?'

'Blessed if I can see what Chitterwick's thinking,' replied Mouse in candid bewilderment. 'I noticed the point myself, and it looked funny to me; I wanted to see if he'd notice it too. But I can't draw any conclusion except that the man must have been a born fool.'

'And he wasn't that,' Mr Chitterwick warned seriously. 'Dear me, no. Very far from it.'

'Well, if you won't tell me, I suppose you won't,' said Judith, with a pettishness which showed her to be feminine enough at bottom. 'Anyhow, will you tell me the other discovery you made?'

'Oh, yes,' said Mr Chitterwick hastily, a little alarmed by this pettishness. 'Of course. And that may prove to be important too. Very important. It struck me, you see, when I was waiting outside during the period of my telephone call, that I had never known fourteen minutes to pass more slowly. From that I passed to the thought of how long, in such circumstances, a quarter of an hour can be. Much longer, I thought next, than one would imagine prussic acid to be in taking effect.'

'Ah!' nodded Mouse getting the point.

'Now, I see here,' continued Mr Chitterwick, adjusting his pince-nez and consulting his timetable, 'that I fixed the time at which I saw the man's hand over Miss Sinclair's cup, as two forty-four; and the time at which I rose to go over to her, and consequently the time she died, as three-six. That gives twenty-two minutes, you see; or, assuming that she did not drink her coffee for as much as seven minutes, a full quarter of an hour. Well, I know it depends on the size of the dose how soon after administration death would ensue, but if the dose was a fairly large one, as is to be expected in such a case, a quarter of an hour seems excessive.'

'Very neat,' approved Mouse. 'Ve-ry neat.'

'But I must look up prussic acid in my Taylor, and also, of course, I must ascertain the size of the dose which was supposed to have been administered. I must confess I have forgotten that.'

'Half a minute,' said Mouse, and fished for his notebook.

'But I do know,' continued Mr Chitterwick, 'that with prussic acid, insensibility, in the case of a large dose, is almost immediate and death very rapid indeed.'

'Half a minute,' repeated Mouse, rapidly flicking pages. 'I've got an idea. Ah, here we are. Sir James Ridley's evidence at the inquest. "Dose estimated at not less than half an ounce of ordinary BP mixture, equivalent to about five grains of anhydrous prussic acid." If you understand what that means.'

'Yes,' said Mr Chitterwick wrinkling his forehead. 'That would be a very fair dose. Very fair indeed. Humph, I must certainly look up my Taylor. This is very interesting.'

'I don't understand,' said Judith, in obvious perplexity. 'If what you're saying is the case, it seems actually to point away from this other man.'

'It does,' admitted Mr Chitterwick. 'That's the extraordinary thing. Or else – '

'That he delayed her taking it,' Mouse supplied, 'until he was clear of the place. Isn't that more likely?'

'Very much so,' Mr Chitterwick agreed readily. 'That is undoubtedly the true explanation. He would, of course, not wish her to become insensible while he was still with her. No doubt he delayed her drinking her coffee until he saw a favourable opportunity, and then left in haste before she had actually done so.'

'Then the point doesn't seem very important after all,' suggested Judith.

'We have to bear in mind every point, however apparently unimportant, when we have so little to go on,' Mr Chitterwick told her rather primly. 'And we mustn't forget that you had one of your own to tell us. Now, what was that?'

'Why, this peering of Miss Sinclair's. I peered at Mouse when we were talking, and at you, and it seemed to me that however short-sighted I was I shouldn't want to peer closely at somebody sitting next to me just in the ordinary way of conversation. What I suggest is that Miss Sinclair was peering because she had her suspicions that the man wasn't Lynn at all.'

'That presupposes that the man definitely was impersonating your husband,' Mr Chitterwick murmured.

'Well, I thought we were quite agreed on that, considering the bogus telephone call and the way he was decoyed to that place where nobody would be able to prove an alibi for him. I thought that if anything was certain it was that the man was definitely impersonating Lynn.' Judith must have been a little overstrung, or she would not have spoken quite so indignantly.

'Yes, yes,' Mr Chitterwick soothed her. 'I have no doubt that probably was the case; I just wished to warn you against taking anything quite for granted to build a theory on. With that proviso, I think that is a very sound point you make, Mrs Sinclair.'

'She wouldn't be able to see him well, you understand,' went on Judith more calmly, 'and something in his voice struck her as wrong. Voices are almost impossible to imitate, you see. So that's why she was peering like that.'

'I think you've probably hit it, Judy,' said Mouse, looking at her admiringly and not at all as one looks at a sister. Mr

Chitterwick intercepted the look and started slightly. God bless my soul, he thought, I do believe the boy's half in love with her; well, no wonder. Mr Chitterwick was not sure that he was not half in love with her himself.

'But it wouldn't carry much conviction, I'm afraid, in court,' Judith sighed.

'Every little helps,' encouraged Mr Chitterwick.

It was past four o'clock. Mr Chitterwick, catching the unusual sight of a waitress passing their table, took the opportunity to order tea.

Over the meal they discussed their immediate movements. Judith was going to take advantage of being in London to see her husband in Pentonville, it having been intimated to her by the authorities that she might do so within reason whenever she wished, and Mr Chitterwick had a few points on which he wished her to question the Major on his behalf and bring back as explicit replies as possible. He noted them down for her, and she undertook to find out what her husband knew.

As for Mr Chitterwick himself, he was going to Scotland Yard. As an honest man he wished to warn Moresby that he no longer felt quite so sure as before of Major Sinclair's guilt. As an unofficial detective he wanted to question that official one about one or two matters on his own account.

Mouse offered to escort Judith to Pentonville, and the three arranged a trysting place in order to reach Chiswick in comfortable time for dinner.

As his taxi chugged down Whitehall Mr Chitterwick reflected, not for the first time, what particularly charming people these were with whom this distressing case had brought him in contact. Judith, of course, was a woman in a million, but to Mouse, too, Mr Chitterwick felt himself peculiarly attracted; he was such a simple soul, and quite unaffected. If there were more dukes like him, thought Mr Chitterwick (who knew rather less than nothing about the others), there would be less talk of absurd social revolutions.

Moresby received Mr Chitterwick with affection and pressed him to a seat. 'Well, sir? Just come along to make sure we haven't let our little bird fly away, eh?'

'No, Chief Inspector,' said Mr Chitterwick, in some embarrassment. 'Er – no. Rather the reverse, in fact.'

'Not come to say you've thought better of it and decided not to give evidence for us after all, I hope?' queried the chief inspector with amusement. 'Or brought the fingerprints of the gardener's daughter, eh, sir?'

'Well, I have come,' said Mr Chitterwick bravely, 'partially to tell you that I do not feel so certain of Major Sinclair's guilt as I did before.'

Moresby's amusement ceased suddenly. He looked searchingly at Mr Chitterwick. 'Those friends of his been trying to get round you, sir?' he asked quite sternly.

'Eh?' said Mr Chitterwick.

'Brought a duke in to help 'em, I understand,' said Moresby in a scathing voice. 'Well, I didn't think you were the sort of gentleman to let himself be got round by a duke.' Moresby spoke as if a duke were some sort of low confidence trick, capable of imposing on only the veriest nitwit.

'You – you know what has happened, then?' said Mr Chitterwick, a helpless feeling invading him, as many better men before him, at the realization of the all-embracing tentacles of Scotland Yard.

'I know where you've been staying, sir, and that they'd brought a duke along to help in the game; and I didn't imagine,' said Moresby, with heavy sarcasm, 'that the game was croquet, even at this time of the year.'

The case put like that, Mr Chitterwick found himself with very little to say. 'I am not proposing to refuse to give my evidence, Chief Inspector,' he replied, with what dignity he could. 'Pray don't think that. I must, in duty bound, recount what I saw. On the other hand, I am naturally anxious not to be the means of hanging an innocent man.'

'No more so than us, sir,' Moresby assured him. 'Now, then, let's talk it over sensibly. What's altered your opinion about our bird?'

Mr Chitterwick was in something of a quandary. It was absurd to answer merely that Major Sinclair's friends gave him a very good character; the character that Major Sinclair's friends gave him mattered just exactly nothing to Moresby. It would be, Mr Chitterwick felt, equally useless to propound his theory that the whole thing was a plot aimed against Major Sinclair and that the man he himself had seen was simply impersonating that unfortunate soldier, having neatly removed him for the period in question from human observation; in the absence of the strongest evidence to support it any Scotland Yard man would excusably regard such a suggestion as fantastic. On the other hand, Mr Chitterwick did not wish to divulge the discoveries he was sure he had made in the Piccadilly Palace lounge that afternoon; they were highly contentious, unaccompanied by any supporting evidence, and would certainly be dismissed by the practical Moresby as bunkum. Mr Chitterwick was forced to fall back on a line of defence in which he did not for a moment believe but which would serve his purpose just as well.

'There are a number of small things, but one in particular which makes me doubt,' said Mr Chitterwick untruthfully, 'whether Miss Sinclair did not commit suicide after all, and that is the question of the poison.'

'Oh, yes, sir?' said Moresby. He wore the air of a university professor endeavouring to listen politely to the observations of the dullest member of his class. That is where university professors differ from schoolmasters, who make no pretence at all of politeness when listening to such observations but simply reach out briskly for their good birch rods.

'From what I remember of the action of the prussic acid,' continued Mr Chitterwick, 'I should have thought it a good deal more swift than in this case, considering the size of the dose. I have been working out the times, and, as near as I can put it, at least twenty-two minutes must have elapsed between the moment when I saw that man's hand over her cup and the moment of Miss Sinclair's death. What I really wanted to ask you, Chief Inspector, was whether you had any evidence at all to show when Miss Sinclair actually drank her coffee?'

'None, sir,' Moresby answered cheerfully. 'That would really be a bit too much to expect. But I can't say it worries us like it seems to you.'

'Well, have you any evidence to show when the man I saw left the lounge?' persisted Mr Chitterwick.

'Major Sinclair?' said the chief inspector innocently. 'Yes, we've got that. He left almost immediately after you were called to the telephone. We've got four witnesses to that, if we want 'em. A party a few tables away noticed both of you go. I wish,' added Moresby with feeling, 'there were more of that kind about, who really do notice things.'

'I see,' said Mr Chitterwick gravely. This was untrue. See was just what Mr Chitterwick could not. Moresby's answer had deepened rather than lessened that particular enigma.

'And what's more,' said Moresby, 'they're prepared to swear that nobody else went near her till you did. But I don't think I should worry if I were you, Mr Chitterwick, sir. There's a bit more evidence come to light since I saw you last. We've got no less than three chemists now, all in London, who recognized the Major from his photographs in the papers and then properly identified him for us as a man who came to their shops trying to buy prussic acid actually the very day before the murder. What do you think of that?'

'God bless my soul!' ejaculated Mr Chitterwick.

'That makes things a bit clearer for you, doesn't it?'

'It certainly is very striking,' said Mr Chitterwick cautiously. 'And did any of the three actually sell any?'

'Well, no,' Moresby had to admit. 'We haven't found the bird who sold it to him yet, I must say, though we've combed the chemists as fine as we can and examined every poison register in London and for fifty miles round.'

'What do you make of that, then?' asked Mr Chitterwick with interest.

'Why, it's my belief that the party who did sell it is lying low. Knows he committed an irregularity, you see (because he can't have got his poison book signed), and knows he'll get into pretty serious trouble if it comes out. You can take it from me, Mr Chitterwick, sir, that we never shall know who sold the Major his prussic acid; but it stands to reason that he got hold of it somewhere. We've got the evidence that he was trying to buy it, you see – that's good enough.'

'Dear me,' said Mr Chitterwick mildly, and soon afterward took his leave. Moresby's farewell was rather less affectionate than his greeting. Mr Chitterwick was left with the impression that so long as he gave the evidence required of him and simply told what his own eyes had seen, Moresby was prepared to forgive him any private fool doubts and worries.

Mr Chitterwick made his way to Charing Cross Road. There was a good half hour before he was to meet the others, and how can half an hour be spent better than gorming over delectable piles of second-hand books?

In the meantime, at Chiswick, in a long, low-ceilinged drawing room, with a spinet on one side of her and a white Persian cat on the other, the mauve ribbons in her cap trembling with pleasure, sat an old lady, waiting to receive the first duke who had crossed her threshold for more than fifty years.

chapter ten

A Fantastic Theory

Mr Chitterwick's first action, after the duties of hospitality had been accomplished and his guests despatched to their rooms to dress for dinner, was to seek out his Taylor and look up the section dealing with prussic acid. What he found there made him shake his head.

Changing, Mr Chitterwick endeavoured to review the situation. That the whole aspect of the case had altered for him as a result of the day's experiment was not to be denied. The fact filled Mr Chitterwick with mingled pleasure and dismay. He was pleased – intensely pleased – that at last something had emerged from the darkness to indicate the Major's innocence; nothing substantial, it was true, a pale, wraith-like appearance; but nevertheless something which one might hope to materialize into definite solidity. He was dismayed because his appearance seemed only to make the case more mystifying than ever; for not only did it tend to clear Major Sinclair, but its tendency was every bit as much in favour of the man who (if the Major was innocent) must have been impersonating him. And that was absurd.

Mr Chitterwick put the difficulty to the others as they sat in the drawing room after dinner.

For the sake of the servants all reference to the case had been avoided during the meal, and afterward Miss Chitterwick had offered to leave the three alone to discuss it. Judith and Mouse refused to hear of her going, pointing out that her experience of life might well throw illumination on some point obscure to those with less years behind them; and nobody hinted that the life of a respectable maiden lady might not include very much experience of murder and the ways of murderers. Positively benign with gratification Miss Chitterwick remained, and her nephew noticed with interest that her manner toward himself was more like that of one human being toward another than he ever remembered.

'You see,' expounded Mr Chitterwick, still a little diffident in the presence of his aunt, 'what I find so baffling is this: Chief Inspector Moresby tells me that this man left the lounge immediately after myself – in other words, a full twenty minutes before Miss Sinclair died. Now whatever else is obscure in the case, this much surely is certain: that this man is the murderer. And that being so, we may assume that he would not leave the lounge until he was assured that Miss Sinclair was on the point of drinking her poisoned coffee. And yet this is what Taylor tells us about the action of prussic acid.' Mr Chitterwick flicked the pages of his well-worn copy of that work. 'Um – um... Ah!... "When a dose of half an ounce and upward of the BP acid has been taken, we may take the average period of death at from two to ten minutes." Um. "It is only when a dose is just in a fatal proportion that we find a person to survive longer." Well!' Mr Chitterwick looked over his glasses at each of the three in turn, his face a picture of perplexity.

'Taylor, you see, puts ten minutes as the limit. The mean period, in other words, is round about six minutes for a dose of the size that we know Miss Sinclair must have taken. Yet here we have twenty minutes. I confess I do not understand it at all.'

Apparently nobody else understood it, either.

'But isn't this the same point that we cleared up this afternoon?' said Judith. 'You remember Mouse suggested that the man probably delayed her drinking it until he was clear of the place.'

'Yes, oh, yes; no doubt he would do that. You see…' Mr Chitterwick ran his eye over the page again. 'Yes, here it is. "It is rare that the appearance of the symptoms is delayed beyond one or two minutes." Um… "Convulsive breathing …when the coma is profound it may be stertorous…" Yes. Yes, I quite agree that he would do his best to find some pretext to leave before the appearance of the symptoms. Indeed, he would have to do so. And in the case of so rapid a poison that would mean leaving before she had even swallowed it. But there is a very great difference between that and leaving a whole quarter of an hour before she did so.'

'Something may have delayed her drinking her coffee,' suggested Mouse.

'For a whole quarter of an hour?' said Mr Chitterwick very doubtfully.

'No woman would put off drinking her coffee for a quarter of an hour,' pronounced Miss Chitterwick with decision, drawing on her experience of Life. 'Nobody but a gairl. Any sensible woman would want it hot.' For some reason Miss Chitterwick had a remarkable contempt for the young of her own sex.

'Just what was in my own mind, Aunt,' observed Mr Chitterwick, in mild surprise at finding his aunt and himself for once in agreement.

'But it's ridiculous to suppose that this man isn't guilty,' said Judith with some impatience, though no one really had supposed anything of the sort.

'Oh, quite,' Mr Chitterwick hastened to assent. 'Ridiculous. Nevertheless, I think we must take it as an established fact that Miss Sinclair did not swallow the poison until, at the very earliest, two fifty-six, and probably a few minutes later. Just at the very time, in fact, that I myself was returning to the lounge.'

'You've got something up your sleeve, Chitterwick,' accused Mouse.

'Nothing, I assure you,' Mr Chitterwick repudiated the insinuation.

'You see some way of getting over the trouble.'

'Well,' said Mr Chitterwick very modestly, 'I have a theory.'

'Good man! I'll admit that this beats me altogether. Let's have it.'

Mr Chitterwick cleared his throat and glanced with some nervousness at his aunt. 'It may strike you as far-fetched. Indeed, it does myself. But really –

'In any case, I think we may say that this is an exceedingly carefully laid and clever plot. Any plot involving impersonation must be so. For instance, I need not ask you, Mrs Sinclair, whether your husband has been trying to buy prussic acid recently; asking for it quite openly in chemists' shops. And yet the police think they have evidence to that effect. I understand that no less than three chemists have identified Major Sinclair as having tried to buy prussic acid from them on the very day before the murder.'

'What!' exclaimed Judith, in a horrified voice.

170

'Further impersonation, you see; designed to make your husband's guilt still more evident. Though in my opinion,' pronounced Mr Chitterwick judicially, 'the criminal overstepped himself there. Really, no one in his senses would do a thing like that if he were really guilty. Although,' he felt bound to add, 'there are plenty of cases on record in which murderers have done just that very stupid thing; though they, of course, were men of very low mentality. Unfortunately, however, the police, I believe, are very little interested in questions of comparative psychology, and the distinction would not appeal to them.

'Nevertheless, there is the fact, which goes in its turn to show the immense care and forethought which must have gone to the making of this plot and its execution. My theory, far-fetched as it may seem to you, nevertheless does allow in all this forethought a place for a consideration which must have appealed with force to so cunning a murderer, namely, the diverting, if in spite of his precautions it ever should fall on him, of suspicion from himself. And I think it is not unreasonable to do that.'

'Is this the theory you hinted at this afternoon?' asked Mouse. 'The one that was going to alter all our ideas about the case?'

'Did I go so far as that?' said Mr Chitterwick in concern. 'Dear me, that was unpardonably rash. It is the same one, yes, but I only put it forward very tentatively, just as a basis of discussion. It occurred to me in the Piccadilly Palace in a flash of illumination, but certainly I should not have gone so far as to say that it actually *will* alter all our ideas; I ought not to have said more than that it *might*. For, really, in some ways it may seem to you quite fantastic. At least, I am convinced that the police would term it so.'

171

'Well, Ambrose, what is it?' gruffly but sensibly demanded Miss Chitterwick.

'Why,' said Mr Chitterwick with becoming diffidence, 'that I was entirely mistaken when I imagined that the man was glaring at me in order to make me look away from him. That he was doing so, in fact, with the express idea of ensuring that my eyes would be riveted upon his every movement.' Mr Chitterwick blushed slightly, as if to apologize for such a preposterous theory.

'Nonsense,' observed Miss Chitterwick briskly, confirming any idea her nephew might have that he was being foolish.

Mouse, however, did not look at all as if he thought Mr Chitterwick was being foolish, while Judith gasped quite audibly. 'What – what *do* you mean, Mr Chitterwick?' she asked.

Still more diffidently Mr Chitterwick tried to explain. 'Well, you know that if a person is looking at you fixedly it is impossible to look away for any length of time. One's eyes keep wandering back to see if the person is still looking. It is quite beyond one's power to prevent them. At least, that is what I have always found. I can't say if everyone experiences the same feeling.'

'Absolutely,' Mouse confirmed. 'Every time. Go on.'

'And the more the other person stares, or glares,' went on Mr Chitterwick, encouraged, 'the more inevitable it is that one must keep on peeping back. Now this man glared at me very fiercely indeed. It is too much to suggest that he was actually ensuring that I should be staring at him just when he wanted – when he could see in the mirror, in fact, that I was actually doing so and should be bound to notice his hand hovering (rather ostentatiously, as it now appears to me) over Miss Sinclair's cup?' Mr Chitterwick drew a breath and looked rather redly round.

'By Jove!' softly exclaimed Mouse.

Judith, however, now seemed rather less impressed. 'Oh, Mr Chitterwick, surely that is too far-fetched, yes.'

'I was afraid you might think so,' admitted Mr Chitterwick with contrition.

'I don't,' Mouse defended his chief. 'But I don't quite see the idea, Chitterwick. Why should the fellow want you to see him putting the poison in her cup?'

'Because he didn't do so,' returned Mr Chitterwick simply. 'Because he poisoned Miss Sinclair in some other way altogether. Because he was so clever that, if suspicion did fall on him, he would have the means to clear himself absolutely and his real method of conveying the poison remain quite unguessed.'

'He could clear himself, you mean, by pointing to the action of prussic acid and showing that it couldn't have been through a dose in her coffee cup administered by him that Miss Sinclair was killed?'

'That partially, no doubt. But, if my theory is true, he would have something else to support that; some piece of solid evidence which would clear him altogether but of which we know nothing at all.'

'Why not?' asked Mouse, relapsing into stupidity.

Judith was quicker to read Mr Chitterwick's expression. 'Why, because – because that piece of evidence would equally clear Lynn! That's what you mean, Mr Chitterwick, isn't it?'

'It is,' Mr Chitterwick admitted, with a modified beam. 'Yes.'

There was a moment of busy silence.

'By Jove!' said Mouse again.

'If I could only think so,' Judith sighed. 'But really, I'm afraid – What do you think, Miss Chitterwick?'

'If Ambrose thinks there's a piece of evidence like that, he'd better find it,' said Miss Chitterwick bluntly.

'And that, I fear, will be an exceedingly difficult task,' lamented her nephew.

Judith looked at him under thoughtful brows. 'Do you intend to tell the police of this idea?'

'I'm afraid they would find it rather fantastic,' Mr Chitterwick confessed.

'I think it would be useless,' said Judith with decision. 'And worse than useless. They're convinced that Lynn is guilty. On that point, without definite evidence, we're not going to move them. Now if there really is anything in this idea of yours, Mr Chitterwick (though I must say candidly that I daren't hope so), it may lead us to just such a piece of evidence. But we must take care that it *is* us, and not the police. If any evidence exists to clear Lynn, I don't want it suppressed; and I'm told the police are quite unscrupulous when they're determined on conviction.'

'Oh really,' expostulated Mr Chitterwick, 'I don't think they would go to such lengths as that, surely.'

Judith looked unconvinced. 'I understand they're quite unscrupulous,' she repeated obstinately, almost angrily.

'Well, it's really for your solicitors to decide whether the theory should be put to the police or not, isn't it?' Mouse suggested mildly.

'For me,' said Judith firmly, and she looked quite capable of taking the responsibility.

'For you, then,' Mouse agreed at once.

Judith spoke without hesitation, 'And I say no. I know solicitors. They wouldn't listen to us. Anything that can be done we'll do ourselves. Yes, Mr Chitterwick?'

'Precisely,' said Mr Chitterwick, and looked a little disappointed that Judith did not seem more impressed with his ingenious theory.

There was a pause, rather an awkward one.

Judith put an end to it speaking in businesslike tones as if to hint that they would now pass from fantasy to fact. 'I asked my husband about the points you raised, Mr Chitterwick. I'd better tell you what he said. I've got it all here.' She rummaged in her bag and extracted a rather crumpled piece of paper, which she studied for a moment. 'He has no idea why the Piccadilly Palace was chosen as the rendezvous. The suggestion did not come from him. He was surprised himself when Miss Sinclair named it.'

'Ah!' Mr Chitterwick crossed his legs and looked up at the ceiling. 'It's possible that I'm wrong, quite wrong; but I can't help feeling this selection of the Piccadilly Palace is significant, if we could only see how. You see, it really isn't the place Miss Sinclair would have chosen herself.'

'You mean, she was prompted?' asked Mouse respectfully.

'It does look like it. But by whom?'

Nobody having any suggestions to offer, Judith passed to the next point. 'Lynn has been allowed to see the phial that contained the prussic acid, and of course he didn't recognize it. I asked him, as you told me, whether he can remember ever handling one like it, and he says he can't, except perhaps one in our own bathroom at Queen Anne's Gate that had some concentrated mouth-wash of mine in it. I took a taxi straight from the prison to Queen Anne's Gate to see if that one is still there. It is; and in any case it's a good deal bigger than the other.'

'I must confess I can't see my way round those fingerprints,' Mr Chitterwick had to admit.

'Fingerprints can be forged, I suppose, can't they?' Mouse suggested.

'Can they?' asked Mr Chitterwick doubtfully. 'Outside a detective story I very much doubt it.'

'I know it's a deadly point,' Judith said tonelessly, 'and I pressed him. It's a very ordinary shape of phial, and I told him he must have handled several; but the only other possibility he could suggest was that it's rather like ones he's seen at Earlshaze in which Miss Sinclair used to have drops for her eyes, but he couldn't swear to the similarity. And even if they were alike, I don't see how it would help.'

'He might have handled one there,' Mr Chitterwick pointed out. 'Would almost certainly have done so. Brought it downstairs for Miss Sinclair, no doubt, or been sent to fetch it from somewhere.' If it were a question of probabilities concerning an aunt no one could speak with more authority than Mr Chitterwick. 'It might well have his fingerprints, you see. We must certainly take up that point.'

'And if they are alike?'

'Try to trace some connection between the two,' said Mr Chitterwick more hopefully than he felt.

'But that would hardly help Lynn, unless we can show that one of Miss Sinclair's phials got into the possession of a third person. And I imagine,' said Judith with a mirthless smile, 'that Miss Goole would not be very helpful if we called to ask her whether any phials lately containing Miss Sinclair's eye drops have disappeared from the house recently in suspicious circumstances.'

'Nevertheless,' maintained Mr Chitterwick stoutly, 'if she could tell us so, and into whose hands, we should know at once the identity of the murderer. In any case we must decidedly not forget the point.'

Judith sighed. 'Oh, such little things... Well, the next point. Lynn can't add anything more to the description he's given already of the man's voice on the telephone. "An exaggerated Oxford accent"; that's all he can say.'

'And did it strike him as odd at the time?'

'Only vaguely, that Eccles should not have got over his youthfully affected drawl even yet; nothing else. Certainly he suspected nothing. Point number four, he can't add anything to his account of what he did during the time he was supposed to have been in the Piccadilly Palace, or suggest any way at all in which his alibi could be proved.'

'Um! Something in that connection has occurred to me, though,' remarked Mr Chitterwick modestly. 'I thought we might at any rate take steps to prove a negative fact if not the positive one. You – er – you do wish to arrive at the truth, I take it? Just the bare truth, whatever it may be?'

'You mean, even if it should turn out that Lynn did poison his aunt, after all?' said Judith calmly. 'Certainly I do, my convictions being as they are.'

'Then, I suggest,' beamed Mr Chitterwick, 'that you offer a big reward, a really handsome one, to anyone who can prove that he or she was on that landing during the period when Major Sinclair says that he was there. If nobody comes forward to claim it you have at least established that the landing was deserted during that very time, and I think that counsel might make a very big point of that indeed.'

There was a pause.

'You – really think that wise?' Judith faltered.

Mr Chitterwick lit a fresh cigarette. 'I understand that you have no doubts,' he said quietly.

Judith threw up her head. 'I haven't! Certainly I'll do what you suggest, Mr Chitterwick. I think it a very good idea.'

'I thought it might be helpful,' admitted Mr Chitterwick immodestly.

But whether it would prove to be so or not nothing else of any importance arose from the rest of the evening's discussion. Mr Chitterwick could not help feeling that the atmosphere was not all it might be. It may have been the presence of his aunt, mostly silent, it is true, but nevertheless acutely felt; it may have been the fact that Judith, whom Mr Chitterwick had hoped to cheer with the progress, interesting if somewhat problematical, that the case seemed to have made, grew undeniably more quiet and depressed as the evening wore on; certainly the general feeling grew less and less hopeful. The impression appeared to be that in all probability Mr Chitterwick's new theory was too far-fetched to be true, and even if it were true it did not advance things, for nobody would ever believe it, nor would they themselves ever be able to prove it. Even Mouse became infected with the prevailing gloom, and the glances he threw from time to time at Judith were anything but brotherly in their intense concern.

It was on this inauspicious note the party broke up, somewhat early, and dispersed to bed.

Under pretext of making sure that his guest had everything he wanted, Mr Chitterwick paid a visit to Mouse's room.

Mouse welcomed him warmly. 'I was hoping you'd come along. Look here, I can't possibly go to bed yet. Could you bear to carry on the pow-wow just between the two of us?'

'I should be only too glad,' returned Mr Chitterwick, no less warmly. 'Indeed it was with some such object... I think we were all a little tired downstairs, perhaps.'

'Things did get a bit damnable, didn't they? Poor old Judy.' Mouse sighed, and then threw a quarter-smoked cigarette savagely out of the window. 'You see, she's far too sensible to build anything on delusions or guesswork, and I'm afraid she thinks things are pretty hopeless.'

Mr Chitterwick dropped gently into a chair. 'She didn't appear to be impressed with the new idea I put forward,' he regretted. 'Of course, it *is* far-fetched; fantastic, one might say; but really, I did feel that – '

Mouse, who was strolling restlessly up and down the room, stopped opposite Mr Chitterwick. '*I* think it's defendable,' he said, almost challengingly. 'Why not? One can argue on behalf of it. I was sorry Judy didn't think more of it. Personally, I shouldn't be at all surprised if you haven't put us absolutely on the right track. In any case, it was damned cunning of you to work it out.'

'Do you really think so?' beamed Mr Chitterwick, artlessly gratified. 'Well, I certainly did hope... But trouble is, you see, that it only leaves us at a dead end again. A different one this time, but just as – er – dead.'

'Does it, though?' Mouse frowned. 'I'm not so sure.' He paused, leaning on the back of a chair and scowling quite ferociously at Mr Chitterwick in the intensity of his thought. 'You know, the more I look at it, the more I feel you've hit the mark.'

'The idea grows on one,' agreed Mr Chitterwick, with gentle pride.

Mouse lit another cigarette. 'You see,' he said between puffs, 'if the fellow wasn't a perfect fool (and it's getting plainer every minute that he isn't) he must have known that glaring like that would only make you look the harder, just as it did. If he didn't want you to look at him he'd have tried to make himself as inconspicuous as possible; avoided catching your eye, shifted his chair round a bit, all that. And then if, as you say, he really was quite ostentatious with his hand over Miss Sinclair's cup instead of being quick and surreptitious; and that mirror – Chitterwick, I'm positive you've hit it!'

'That is exactly how it strikes me,' nodded Mr Chitterwick vigorously.

'Well, let's see exactly what that gives us.' Mouse looked very earnest indeed and very young as well.

Mr Chitterwick's heart grew still warmer toward him. He was almost as anxious to solve the case on Mouse's behalf as on Judith's own. And having tucked away somewhere behind his criminological and stamp-collecting passions a strong feeling for romance, hitherto ungratified, it touched him to see the desperate eagerness with which this young man was bent on saving from the gallows the husband of the woman with whom he was, undoubtedly, in love, thus robbing himself for good and all of any possibility that might exist of getting her for himself.

He recapitulated exactly what, in his opinion, his new theory gave them.

'Yes,' Mouse nodded, 'this idea of yours about the action of prussic acid doesn't really help Lynn much at present, of course, because it's impossible to prove when Miss Sinclair swallowed her coffee; and through counsel ought to make a nice point of it, the jury can't be expected to attach much importance to psy – psychological possibilities.'

'Or the judge' lamented Mr Chitterwick, thinking of a recent and now notorious miscarriage of justice, brought about in very large measure by the learned judge's sturdy refusal to recognize any such un-British values. 'The legal mind, you know,' he added, as one apologizes for an unsightly boil on a child's face.

'But the other thing, the piece of evidence which you think exists to clear this man, and Lynn with him – '

'Well,' modified Mr Chitterwick, 'I can't really say with confidence that it exists at all, you know; only on the balance of probabilities. And even if it does, I should doubt whether it would clear either of them from suspicion, and very grave suspicion. In my opinion,' ruminated Mr Chitterwick, 'all it would do would be to introduce such an element of uncertainty as to make it impossible for a jury to say beyond all reasonable doubt that Miss Sinclair did not commit suicide (for it is little beyond my own evidence, you see, that really establishes that she did not), with the result that the police, recognizing the extreme difficulty of obtaining a conviction, would probably not prosecute. But beyond that I think it would be injudicious to go.'

'Well, at any rate,' said Mouse with some impatience, 'it would save Lynn's neck.'

'Oh, yes,' assented Mr Chitterwick, who seemed rather to have lost sight for the moment of the main point, 'I think we might say it would do that.'

'Well, what about concentrating on that, then?'

'It would be remarkably gratifying to find the real murderer as well, though,' sighed Mr Chitterwick. 'Even if we were able to ensure Major Sinclair's acquittal, you see, suspicion of having poisoned his aunt would still rest on him; and with so many people suspicion is tantamount to certainty.' Mr Chitterwick's tone apologized for the base tendencies of so many people.

'Yes, of course. But let's clear Lynn first. I vote for directing our forces to seeing whether we can unearth any piece of evidence to do that.' Mouse was so determined to carry his point, which at least was reasonable enough, that he took Mr Chitterwick's agreement for granted. 'Now, how are we going to do that?'

'We must put ourselves in the criminal's place,' promptly replied Mr Chitterwick, who had not read so many detective stores for nothing, 'and see what he would do.'

They put themselves, presumably, in the criminal's place, and Mouse, at any rate, saw nothing. He said as much.

'Nor do I,' Mr Chitterwick confessed. 'Dear me, this is extremely baffling. I wonder – I wonder whether we are possibly becoming too muddled. I feel that I may be, for one. Do you know what I feel inclined to do, Mouse? Retire to the study and put the whole case into writing, tabulate what conclusions we have agreed on as certain, what conclusions are still speculative, what deductions may legitimately be drawn from every one of the very few points that the case presents, and from that,' said Mr Chitterwick, recalling the brilliant methods of some of his collaborators in his last case, which had led them to such surprisingly wrong conclusions, 'endeavour to form some idea of the mental processes of the murderer which might enable us to estimate those of his actions which remain unknown to us.'

'That,' said Mouse with some awe, 'is a dashed good idea.'

So Mr Chitterwick retired to his aunt's study.

He seated himself at his aunt's table and recklessly grasped his aunt's favourite pen. He wanted first of all to jot down an idea which had occurred to him within the minute. 'If *I* were the murderer,' wrote Mr Chitterwick improbably...

chapter eleven

Mr Chitterwick Solves the Problem

Having got his notes, Mr Chitterwick proceeded with his summary as follows:

General Conclusions.

That this is a carefully planned murder, probably prepared for a considerable time, involving impersonation and a deliberate attempt to throw the blame on another person.

That, if this object is gained and Major Sinclair is hanged in accordance with the murderer's intention, a double murder will have been achieved. (That Major Sinclair himself is innocent is the basis on which these remarks are made.)

That the chief object of the murderer is the death of Miss Sinclair.

That the fixing of the crime on Major Sinclair and his subsequent death is an extremely important objective, but subordinate to the safeguarding of the actual murderer in the event of suspicion ever attaching to himself. (This, assuming that my theory of the murderer's behaviour is correct.)

That, in this event also, my connection with the case is due solely to the three facts that I was alone, that I was in a position to observe the murderer's actions, and that he could see me in the mirror. Any other person fulfilling these conditions would have done equally well. (NB This explains the choice of the Piccadilly Palace from the murderer's point of view, as at that time it would be almost certain that someone would be there who could do so. Indeed, from the murderer's standpoint the Piccadilly Palace is ideal for the achievement of his various objects. But apparently Miss Sinclair, and not the murderer at all, chose the Piccadilly Palace. There should be helpful significance here.)

That, in this event, further, a vital piece of evidence which would almost certainly acquit and perhaps exonerate Major Sinclair, remains to be discovered.

That in this event, I myself, the police, and everyone else, have fallen into a trap very cleverly laid by the murderer.

That, after serious consideration, I have decided that my theory is correct, and the remainder of these remarks will be based on that supposition.

Deductions from the Administration of the Poison.

That the vehicle in which the poison was administered has probably not yet been discovered. That it was in the coffee seems extremely doubtful. (Was anything else ordered by Miss Sinclair, perhaps, or by the man with her? e.g., a liqueur? Such a liqueur as kirsch or kümmel would probably disguise both the taste and smell of prussic acid. Inquiries must be made on this point.)

That, as the murderer left the lounge very shortly after myself and would not do so until he had made sure that the swallowing of the poison by Miss Sinclair was certain, then the means of administration must have been to hand at just about the very moment when I was called to the telephone. (NB Perhaps the waitress who called me could help on this point.)

That, as it seems probable, if not certain, that the poison was not swallowed by Miss Sinclair till at least ten minutes later, then the vehicle containing the poison must either have been a drink of a cold nature (such as the liqueur), or else something which the murderer knew Miss Sinclair would be taking before she left the Piccadilly Palace, such as a dose of medicine. (Make inquiries about this.)

That some means must have been adopted by the murderer to ensure her remaining there after he himself had gone. No doubt he simply made some excuse to leave her temporarily, and she was expecting his return.

Deductions from what I Saw of the Interview.

That Miss Sinclair had her doubts at one time that the man really was her nephew, but that he was able to remove any such doubt. This explains her peering at him doubtfully at first (as suggested by Mrs Sinclair) and subsequently talking to him with animation.

That the leaving of one pair of spectacles behind and the breaking of the others happened most fortunately for the murderer; so fortunately that design rather than luck would seem to be behind it. (NB This might be a most hopeful line of investigation.)

That the man I saw with Miss Sinclair was not Major Sinclair is supported by the feeling I had, on seeing the latter later at close quarters, that he differed, though only very slightly and very subtly, from the impression I had formed of him earlier; namely, that he was somewhat older, somewhat broader, and possessed of rather more natural dignity. These differences, though far too slight to affect the question of identification, do remain in my mind.

That the impersonator had, after all, not so difficult a part to play as one might think. Not only could Miss Sinclair not see him very well, but during the interview it was she who did nearly all the talking; he had little to do but listen. Assuming that he had some such excuse ready, such as a sore throat, to account for his altered voice, there is no reason, so far as Miss Sinclair is concerned, why he should not have carried off the deception successfully.

That, on examining my own memory as closely as possible, I am more than ever of the opinion that the murderer's action with regard to Miss Sinclair's cup may be described as ostentatious rather than surreptitious. His hand remained in position over it much longer than would be necessary just to drop something in, or even pour a few drops from a phial. He would, of course, be expected to jerk the poison in with the greatest possible despatch.

That, endeavouring to the best of my ability to re-enact the scene in my own mind, I am strongly inclined to think that after directing Miss Sinclair's attention to the distant object and continuing during the next few moments to do so, the murderer did not keep his gaze fixed as one would expect on the cup over which his hand was poised but glanced up once or twice. This confirms my theory that he was glancing up at the mirror to make sure that I was still watching him. (NB I could not possibly swear to this impression, but on balance it remains with me.)

Deductions from the Phial.

That the murderer must be a man, not only in touch with Miss Sinclair (to know of the appointment for half-past three in the Piccadilly Palace), but also, in view of the fingerprints, with Major Sinclair also.

That the fact that the murderer was able to obtain an impression of Major Sinclair's fingerprints on the phial may be of the greatest assistance in checking his identity.

That it is quite possible that the phial is not only a trap to incriminate Major Sinclair, but also a trap for the police too, and that the poison was never administered from it at all. In that case…

At this point in his task Mr Chitterwick sat bolt upright in his chair, and his mouth dropped open. He gazed with unseeing eyes at the blotting paper in front of him, and his jaw sagged lower and lower; the pen dropped from his fingers and made a large blot on the immaculate neatness of his manuscript. He continued to present this remarkable picture for nearly a whole minute. Then he literally bounded up from his chair, dashed out of the room, tore upstairs, and burst open the door of the ducal chamber without so much as a single respectful tap.

'Mouse,' he squeaked, 'I – I have been guilty of the most unpardonable blunder. I – I – Really, I cannot imagine how I can have overlooked such a glaring piece of evidence.'

Mouse had been sitting gloomily in a chair poring over his notebook prior to Mr Chitterwick's unceremonious intrusion. Now he jumped up, no less excited. 'What?' he deman-ded. 'You haven't cleared Lynn, have you?'

Mr Chitterwick beamed at him triumphantly over his glasses. 'Well, perhaps not altogether. But I think so. I think so. At the very least, I may say I have destroyed a particularly damning fact against him. That piece of evidence which was to render a conviction impossible! It's been staring us in the face all the time – you, me, the police, everyone. And yet nobody saw it, and probably never would have, had we not had our own convictions about the case. Dear me, dear me.'

'What is it then, man?'

'Why,' said Mr Chitterwick, 'that phial. If the man impersonating Major Sinclair left the lounge just after I did, when Miss Sinclair was alive and well (a fact we can surely prove from those same witnesses who saw him go), how could he possibly, and equally, for the benefit of the police, Major Sinclair himself, have placed the phial in her already nerveless fingers?'

The two men looked at each other.

'Oh, neat,' whispered Mouse. 'Dam' neat.'

'So simple,' crowed Mr Chitterwick, 'and yet so subtle.'

'This lets Lynn out,' Mouse grinned.

'I really believe it does,' Mr Chitterwick grinned back. 'It would be quite impossible for the jury, you see, to exclude the possibility of suicide beyond all doubt. Well, well.'

They stared at each other again.

'Then who,' said Mouse, 'did put it there?'

Mr Chitterwick's jaw dropped lower than it had done in his aunt's study. His glasses fell off his nose, and he positively goggled at the other.

'God bless my soul!' gasped Mr Chitterwick. 'I – I never thought of that.'

The proceedings of the next half hour may perhaps be best expressed as follows:

Back in his aunt's study, Mr Chitterwick, though with some difficulty, proceeded with his summary.

The question posed by Mouse had disconcerted him considerably, and the two of them had discussed possible answers to it for some time. Had the murderer an accomplice? That was a possibility which Mr Chitterwick had examined before, and rejected; the job had looked to him like a one-man affair. Since Moresby's statement that his four witnesses were ready to swear that no one at all had visited the old lady's table between the red-haired man's departure and Mr Chitterwick's own arrival, the possibility of an accomplice had seemed quite ruled out. It still seemed so; yet who, as the red-haired man could not conceivably have done so, had placed that phial in Miss Sinclair's already unconscious fingers?

After half an hour's discussion no credible explanation had emerged. In the end it was left at the agreement that, shelving the matter of any such explanation for the time being, Mr Chitterwick must have the two vital points definitely and irrevocably confirmed by an unsuspecting Moresby, that his four witnesses really were convinced of that fact and that Miss Sinclair really must have been unconscious when the phial was slipped into her loosely clenched hand. With that, at a few minutes past one o'clock, Mr Chitterwick had again taken his leave.

It was not till more than an hour later that his summary was completed. Mr Chitterwick had intended to proceed with the remainder without taking account of this latest momentous question, simply recording the state which the case had reached before that had been posed; but even as he wrote, speculations and possibilities occurred to him which he had to incorporate. Reading it through to himself, he decided that he had produced on the whole a not unhelpful document.

Deductions Regarding the Murderer.

That he must be an exceptionally intelligent, capable, and self-reliant man. To work out a plan in which a murder is made to look like suicide and yet with such a small degree of clumsiness that the police will be bound to see through it without, however, suspecting that they are meant to do anything of the sort, and at the same time to throw all suspicion on another person, and then to put that plan into operation without a hitch, implies a combination of intelligence and determination almost unsurpassed in the records of crime.

That he must have an interest in the deaths of both Miss and Major Sinclair, the former most directly, the latter less urgently. (NB This narrows the field of suspicion and search to a most remarkable degree.)

That he must have been in contact with Miss Sinclair, either personal or by correspondence, or with a member of her household, and similarly with Major Sinclair (*vide supra*). (NB This also should prove an invaluable pointer.)

That both to plan and successfully to carry through so close an impersonation he must have had some previous experience on these lines; it is obvious that he has confidence in his powers as a mimic.

That from his voice on the telephone he would seem to be a man of culture and breeding. (NB His representation of himself as Eccles gives further proof of his cognizance of Major Sinclair's affairs. Might he be looked for among the friends of Sinclair's Oxford days? But what interest could any such friend have in Miss Sinclair's death?)

That we have a fair idea of his physical appearance. He *must* be a big man, tall, and only slightly less broad than Major Sinclair himself, if at all, with an unmistakably aquiline nose, and very much like Major Sinclair in face. He *may* have red hair (though this might equally have been a wig), a pronounced drawl (though this might have been adopted to suit the representation as Eccles), be several years younger than Major Sinclair (this is only my impression, and I could not swear to it), and be somewhat slipshod in his manners and personal bearing (this again is only my impression, and a vague one at that).

That from all these indications it should not be impossible, or even difficult, to identify him should suspicion from other sources be strong enough. (NB The nose, of course, is the real test.)

Speculations Regarding the Murderer's Methods and Intentions.

That one difficulty may be the probability that the full benefit to himself would not become apparent until after Major Sinclair's execution.

That in view of the other ingenuity shown in his plan, a particularly ingenious method of administering the poison (and also of ensuring the marked phial being found in Miss Sinclair's possession) remains to be discovered.

That if, as we have seen, the murderer could not have placed the phial in Miss Sinclair's hand while he was still with her and under the observation of the four witnesses, he may equally have found some method of substituting a poisoned coffee cup on the table for Miss Sinclair's own; in other words the poisoned cup may be just as much of a trap as the phial itself, and the fact that it was poisoned must not be taken as proving that the coffee was the vehicle by which the prussic acid was administered; and in this case, the real vehicle would have been removed at the same time.

(Dear me, thought Mr Chitterwick at this point, this is becoming extremely involved; but really, with such an ingenious mind...)

That the whole plan seems to have had as its aim not only the deaths of Miss and Major Sinclair, but above all security for the murderer. One might almost say that 'Safety First' was the latter's motto, and if Miss Sinclair could not have been poisoned with perfect security (or apparently perfect security) for the criminal, he would have been ready to drop the whole affair at any point. If that is the case, one must look for a means of introducing the phial into Miss Sinclair's hand which would not appear to involve the murderer at all. An accomplice might be indicated here; but not only have we evidence that no accomplice approached her, but it is my estimate of the cautious mentality behind this crime that the necessity of trusting an accomplice would be entirely ruled out. If *I* were the murderer I should have been satisfied with the affair up to the time of leaving the table; the phial I should regard as a master card to be played only if certain circumstances permitted, and in perfect safety to myself; that circumstances apparently did so permit might possibly help to show (*a*) what those circumstances were, (*b*) how this very difficult task was accomplished.

That the murderer's motive, at present obscure, might be found by an examination of all persons who would benefit by the joint deaths of both Miss and Major Sinclair.

That in view of the clever way in which Major Sinclair was deprived of his alibi we may suppose that the murderer would not have overlooked the question of an alibi for himself. We should be prepared to find that he has one, and a good one, which will need to be broken down.

That we may expect the murderer to be vehement in defence of Major Sinclair, and anyone so vehement, whose physical characteristics correspond roughly with what we know of the murderer's, may be viewed with the greatest suspicion.

Obscure Points Requiring Explanations.

Why the interview was arranged by Miss Sinclair for the Piccadilly Palace.

How the poison was administered.

How Major Sinclair's fingerprints were obtained on the phial.

How the phial was conveyed to Miss Sinclair's hand.

Why Miss Goole is disguised.

'Not unhelpful, no,' murmured Mr Chitterwick, and read the whole thing through again.

'Yes, that's the truth, undoubtedly,' observed Mr Chitterwick, at the end of another five minutes. 'The difficulty, no doubt, will be to prove it. Dear me, what a depraved creature he must be.' Mr Chitterwick shook his head sadly over the unnamed creature's depravity and, gathering his sheets up into a neat stack, folded it across the middle and carried it soberly up to bed with him.

chapter twelve

A Little Detecting

After profound meditation in the small hours of the morning
Mr Chitterwick had arrived at the decision to say nothing to
Judith and Mouse of his own private conviction that he had
solved the problem. That conviction had still to be tested,
and Mr Chitterwick was diffident enough to recognize the
possibility of its falling down badly. In that case he had no
wish to raise hopes which might only be crushed later, and
slightly guilty though he felt in doing so, particularly as
regards Mouse, he thought it better to confine to the dark
lantern of his own consciousness the illumination which he
felt had been vouchsafed him.

The next morning, therefore, he was exceedingly
cunning. Saying at breakfast, and even with an air of
carelessness, that as there were one or two points he wished
to look up, matters simply of dull routine such as fall to every
amateur detective, he would not return with them to
Dorsetshire that day; he intimated that there was nothing
whatever to detain the other two in London. Mouse offered
eagerly to stay up too and help him. Miss Chitterwick, who
had broken the custom of years and appeared at her own
breakfast table, gruffly extended invitation after invitation,

each more pressing than the last, to her guests to remain at least another night; but Mr Chitterwick, who wanted a free hand and was really alarmed lest he might let some of his great ideas slip out if the opportunity remained with him to do so, succeeded in shepherding them gently off the premises by eleven o'clock, with the hypocritical promise of following them down to Dorsetshire the very instant he discovered anything of importance.

Before they went he did, however, show them his summary, both out of mere fairness and also because he was much interested to see whether either of them would arrive at the same tentative conclusion as his own. Both of them read it with interest and agreed that it was quite a remarkable document and would probably be of the very greatest service; but though they commented freely on some of the points raised in it, neither appeared to notice the particular significances which had so struck Mr Chitterwick.

The rest of the morning that astute detective spent on his matters of routine. Moresby had to be seen and, without being made suspicious, delicately questioned as to the phial in the dead woman's hand. The result was quite satisfactory. Moresby was not suspicious at all, only jocular; he seemed now to derive such hearty amusement from the idea of Mr Chitterwick investigating things on his own account that he was ready to part with any information required for the sake of an extra laugh. Moresby, it seemed, now regarded Mr Chitterwick not only as a performing pet but as a pet performing a particularly hilarious turn. Mr Chitterwick's conscience, it appeared to Moresby, was a wow.

Mr Chitterwick beamed his acquiescence in this view. He did not mind in the least in what capacity Moresby regarded him and his conscience so long as the chief inspector was willing to assure him, as he did, that the police doctor had definitely stated, with a view to excluding the suggestion of suicide, that the phial must have been placed in Miss Sinclair's hand by some other person after she had lost consciousness, and could not possibly have been in her own grasp when she did so. Moresby also very kindly confirmed in the strongest terms (between guffaws) that his four witnesses, who were now six because he had succeeded in finding two more people at another table, were all ready to swear by their immortal souls that no other living soul had approached Miss Sinclair's table between the red-haired man's departure and Mr Chitterwick's advent.

Mr Chitterwick marvelled that the relation between these two facts, the perfectly obvious inference which there was really no gainsaying, should miraculously remain hidden from Chief Inspector Moresby – oblivious of the fact that it had up to a few hours ago remained equally hidden from himself.

If Mr Chitterwick had had time he might also have found a moment to marvel at these six witnesses, who were all ready to swear to such a trifling incident that had happened weeks ago. Doubtless they were perfectly correct in such readiness, but if so what an enviable attention to detail must have been theirs. They were of the same breed as that which infests semi-detached villas and makes life miserable for the occupants of their twin. Never can the latter poke their innocent noses out of the front door or back, garden gate or French window without being aware of another nose pressed whitely against one of their twin's windows and two piercing eyes following avidly their every movement; and never do the owners of those piercing eyes walk past the front of their twin's house, or even out into their own back gardens, without gorming up at the other's windows in an effort to penetrate the modesty of the curtains and violate every secret that any of the rooms may hold. A noisome type.

Mr Chitterwick, however, who had never had experience of a semi-detached villa, marvelled uncomprehendingly.

Close acquaintance with crime certainly does enlarge one's horizon. For about the first time since he went to live with her Mr Chitterwick had not implicitly asked his aunt's permission to absent himself for a meal. He had simply and calmly, and without even realizing the magnitude of the step he was taking, announced that he would not be in to lunch. Miss Chitterwick, subdued by her nephew's familiarity with the Great, had meekly accepted this pronouncement.

Having satisfactorily concluded this interview with Moresby, therefore, Mr Chitterwick took himself and his amusing conscience out to lunch. He chose the Piccadilly Palace, as he had business there afterwards. Having demolished in the immense dining room a sizeable meal (not excluding poulet rôti salade) for the ridiculous sum of two shillings, Mr Chitterwick betook himself to the lounge and seated himself at the very table where Miss Sinclair had met her death. It was not the instinct of morbidity which causes perfectly respectable citizens to gaze for hours up at the uninteresting exterior of a house in which a particularly unpleasant murder has been committed that caused him to do so; simply a wish to get hold of the waitress who had served Miss Sinclair with coffee.

Mr Chitterwick was in luck. From her lurking place afar the waitress spied him and recognized him as a (technical) friend. Their police-station companionship caused her to do for Mr Chitterwick what she would never have done for any ordinary patron. She came forth to serve him.

She even set the seal on her action by accosting him by name. It is only the most favoured of mortals whom a waitress at the Piccadilly Palace will accost at all, let alone by name. 'Good afternoon, Mr Chitterwick,' she said, in sombre, conspirator-like tones. 'Can I get you anything?' From her voice one would have gathered that she and Mr Chitterwick were the principals in the perpetration of a murder instead of in its discovery; the secret understanding between them was so evidently a guilty one.

Mr Chitterwick intimated a craving for coffee. The waitress nodded portentously, as if a cup of funereal coffee were the only thing that would adequately meet the occasion, and retired with solemnity to obtain it, regardless of the becks and calls and wreathed smiles that were showered on her from all sides by other thirsty inhabitants of her tables.

Mr Chitterwick had taken the opportunity to commit her to memory. Though he had seen her, and even exchanged a word or two with her, in the police station, his state of agitation at that time had been such that he could not have remembered a minute afterward whether her hair was gold, or brown, or bright pea green, while his impression of her at the inquest and before the magistrate was of the vaguest. He had recognized her this time as she approached him, but only just. Now he noted meticulously that she was not very young, thirty-two or three at the least, with a very plain face, pale frizzy hair, a thin mouth, and watery blue eyes.

With surprising alacrity the coffee arrived, and the waitress lingered. 'Come to have another look at the place, Mr Chitterwick?' she asked with due gravity, oblivious of the clicking fingers all round her.

'Well, as a matter of fact,' said Mr Chitterwick, 'I came to see you. Is there anywhere – er – fairly private where I could have a word with you?'

'We ought to have a word together,' approved the waitress, 'and that's a fact. Yes, there's plenty of places. Will you finish your coffee first, Mr Chitterwick?'

'Whatever is most convenient to you,' accommodated Mr Chitterwick.

The waitress looked round with distaste at the wielders of the clicking fingers. 'I suppose I'd better see to some of these folks first,' she sighed. 'Hark at 'em! Never give a girl a minute's peace, some people wouldn't. All right, all right,' she added to a white-haired country clergyman who was clicking with particular frenzy. 'I'm here, aren't I? Well, what is it?'

She departed with dignity, under a shower of orders. Mr Chitterwick was conscious of a sense of superiority, as a royal favourite among a host of lesser courtiers.

In the course of time Mr Chitterwick drank his coffee, the owners of a selected number of the clicking fingers were appeased, and Mr Chitterwick followed the waitress out of the lounge, down a number of passages, and into a very large room, which was explained to him as a private dining room not in use for the day where they could rely on being undisturbed. The waitress sank into a chair and kindly waved Mr Chitterwick into another, remarking that they need not hurry themselves, as one of the other girls had undertaken to keep an eye on her table for a few minutes; the air of conscious importance with which she spoke was evidently the measure of the rise she had made in her confreres' estimation through her participation in the tragedy.

'Thank you, thank,' murmured Mr Chitterwick, lowering himself into the chair indicated. 'Now, let me see. Oh, yes. What I wanted to ask you was this: do you remember whether Miss Sinclair, the unfortunate lady who was poisoned, or the man with her, ordered anything at all besides the two cups of coffee?'

'Anything else? No, that they didn't. Oh, Mr Chitterwick, it is terrible, isn't it? To think of that man, sitting there as innocent as you like, and then putting poison in her cup that way. I can tell you, I hardly got a wink of sleep for nights after, thinking of it. And how I'm going to get through giving evidence in court – well! Before the magistrates was bad enough, didn't you think? But – '

'You're quite sure,' persisted Mr Chitterwick, 'that neither of them ordered anything in the nature, let us say, of a liqueur?'

'Not a thing. I should know quick enough if they had. Deary me, if I could 'a' known as they sat there what – '

'They couldn't have ordered anything from one of the other waitresses, perhaps?'

If any of the other girls had served them, I should have heard about it quick enough, I can tell you, after we knew what'd happened. No, Mr Chitterwick, you can take it from me they ordered nothing but that coffee he put the poison in. Goodness gracious me, if I'd thought I'd ever be mixed up in...' She detailed the thoughts she had not had at considerable length.

Mr Chitterwick waited for the first pause to proceed to his next question. 'Well, if they didn't order anything, do you remember whether you cleared anything away from the table besides the man's coffee cup? Did he give you anything with that?'

'No, there was just the cup; that's all. Beckoned me over, he did, and – '

'You didn't remove anything from the table a few minutes later, after he'd gone? An empty medicine bottle, perhaps, or something of that nature? A piece of paper, even?'

'And why should you think I did?' asked the waitress, with evident suspicion. 'I've told the police all I did, times enough, and I'm sure I don't understand why you should think I haven't.'

'I don't think anything of the sort,' said Mr Chitterwick hastily. 'Dear me, no. Quite the reverse. I'm quite certain you told them everything you remembered doing, just as I did myself. All I want to find out is whether perhaps some quite trifling thing, like picking a piece of waste paper off the table or the floor as you passed, may have escaped your memory. I can assure you, I have remembered several trivial incidents of that nature from time to time since I gave my first report to the police, so it would be quite natural – '

'Well, what do you want to know for, anyway?' asked the waitress, her suspicion allayed but not altogether dispelled.

Mr Chitterwick adopted a confidential air. 'Well, you see, it's like this. Some doubt has arisen whether the poison was actually given to Miss Sinclair in the cup at all.'

'But it smelt of poison, the doctor said. I heard him, at the inquest.'

Oh, yes. But that's just the point. It isn't certain that that cup isn't a clever trap, laid by the murderer to put us off his track and make everyone think Miss Sinclair had committed suicide. It's a question of – er – the action of prussic acid, you see.'

'Well, there, now, he's a cunning one all right,' said the waitress admiringly, now quite mollified. 'Upon my word, I could quite believe it, I could. And if they can't find out what the poison was really in he may get off, after all?'

'Something like that,' agreed Mr Chitterwick.

'Well, I'd tell you if I could, I'm sure, because, though I'm not much of a one for bloodthirstiness meself, I do think hanging's too good for *him,* and that I will say, major or no major. Poisoning his poor old aunty like that! But there, what's the use? I never went near the table, not after I'd taken his cup just as he was getting his things together to go out, and that I know as well as I know I'm sitting here. No, Mr Chitterwick, I'm sorry I can't help you, but whatever there was on that table was still there when the police and you were there afterward.'

'And as far as you know, no one else went near the table either, after he'd gone out?'

'The police asked me that, and I told 'em I couldn't swear to it, not wishing to take my Bible oath on anything I couldn't say for positive certain; but I'll tell you what I told them, and that is that no one went near it while *I* was looking, at any rate.'

'I see,' said Mr Chitterwick, and felt thoroughly disappointed. On neither of the two major points he had noted down for inquiry had he been able to obtain any helpful enlightenment at all.

There was a pause, while he wondered if there were anything else on which he ought to question her.

'It's funny you should have mentioned a lickure just now, though,' said the waitress slowly.

'Eh?' ejaculated Mr Chitterwick.

'I said, it's funny you mentioned that about a lickure, because – well, 'sa matter of fact that has reminded me of something.'

'It has? What?'

'Well, reely,' said the waitress coyly, 'I don't know that it's worth telling you, I'm sure.'

Mr Chitterwick's reply was calculated to leave her in no doubt that it was very well worth telling.

'Well, then I didn't say anything about it to the police because for one thing I wouldn't have thought it worth the while, and for another it'd quite slipped my memory; but I do remember now thinking at one time that I'd seen a lickure

202

glass on her table. It was your mentioning that about a lickure that brought it back to me.'

'You – you did see a liqueur glass on Miss Sinclair's table?' clucked Mr Chitterwick, puce with excitement.

'Well, that's what so funny. I couldn't have reely, because when I went to look for it only a minute afterward it wasn't there, so of course I must have been dreaming. But it was funny, you mentioning that about a lickure, wasn't it?'

Disregarding the humour of the situation, Mr Chitterwick set about obtaining the facts. It was a delicate task, because he was unwilling to let his companion guess the supreme importance he attached to her story. As she evidently thought herself to have suffered from a minor hallucination, it was a good deal better to leave her under that impression; Mr Chitterwick did not want a report of this interview to reach Scotland Yard just yet. To dig the facts, however, out of the mass of irrelevance and anecdote with which the woman chose to embroider them required all the tact and patience Mr Chitterwick possessed.

He succeeded at last, and the story of which he then found himself in possession was as follows:

Not long after Miss Sinclair's companion had left her the waitress was passing fairly close to the table to receive an order from somebody a few yards away and, knowing there was still a coffee cup to be collected, glanced casually at the table as she went by to see if the cup were empty, in which case she would have picked it up on her return a moment later; it was not quite empty, so she did not pass the table again on her return journey as it was some little distance out of her direct way. She vaguely fancied afterward that she had seen a full glass of some white-looking liqueur standing by the cup. On repeating the journey to fulfil the other customer's order about five minutes later she had taken the short route each way and had therefore not passed close enough to Miss Sinclair's table to be able to see whether the cup was then empty or not; she had, however, looked at the table itself and noticed that there was no liqueur glass on it, as she had imagined. The incident had then faded from her mind.

Those were the bare facts. By his cautious questioning Mr Chitterwick was able to add something to them.

She was sure it had happened after the man had gone, because he was evidently on the point of leaving when he had beckoned her over to take his own cup, and this must have been a good five minutes afterward, if not more; besides, she had noticed that the old lady was then alone. The presence of the liqueur glass on the table had not really struck her till she was back in the service quarters; she had then realized that it was odd, because she knew that she herself had not taken an order for a liqueur at that particular table, or delivered one; it was not, however, as odd as it might have been, for some of the more good-natured waitresses did occasionally take and fulfil orders at tables not their own if the customer seemed particularly pressing or the correct waitress particularly busy; and lastly her impression that there was a glass on the table had been so vague that she was really not at all surprised to find that there was nothing of the sort and that she must have been completely mistaken.

Mr Chitterwick contrived to hide his elation and, as there was nothing more to be learned from this particular witness, proceeded to his next objective.

'Thank you, thank you. Now there is just one other thing. It is not particularly important if there is any difficulty about it, but I should rather like to have a word with the waitress who called me to the telephone. Do you think that could be managed?'

'Well, I don't see why not, I'm sure,' said the waitress amiably (the more so as Mr Chitterwick was now fumbling, rather diffidently, with his note-case). 'Now which one would that be, I wonder. She hasn't been called as a witness, that I know. I'm the only one here they want for that. Could you describe her, Mr Chitterwick?'

But that was just what Mr Chitterwick could not do. So far as her face was concerned his mind was a complete blank. For the first time he realized that one very seldom does look a waiter or waitress directly in the face, unless with the object of learning whom to summon later. He had not the faintest idea what she looked like. The nearest he could get to a description was that, so far as he remembered, she was tall rather than short, perhaps dark rather than fair, and on the whole, he was inclined to think, not bad-looking. As a working description of an unknown young woman, this did not take them very far.

But that was as far as they did get. The waitress herself went off to make inquiries in the service quarters but had to return empty handed; Mr Chitterwick was posted in a seat near the service door where he could see every girl as she passed in or out, but though one or two struck him as possible, on being interrogated by his assistant these all proved blanks. In the end it was left that the waitress, now fortified with a ten-shilling note, would make further inquiries, not only among the girls still in the hotel's employment, but also of any who might have left it since that date, and let Mr Chitterwick know the result.

As he walked slowly to the entrance lobby Mr Chitterwick reflected how very unobservant he must be, for he had seen the girl not once only but twice, in the lounge and later in the vestibule, yet on neither occasion had he really taken her in.

Suddenly he stopped dead in his tracks, and turned quite old-red-brick-coloured.

'God bless my *soul!'* breathed Mr Chitterwick.

A blinding flash of thought had just struck him. It was impossible, of course. Oh, quite impossible. Out of the question. Ridiculous. Oh, why bother?

Still...

'Now, what *was* that number?' murmured Mr Chitterwick distractedly. 'I shall never remember it, of course. Never. Never. How could one hope to? Dear me, dear me.'

But memory is a peculiar affair. It will refuse to record a perfectly good face with which one has actually talked; it will take careful note of the most unimportant thing in the world, a number casually mentioned in a hurriedly spoken sentence.

'473!' almost crowed Mr Chitterwick in triumph. 'God bless my soul, 473.' And he dived for the office, on the counter of which squatted the enormous hotel register.

Flicking feverishly back through the weeks, none saying him nay, Mr Chitterwick found that which he sought. He grabbed an old envelope from his pocket and made the following note:

12 June. No. 473. Jas. Hall Ings, 47 Southowram Villas, Ashton-under-Lyne.

'Dear me,' murmured Mr Chitterwick distractedly. 'Ashton-under-Lyne. What a very long way to have to go. But I must. I must. Er – have you a timetable showing the trains to Ashton-under-Lyne, if you please?' he added with humility to the young woman behind the counter.

'Timetable, apply to the hall porter,' replied the young woman severely.

Chastened, Mr Chitterwick betook himself to the hall porter.

That evening at dinner, by way of setting the seal on his new independence, Mr Chitterwick announced to his aunt his intention for the morrow, simply, and without vouchsafing a single reason. Miss Chitterwick did become a little restive at that, pointing out with justice that people, real People, simply do not go to Ashton-under-Lyne; but a single reference to the Duke quietened her. Mr Chitterwick's emancipation was complete.

It cannot be said that Mr Chitterwick really enjoyed his visit to Ashton-under-Lyne. To some individuals Ashton-under-Lyne may represent everything that is gayest, most beautiful and most desirable in the human cosmogony; and who shall say that they are wrong? These things are a matter of comparison, and one whose outlook had hitherto been limited to Sheffield might well think all this and more of Ashton. But if there are such persons, Mr Chitterwick very soon discovered that he was not one of them. To him Ashton-under-Lyne explained in three minutes more of our prevailing industrial discontent than he had been able to understand from other sources in thirty years.

We will pass briefly over his visit. Catching an early morning train, he had been decanted just before lunch into the smoky haze that sits upon Ashton and its neighbours like a mute on a hearse. He had eaten that meal at what was reputed to be one of the best hotels in the town, where he was served worse and charged more exorbitantly than ever in his life before; he had then taken a taxi to the depressing street in which Southowram Villas, a long and murky row of semi-detached houses, each separated from the sidewalk by a six-foot strip of moribund vegetation, was distressingly situated. Knocking at the door of No 47 he was informed that

Mr Ings was not at home. Where was he? Probably at the Mission Hall. Where was the Mission Hall? First on the left, second on the right, third on the left, and that brought you out straight opposite it.

First on the left, second on the right, and third on the left trudged Mr Chitterwick, supported by the thought that he really was doing some indubitable detecting at last, and came out opposite a blot on civilization consisting of a red (or once red) corrugated-iron erection with dirtier windows than one would have thought possible. There was a notice board outside, and studying it Mr Chitterwick absorbed the information that on the following Sunday Mr Jas. Hall Ings would preach to his flock of the All-Square Gospel Church on the somewhat peremptory subject of 'Repent or be Damned.'

Inside this excrescence even on the face of Ashton was lurking Mr Ings, no doubt doing a bit of repenting in advance. A tentative knock with the head of his walking stick by Mr Chitterwick, that reverberated on the corrugated iron like a whole succession of last trumps and must have considerably started the All-Square Gospeller inside, brought the latter to the pitch-pine door. He was a gaunt, tall man, with a semi-bald head and a straggling, discouraged-looking beard, and for some obscure but no doubt holy reason of his own he wore an aged frock coat and a stiff polo collar whose stud supported by a clip a made-up pale-blue bow tie, leaving a long stretch of stringy throat nude to the interested observer; he peered with mild inquiry at Mr Chitterwick over a pair of steel spectacles.

'You are Mr James Hall Ings?' nervously accused Mr Chitterwick.

'I am, brother,' admitted the Gospeller.

Mr Chitterwick staggered slightly but recovered himself.

'I – er – hoped to catch you when you were staying at the Piccadilly Palace last June,' he said with complete untruth.

'Indeed?'

'Yes. You – er – you were there, were you not?'

'I was, brother,' said Mr Ings, with a good deal of solemnity. 'Why should I deny it? I went up to that city of unrighteousness to attend a conference called by our founder, Dr Ezra Drigglington, whose name is no doubt familiar to you, alleluia.'

'I – I beg your pardon?' stammered Mr Chitterwick, under the momentary impression that he had been called a rude name.

'I said, no doubt the name of our holy founder is familiar to you, praise the Lord. But come inside, brother, if you wish to see me; come inside.'

'No, thank you,' said Mr Chitterwick hastily. 'There is really no need. I have just run down from London, you see, to – to – That is, I wished to present your fund with – You – you have a fund?'

'Several, brother,' replied Mr Ings complacently.

'Exactly. Precisely. Then I just wished to present your fund – that is, one of your funds, with this. A slight token of... Exactly. Not at all, not at all. Good-afternoon.' And, having thrust a pound note into Mr Ings' surprised but ready hand, Mr Chitterwick returned as quickly as he could to London.

I feared so, I feared so, ruminated Mr Chitterwick later as with a sigh of contentment he watched the outskirts of Ashton slide forever out of his sight. Dear me, this is very upsetting. Really, I had thought I was within measurable distance of... And now this makes it much more puzzling than it was before. I shall have to think very hard indeed.

And Mr Chitterwick settled himself down in his corner and thought.

chapter thirteen

Clay Feet to a Paragon

The next three days Mr Chitterwick remained in London in a state of considerable agitation. Each day he knew he was breaking into smaller fragments the promise he had made to Mouse to follow the other two down to Dorsetshire as soon as he had discovered anything of interest; each day he could not make up his mind to fulfil it. Personally he was of the opinion that he had discovered something very important indeed, but, unable to look on one side of any picture only and disregard the other, he could not but harbour an uneasy feeling that he had unearthed nothing more substantial than a mare's nest, built out of a chance remark which might or might not have held the significance that he had read into it. If he was right, then he had gone some considerable way toward confirming his private solution of the problem; and, to support his theory, such a solution as he had in mind, while still leaving another puzzle to be deciphered, did explain what both he and Mouse had felt to be the crux of their case, namely, the question of how the phial had been placed in Miss Sinclair's unconscious hand.

Ought he to see Moresby and put his new ideas before that sceptical official? But they were nothing more than ideas; there was practically nothing to support them; he had not been able to take the first step toward proving them. And would Moresby be impressed by a collection of mere ideas, however ingenious? To Mr Chitterwick's mind the question answered itself.

Ought he to see the solicitors for the defence and tackle them? Mr Chitterwick did not know much about solicitors, but he had no difficulty in supplying from his imagination the gap in his knowledge. The solicitors would be jealous of an outsider's intrusion. They would be dry, legal – demand facts; and Mr Chitterwick had practically no facts to give them.

Ought he not to talk the whole thing over with Mouse and Judith, regardless of raising hopes that might never be substantiated, and put the responsibility of proof and future action upon them? After all, that was the obvious thing to do. It was their problem and not his. Nevertheless, Mr Chitterwick would have liked something just a little more tangible to lay before them to strengthen his theory. He spent the greater part of the three days looking for it, poking about here and there, making fruitless inquiries, annoying a great many people with apparently irrelevant questions, but all without result; beyond the negative fact that no trace at all could be found of the waitress who had summoned him to the telephone, nothing emerged that helped in the least to confirm his ideas.

And then Mouse and Judith obligingly resolved his difficulty for him by appearing on the fourth morning at Chiswick and demanding lunch of a delighted Miss Chitterwick.

As soon as Mr Chitterwick saw them he knew exactly what he should do: tell them exactly his new theory of how the crime was accomplished, and, pending confirmation, continue to conceal his opinion that he had arrived at the person of its perpetrator. How simple.

Having therefore hinted mysteriously at lunch of important developments, he withdrew them after the meal to his aunt's study as being a place more fitting for momentous disclosures than a mere drawing room. It says much for Miss Chitterwick's strength of mind that, bursting with curiosity though she was, she refused with resolution this time to attend the conference, saying she had no wish to learn things which everyone afterward might regret having divulged to her.

Mr Chitterwick beamed upon the intent faces of his two coadjutors, crossed his legs, leaned back in his chair, and cleared his throat.

'The particular problems on which I have been concentrating since I saw you last,' he began, in somewhat didactic tones, 'are the administration of the poison and the introduction of the poisoned phial into Miss Sinclair's hand. Now you will remember that in the summary of the case which I drew up the night before you left here, I expressed the strongest doubts as to whether the coffee had been the vehicle of conveying the poison at all, in spite of the fact that the dregs in the cup were strongly impregnated with prussic acid. I had formed the tentative opinion that that cup might be yet another trap for the police.

'I therefore paid a visit to the Piccadilly Palace in order to ask the waitress who had served Miss Sinclair a few questions. I need not detail now the inquiries I made; it is enough to say that they did actually succeed in reminding the waitress of a circumstance she had quite forgotten. That circumstance was that she had actually fancied that she did see, at one period, a glass on Miss Sinclair's table containing apparently some liqueur of a white colour.'

'Jolly good,' cried Mouse, smiting his knee. 'Just as you guessed.'

'Exactly,' beamed Mr Chitterwick, and went on to describe just what the waitress had told him.

'This seemed to clear up one point, you see,' he continued. 'I had no doubt that the waitress really did see that glass of liqueur, and that it really was the vehicle in which the poison was administered. But, as again you will see, all this simply presented another puzzle to be solved: who served Miss Sinclair with that glass of liqueur?

'That it could not have been one of the regular waitresses I felt certain. This particular girl seems to have derived a certain amount of – er – kudos through her connection with the tragedy, and I have no doubt at all that any other who could lay claim to a similar distinction would have come forward at once to share her honours; for the same reason it is inconceivable that the incident could have slipped the memory of the girl who had done so. On the other hand, we have a large and decided body of evidence to the effect that nobody at all went near Miss Sinclair between the man's departure and my own move. Those were the Scylla and Charybdis of the new problem.

'Now, according to Chief Inspector Moresby those witnesses of his are very positive on this point, and the evidence of the first four is certainly remarkably confirmed by that of the fresh two. We may take it as pretty sure, I think, that they honestly believe themselves to be speaking the truth. On the other hand the facts indicate that they are mistaken. How are we to reconcile this discrepancy?' Mr Chitterwick looked inquiringly at his audience.

The audience looked at each other, and Mouse spoke for both. 'Don't ask me,' he said helplessly.

'I asked myself,' proceeded Mr Chitterwick. 'Not once, but many times. And at first I must admit I could find no answer at all. Then all at once, just as I was on the point of leaving the hotel, a remarkable idea occurred to me. Or perhaps I should say, more accurately, two separate ideas, but so blended together that it took me a moment or two to disentangle them. The first one was this: Might not all these witnesses have actually *seen* something which they did not, so to speak, perceive?' Again Mr Chitterwick paused.

'What exactly did you say, Mr Chitterwick?' asked Judith.

'Don't quite get that,' mumbled Mouse.

Mr Chitterwick looked slightly distressed. 'Dear me, I am afraid I am explaining this rather badly. But it is difficult to put in general terms. Perhaps I may express it something like this: Could the eyes of those witnesses have rested on something so commonplace that their brains refused to register the impression? In other words, could they be quite correct in stating that no other visitor to the Piccadilly Palace approached Miss Sinclair during the critical period, and yet incorrect in stating that no *person* did?'

'Put it in words of one syllable,' Mouse begged. 'I must be terribly dense today.'

'You still don't see my meaning? Then I'll state it bluntly. Suppose it was a waitress who went up to Miss Sinclair. That would be so commonplace an occurrence in that particular locality that the witnesses, although seeing it perfectly well, might retain no impression of it at all and be quite ready to swear that *nobody* had done so. I think,' said Mr Chitterwick diffidently, 'that that is a feasible suggestion.'

'It's very ingenious,' said Judith, not exactly grudgingly but as if not yet quite convinced.

'But doesn't it still leave you up against the trouble that it couldn't have been a waitress after all?' Mouse asked, evidently suspending judgment.

'It does, yes; and that is where the second part of my blended idea comes in. You will see how the two parts work in together. This was my second idea: Suppose the murderer had a female accomplice, disguised as a waitress!' Mr Chitterwick beamed round in undisguised pride.

This time Judith was impressed as well as Mouse. She sat up sharply in her chair and looked at Mr Chitterwick with big eyes. 'Have you any evidence to support that?' she asked, almost peremptorily.

'Only negatively, I am afraid,' lamented Mr Chitterwick. 'But, as you will see, so far as argument goes there is everything in its favour. Just think how that fact would simplify matters. Why, it solves nearly all the small puzzles connected with the actual death of Miss Sinclair. The serving of the liqueur, the removal of the glass after it had served its purpose, the pouring of a few drops of the poison into the empty coffee cup, the placing of the prepared phial in Miss Sinclair's hand, to say nothing of the death occurring so long after the man's departure and his subsequent ability, should it ever come to the point, to clear himself of the crime. Why, all those little difficulties disappear like magic.'

'But how could such a thing have been done?' asked Judith, who had become quite tense. 'I quite see that it should simplify matters from our point of view, but – but surely the difficulties would have made it impossible. How could anyone have masqueraded as a waitress for two minutes without being detected? It's a marvellous idea, but – ' She shook her head regretfully.

'Really, I don't think it would be impossible at all,' argued Mr Chitterwick with energy. 'I have devoted considerable thought to the point, as you may imagine, and the more I ponder on it the easier I feel the plan would have been to carry out. Just consider. The accomplice has not to mingle with the other waitresses at all. A careful timetable would of course have been made in advance, or some arrangement whereby she would need to spend only the minimum amount of time in the danger zone, so to speak. She would be concealed somewhere, no doubt, till the man emerges from the lounge and tells her that everything is ready, and after that all she has to do is to carry the glass in on a tray (and who is going to question that?), deliver it to Miss Sinclair, wait until the latter had drunk the requisite amount of it (that would be the only really dangerous period), remove it, and at the same time slip the phial that she had with her into Miss Sinclair's hand, and make good her retreat. What could be simpler?

'It would be difficult in a smaller place, I admit, but in the lounge of the Piccadilly Palace, without even considering the restaurant and grillroom, there are so many waitresses that they can hardly all know each other even by sight. New faces are appearing every day. She would choose her moment of course when the correct waitress for that table had just gone to the service quarters. It would be easy for her to do so. She would only have to walk about busily with her tray, and no one is going to question her presence. It seems to me a plan that is ingenious only in its utter simplicity.

'I am taking certain things for granted, of course, such as that the man would have prepared the way for a liqueur to arrive and ensured Miss Sinclair's drinking it, and that the amount of poison contained in it would have been enough to ensure death after quite a small sip. I can see no other obstacles. The phial she would hold by its cork, to avoid fingerprints. Any stooping over Miss Sinclair could have been effected under the pretence of picking something up from the floor, or some such subterfuge. I am convinced this is the truth about the way the murder was committed.' Mr Chitterwick was quite red in his earnestness.

'I agree,' said Mouse solemnly. 'I think you've proved your point, Chitterwick. By jove, we shall owe you something by the time we're through with this affair.'

But Judith, it seemed, was not quite so readily convinced. 'But how could she have got into the clothes, Mr Chitterwick? She could hardly have changed on the premises, surely, and it would have been far too dangerous to arrive ready dressed for the part. I'm afraid I can see a good many more difficulties, from the woman's point of view, than may have occurred to you.'

'That one had, however,' said Mr Chitterwick, more mildly. 'The question of adopting her disguise I have certainly considered. Here I must admit I'm on merely supposititious ground; but putting myself so far as one can in her place, one course seems to me to stand out as quite obvious, and that would be to hire, *in propria persona,* a room in the hotel. She could then change there in security and wait safely until the man came to tell her the coast was clear; while he, for his part, could adopt there any disguise, such as a wig, which he had found necessary, and prepare the various poisoned utensils. In my opinion that course is so obviously advantageous that, assuming I am not completely mistaken from beginning to end, this is almost certainly what occurred.'

'Let's hope so,' said Mouse. 'She can be traced and identified if she did.'

'Yes,' agreed Mr Chitterwick, though somewhat dubiously. 'So I had thought too, and have even gone so far as to examine the register with that intention. But the Piccadilly Palace is a very large hotel. There are over a thousand bedrooms, and all occupied every night. On that particular day no less than two hundred and seventeen women, according to my calculations, were occupying single rooms there. To pick this particular one out of that number, would, I fear, be quite beyond an amateur detective's powers.'

'Oh!' said Mouse.

'We must try to discover her identify by other means: her association with the murderer, for instance.'

'Having first discovered who the murderer is,' put in Judith, somewhat drily.

'Yes, of course,' said Mr Chitterwick, and looked a little guilty. 'Having first discovered that, no doubt.'

'And having discovered, too, that there ever was such a person at all,' added Judith, who still seemed sceptical. 'As I said, Mr Chitterwick, it's a very ingenious theory of yours, but I can't see that there's the faintest jot of evidence to support it. Of course, it does simplify some of our problems, but we mustn't regard as fact, or even as probable fact, everything that does that, must we?'

'Oh, no; certainly not. But you see, there *is* a tiny shred of evidence to support it.'

'There is?' Judith was alert again. 'What, then?'

'Well, as I think I mentioned, only a little bit of negative evidence, and indeed it may turn out to be nothing more than a coincidence after all, but this is how it struck me. The waitress who called me to the telephone spoke to me in the vestibule afterward, asking if I had got my call. There was nothing odd in that, of course. When I remarked that it seemed to have been a mistake, and there was apparently no call for me at all, she asked me if I was not Number 473;

when I said I was not, she observed casually that I was as like Number 473 as two peas. And that,' apologized Mr Chitterwick, 'is really all the evidence I can produce.'

The other two looked puzzled. 'I don't quite see it,' said Mouse.

Mr Chitterwick started. 'Oh! I beg your pardon. Of course. I haven't explained, have I? Why, I searched the register to find out who was occupying room Number 473 that night, and was able to discover that the man in question is no more like me than – than a vegetable marrow. That is,' said Mr Chitterwick meticulously, 'if I really do resemble a pea. I had to make a special journey to Ashton-under-Lyne to do so,' he added with feeling.

'Ah,' nodded Mouse, 'I begin to get you. And you think she was the accomplice, then?'

'If there ever was one,' assented Mr Chitterwick, with a diffident glance in the direction of Judith.

'But I still don't understand at all' Judith cried. 'I may be very dense, but why should this problematical woman send you maliciously to the telephone for a call that didn't exist? That's what you seem to be inferring, Mr Chitterwick.'

'Why, you see,' explained Mr Chitterwick with some hesitation, 'I think one could understand that, couldn't one? I had already played my allotted part in witnessing what I had been meant to witness; I had to be got rid of before I witnessed what I was not meant to see, namely, the actual administration of the poison. Then I had to be brought back so that I should observe the actual death of Miss Sinclair, in which case I should not be likely to forget what I had already seen and would come forward as the chief witness against your husband; which, of course, is what actually happened.'

'It seems terribly complicated,' Judith said doubtfully.

'I think it's quite simple really,' pleaded Mr Chitterwick.

There was a pause while they contemplated the possible complication of simplicity of these manoeuvres.

'But unfortunately you can't describe this woman at all?' Judith challenged.

'I'm afraid,' said Mr Chitterwick humbly, 'that is so. Really, I seem to remember very little indeed about her.'

'What do you remember?' asked Mouse.

Mr Chitterwick searched his treacherous memory. 'Well, I appear to have the impression that she was fairly tall, and perhaps dark, and I don't think she was ugly or I should probably have noticed it. Though, really, I'm quite doubtful whether I ever looked her in the face at all. Probably not.'

'It's a pity you didn't,' Mouse regretted. 'A woman can't disguise her face, you see. She may put on different clothes and so on, but she can't stick on a false beard, can she?' He appealed to Judith, but though she looked at him thoughtfully she did not answer.

'But she can put on a pair of horn-rimmed spectacles,' remarked Mr Chitterwick, with more reminiscence than significance.

Mouse sat up in his chair. 'Good heavens, Chitterwick, you're not suggesting that – ?'

'Dear me, no,' protested Mr Chitterwick. 'I assure you, it was merely a chance remark. Such a thought had never entered my mind.'

Before anyone had time to elaborate this interesting theme there was a knock at the door. 'The telephone, sir,' said the parlourmaid.

Mr Chitterwick made his apologies and withdrew.

If any further proof were needed of Mr Chitterwick's new independence, it was in this installation of the telephone. He had simply overridden his aunt's acid objections and insisted. For one in almost daily touch with Scotland Yard (as Mr Chitterwick had pointed out) a telephone was quite indispensable.

And appropriately enough it was Scotland Yard that wanted him now. Moresby's voice came over the wires. 'That you, Mr Chitterwick, sir?'

Mr Chitterwick intimated that it was.

'You sent us some fingerprints a little time ago, didn't you?'

Mr Chitterwick's heart gave a convulsive jump. 'Yes, Chief Inspector, I did.'

'And we couldn't trace them in our records. Did you send one of those photos I had done for you to America, sir?'

'Y-yes,' said Mr Chitterwick breathlessly. 'I did. Why?'

'I should like to know, sir, whose prints they are.'

'Why, Chief Inspector?' positively squeaked Mr Chitterwick. 'Have you – have you heard something from America?'

'They thought it better to cable me direct, sir,' replied Moresby guardedly.

'But why? What did they tell you?'

'Umph! That's confidential, Mr Chitterwick, you'll understand. No need to bother you with that, sir,' said Moresby in unctuous tones. 'All I want to know from you is whose they are.'

Almost dancing with excitement though he was Mr Chitterwick nevertheless managed to keep his head. 'But – but that's confidential too, Chief Inspector. Most confidential. I'm afraid... Oh, quite impossible.'

'Meaning, I suppose, sir,' came Moresby's voice wearily 'that you refuse to tell me unless I tell you what America says?'

It may have been because he was not confronting the chief inspector face to face that Mr Chitterwick managed to speak with such firmness; the telephone is a wonderful stimulant. 'Certainly. That would be only... In fact, I must insist that if I am to... Yes, certainly.'

'Very well, Mr Chitterwick,' said Moresby resignedly. 'Though of course you'll understand that we could have found out quickly enough for ourselves if it had been necessary. Still, there's no real reason why you shouldn't know; and if it's the party I suspect you may go so far as to drop a word of warning in the right quarter, if you like. America notifies us that these prints belong to a very shady character, suspected of having had a finger in more than one jewel robbery over there, whose owner they've never been able to identify; and even now they've got nothing definite against her, though they advise us to keep a pretty sharp eye on her over here. They got the prints off a jewel case that had been rifled, but they didn't correspond with those of any member of the household, and they could never find the owner of them. But they believe she takes a position as lady's maid or something like that to a rich woman to get opportunities of robbing her employer's friends; much too fly to rob the employer herself.'

'Good gracious me!' gasped Mr Chitterwick.

'Now, then, sir, if you'll tell me whether the name begins with a G or not, I fancy that'll be enough, over the telephone. Eh?'

'It does Chief Inspector; you're perfectly right. God bless my soul!'

It was a seething Mr Chitterwick who returned to the study with his momentous news.

'Good Lord!' exclaimed Mouse, with blank astonishment. 'That paragon of all the virtues!'

'I never did trust her,' cried Judith, true to her sex.

They looked at each other.

'My hat!' Mouse breathed, in a somewhat strangled voice. 'What – what about that chance remark of yours now, Chitterwick?'

'And – she must be used to playing a part,' said Mr Chitterwick soberly.

It was Judith who, quite unexpectedly, appointed herself counsel for the defence. 'We mustn't let ourselves be led away by side issues,' she said, with brisk common sense. 'Because a woman may be a thief that doesn't make her the accomplice in a murder. Besides, trying so far as I can to look at it all without prejudice, Mr Chitterwick has yet to convince me that such person as that accomplice exists at all.'

'It was only conjecture,' murmured Mr Chitterwick. 'Purely inductive conjecture.'

'I'm betting on it myself,' Mouse said firmly. 'And what's more, I'm betting Chitterwick's found her.'

Mr Chitterwick looked at Judith. 'Really, Mrs Sinclair,' he beamed, 'I think I have.'

Judith did not smile back. 'But Miss Goole!' she muttered, rather incredulously.

'She's dark, she's tall, without those spectacles she might not be bad-looking,' almost chanted Mouse. 'Oh, we've found her all right.'

'Well, I hope so, certainly.' Judith sighed, and relapsed into a reverie.

Mouse turned to Mr Chitterwick. 'Have you got that summary of yours handy, Chitterwick?'

'I have it here,' said Mr Chitterwick promptly, and drew it from his breast pocket.

Mouse turned over the pages. 'Here we are. "Obscure Points Requiring Explanation." Listen to me Judy, and I'll dot Chitterwick's i's and cross his t's for you. I think you'll agree this clinches it.

'"Why the interview was arranged by Miss Sinclair for the Piccadilly Palace." It wasn't. It was arranged by Miss Goole, who simply typed in "Piccadilly Palace" in Miss Sinclair's letter to Lynn instead of the place that had really been arranged; when Lynn's letter arrived to say he would meet her there, she would have some explanation to suit. Point No.1.

'Point No. 2. "How the poison was administrated." Well, we know that now, thanks to Sherlock Chitterwick here.

'Point No. 3. "How Major Sinclair's fingerprints were obtained on the phial." Miss Goole as the accomplice clears that up too. Lynn said the phial was like the ones that Miss Sinclair's eyedrops were in, didn't he? Well, then.

'Point No. 4. "How the phial was conveyed to Miss Sinclair's hand." Sherlock's explained that. And Point No. 5. "Why Miss Goole is disguised," stands to reason. There you are, you see. Every single difficult point cleared up. Doesn't that absolutely fix that hag as the accomplice?'

'It's more convincing than I thought at first,' Judith admitted.

'And here's another possible pointer,' continued Mouse, upon whom the mantle of inspiration seemed to have fallen. 'The Goole is a jewel thief. What about Miss Sinclair's jewels? Haven't any been missed since her death?'

But at that Judith shook her head with decision. 'Not so far as I or anyone else knows. I've had to have an inventory made out, of course, for proving the will, and everything of which there's any previous record is there.'

Mouse looked disappointed. 'Oh! I should have thought, once a jewel thief, always a jewel thief. And with such a wonderful opportunity. Wouldn't you Chitterwick?'

'Criminals are well known to be remarkably tenacious in their habits,' pronounced that authority. 'I should certainly have thought... You might do well to look into that point perhaps a little more closely, Mrs Sinclair.'

Judith intimated that she would do so.

Mouse and Mr Chitterwick embarked on an excited discussion of the light that had been thrown on the whole case by this development, the former maintaining that the identity of the accomplice must prove a pointer toward the person of the real murderer, the latter agreeing with great heartiness and continuing to conceal his own private conviction of who that person must prove to be; Mr Chitterwick did not believe in jumping his fences till he had had a good look for possible ditches the other side.

'Mr Chitterwick!' said Judith abruptly. She had relapsed into her interrupted reverie and taken no part in the discussion that had been proceeding. 'Mr Chitterwick, I've been thinking this over. We must keep it to ourselves.'

'To ourselves?' said Mouse in surprise. 'But – '

'To ourselves,' Judith repeated firmly. 'That is, for the present. However convincing it all may sound, you see, we've actually proved nothing at all. And I know exactly what the police, and even Lynn's own solicitors, will say. Proof, proof, proof! We *must* go some way toward proving our case before we let out a thing about it to another soul. Don't you agree, Mr Chitterwick?'

Mr Chitterwick considered for a moment. 'I do. Quite decidedly. A premature disclosure might be fatal. At all costs,' said Mr Chitterwick, relapsing into unwonted slang, 'we must not risk scaring our birds.'

'Perhaps you're right,' Mouse admitted reluctantly. 'But it does seem rather tough on Lynn. Couldn't Judy just drop him a hint that we've practically cleared him already and we're just waiting to clinch our case?'

Mr Chitterwick looked doubtfully at Judith. 'It would be inadvisable.'

'Quite,' Judith agreed. 'It's very hard on Lynn; but he'll understand later.'

On that basis the matter was left. Mr Chitterwick contrived to hint, without saying anything definite, that he already saw one or two lines of inquiry which might prove helpful in establishing the identity of the murderer, but that they could not be followed up for a day or two at least. The conversation became general.

'By the way,' Mouse remarked casually a little later, 'the missing heir lands tomorrow, Chitterwick.'

'Indeed?' said Mr Chitterwick with interest. 'At Liverpool?'

'No, Southampton. I'm taking the Bentley down there to meet him, with Judy.'

'And bring him up to London?'

'No; Agatha's idea is that he had better come direct to Riversmead, so that Judy and the rest of us can get to know him in peace and comfort. Good scheme, I think. He'll be better parked there than raising Cain in London.'

'Is he likely to raise Cain in London?'

'Judy rather gathered from his letter that he intends to move heaven and earth to get Lynn cleared. Eh, Judy?'

'He certainly seemed quite enthusiastic,' Judith said drily. 'An impetuous person. I gathered.'

'And at the cost to himself of a large fortune,' said Mr Chitterwick, equally drily. 'Not only an impetuous person, one would say, but a most altruistic one. I should quite like to meet him.'

'Well, that's simple enough. We're staying in London tonight. Come down with us tomorrow.'

'Shouldn't I be in the way?' Mr Chitterwick demurred.

'Of course not. Agatha's expecting you back at Riversmead any time you want to come. There's a bedroom at your disposal there, you know, whenever you want to pop down, and a trencher on the ancestral board.'

'That is exceedingly kind of your sister,' said Mr Chitterwick warmly.

'It's little enough, considering what you're doing for us,' returned Mouse, with equal warmth.

Both men turned slightly red and looked extremely uncomfortable in the manner adjudged correct by the Englishman at the least hint of a suspicion of sentiment. Mr Chitterwick turned off the awkward moment by mumbling something about in that case he must insist that Mouse and Judith stayed where they were for the night, which Mouse and Judith mumbled back that they would be delighted to do so and it was exceedingly kind of him, but wouldn't it be too much bother for Miss Chitterwick? Whereupon, and as the discussion seemed to be at an end, Mr Chitterwick went off to fetch that lady to assure her guests in person how remarkably little trouble it was to put up for the night a duke and his adopted sister.

Or rather, as Mr Chitterwick had some reason to think during that same evening, a duke and the lady who had adopted him as a brother; for though Judith's attitude was nothing more than the casual affection of sister to brother, that of Mouse was anything but complementary. Mr Chitterwick found himself sighing more than once over the pity of such an estimable and charming young man having fallen in love so helplessly and so hopelessly. But such, no doubt, reflected Mr Chitterwick with altruistic philosophy, is the way of the world.

It was not until the end of the evening that any further contribution was made toward the progress of the case, and then it was Mr Chitterwick who made it. He sat up suddenly in his chair and gave vent to an exclamation which made the rest of the company, who happened at the moment to be peacefully discussing the intensive cultivation of mushrooms, jump nimbly in their seats. 'God bless my eternal *soul!'* positively boomed Mr Chitterwick.

'Ambrose!' exclaimed his scandalized aunt.

'Good gracious me! Well, of all the...! Good heavens!' continued to ejaculate Mr Chitterwick, seemingly lost in a daze of wonderment.

'What?' demanded the others.

Mr Chitterwick seemed to come to his senses, or some of them. 'I've just realized... I probably told you that Miss Goole seemed to remind me of somebody, but I couldn't... Really, memory does play the most surprising... I've been racking my brains ever since, trying to remember who... And now, thinking about mushrooms of all things... Now what connection *could* there be between that girl and mushrooms?'

'What girl?' patiently asked Mouse, exchanging a smile with Miss Chitterwick as they both contemplated Mr Chitterwick's bewildered face.

'Whom does Miss Goole remind you of?' as patiently asked Judith.

Mr Chitterwick started slightly. 'Oh, yes. I beg your pardon. Why, there was a girl in the Piccadilly Palace lounge. Quite a pretty girl. She happened to catch my eye. I mean,' amended Mr Chitterwick hastily, conscious of his aunt's gaze, 'I mean, I happened to notice her and thought what a pretty girl she was, before I began to – to study Miss Sinclair. It was only a passing incident. I've never thought of it from that moment to this. I don't think I even glanced at her again. How long she stayed there I haven't the faintest idea. I found Miss Sinclair so much more interesting, you see.' He paused and looked vaguely at the others, evidently thinking hard.

'And Miss Goole reminds you of that girl?' Judith asked quietly.

Mr Chitterwick gazed at her for a moment as if weighing his words; then he seemed to make up his mind. 'That girl *was* Miss Goole,' he said firmly.

There was a short silence, such as follows a momentous announcement. Then Judith laughed shrilly. 'Yes, I think that does clinch it, as Mouse would say. My God, I'll – ' Mr Chitterwick, looking at her in consternation, was astonished at the expression of vindictiveness on her usually calm features – one might almost say malignant vindictiveness, as if she would positively gloat over the sight of Miss Goole being torn in pieces under her very eyes; the knuckles of her hands as she gripped the arms of her chair were white; she was obviously on the verge of hysteria.

Slowly she regained her usual grip on herself, the tension of her attitude relaxed, and she smiled uncertainly. 'I'm sorry,' she said in a shaky voice, passing her hand across her forehead. 'I try not to show it as a rule, but all this business is rather a strain on me, you know.' She stood up, swaying a little. 'I think, if you don't mind, Miss Chitterwick, I'll go to bed.'

'Of course, my dear,' said Miss Chitterwick, rising too and speaking in unwontedly gentle tones. 'We quite understand. And I'll come along soon and bring you something soothing.'

Mouse had jumped up and slipped his arm round her waist. 'Come along, Judy, old girl. I'll help you upstairs.'

Judith looked round with tragic eyes. 'I'm so sorry,' she repeated. 'I hate making an exhibition of myself, *and* a nuisance. Goodnight.' She walked out of the room, leaning heavily on Mouse.

Mr Chitterwick, who realized that he had just been permitted a glance at a raw human soul, looked and felt like a small boy caught stealing jam.

chapter fourteen

Rough House

The journey the next day from Southampton to Dorsetshire was, so far as Mr Chitterwick was concerned, a silent one. Mouse was occupied with driving, Mr Chitterwick was occupied with his thoughts; in the back seat, exchanging rather stilted politenesses, were Judith and the new cousin.

It had not been a difficult task, as the three stood on the quay and watched the passengers threading their way down the gangway, to pick out the object of their search. Whatever his father might have been, the stock had evidently been unable to stand up against that of the Sinclairs; the nose which preceded the new cousin down the gangway would have marked him out as a Sinclair whatever the accident of his name. As a matter of fact, this was Benson.

Mr Chitterwick had marked his appearance with a good deal of interest.

Harold J Benson, then, had proved to be a man in his late twenties, and the possessor not only of the Sinclair nose but the Sinclair physique too. He was large and sturdy, with grey-green eyes and a lot of tow-coloured hair, which he wore in a strange roll over the middle of his head, giving him the appearance rather of a cockatoo than of a parrot; the only particulars in which he deviated from the traditional Sinclair appearance, apart from the roll of tow-coloured hair, were his somewhat receding forehead and chin, the latter perhaps a legacy from his father – the only one he had received.

He had wrung Judith's hand till the tears came into her eyes, then Mouse's and then Mr Chitterwick's, while he assured the three of them with the utmost enthusiasm how pleased he was to meet them, how sorry he was that it should be in these circumstances, and how he was going to instill such pep into Scotland Yard and the whole Metropolitan Police Force that they wouldn't be able to see their eyes for tears before he'd done with them. His audience, at that moment,who could hardly see their own for the same reason, agreed vaguely, and hoped in silence that Mr Benson would shake hands with the whole Metropolitan Police Force too.

Still telling them at the top of a pronounced American voice (the most American voice Mr Chitterwick thought he had ever heard) his ideas for instilling pep into Scotland Yard, promising Judith that her husband should be hanging up his hat in the little old back porch again within three days, observing to Mouse how tickled to death the folks would be way back to hear that he'd no sooner set foot in England than up runs a real he-duke and grabs his mitt and calls him brother, and remarking parenthetically to Mr Chitterwick that a duke didn't look too different from other folk, which seemed a bit tough on the dukes, he led them through the customs sheds, ushered them into their car, and was, Mr Chitterwick felt, within an ace of offering to show Mouse a better way of driving it. In short, Mr Harold J Benson presented a perfect replica of the popular English idea of the travelling American – so perfect that Mr

Chitterwick, who had always thought this idea to be more in the nature of a caricature than a replica, marvelled greatly at finding it actually translated into flesh and blood.

At Riversmead Priory he remained no less true to type. Mr Chitterwick, who remembered only too well his own embarrassment at being pitchforked into the middle of a set of complete strangers, envied exceedingly the easy assurance with which Mr Benson wrung his hostess' hand (while Judith looked on with malicious amusement), clapped his host on the back, thereby causing that elderly nobleman to stagger convulsively, made a small speech thanking the entire party for (*a*) their devotion to his cousin Lynn's interests, (*b*) their kind welcome of himself, and (*c*), he need hardly add, their sympathy with his cousin Lynn's plucky little wife in this terrible misfortune, and addressed the butler (that same fish-eyed, magnificent butler who had so seared Mr Chitterwick's soul on the night of his arrival) as 'Bo.'

The rest of the party gazed after him with starting eyes as he clumped in his thick-toed shoes after the footman to his room.

Then Agatha began to giggle. 'He – he's just like the comic American in a bad farce,' she said in a stifled voice. 'He might have stepped straight off the stage.'

'That,' said Mr Chitterwick thoughtfully, 'is just exactly what he has done.'

'What did you say, Mr Chitterwick?' asked Judith, looking at him curiously.

'I – only that I understood that that was exactly what he had done,' explained Mr Chitterwick, in some confusion. 'You did mention that he had been on the stage at one time, did you not?'

A muttering growl was audible from the direction of Lord Milborne. 'And to think of *that*,' muttered the growl, 'coming into Earlshaze.' One gathered that in Lord Milborne's opinion that was the worst tragedy of the lot.

They turned solemnly into the house and dispersed to get ready for lunch. There was at least half an hour before the meal, but, as Judith said, dispersal seemed the only possible thing.

At that meal, however, it may be said at once that Mr Benson showed himself much improved. It may have been that his surroundings and the company in which he found himself were beginning to overawe Mr Benson, it may have been (and this Mr Chitterwick considered quite possible) that somebody had managed to convey a warning hint to him; in any case, he made no more speeches, his enthusiasm was patently damped, and even the breadth of his American accent had narrowed perceptibly. After all, there is nothing like a well-bred English household for making a guest feel thoroughly uncomfortable.

If the truth must be told (and presumably it must) it was Mr Chitterwick who displayed himself after lunch as one of the worst types of rank bores. It appeared that Mr Chitterwick was that fiend in human form, an enthusiastic amateur photographer. Hitherto he had kept this mania under control; now apparently it had to find an outlet. Regardless of all decency and the undisguised reluctance of his victims, he produced a camera and insisted on marshalling them on the terrace and photographing them a surprising number of times, both in groups and even singly, prattling artlessly the while about his fondness for souvenirs of all the places he had stayed in and all the people he had met, and gloating quite shamelessly over the valuable additions he would now be able to make to his albums. Lord

Milborne did not try to conceal the pain with which he watched his wife abetting Mr Chitterwick in this ignoble pursuit as, hardly less insistently than the chief torturer, she ordered the other victims about and posed them delightedly for his delectation. It was not a pleasant quarter of an hour.

Flushed but triumphant, though taking some pains to avoid his host's eye, Mr Chitterwick retired with the two rolls of films he had taken, carrying a reluctant Mouse with him under pretext of helping him develop them. As soon as they were out of sight of the others, however, he led the way not to the bathroom but to his own bedroom, where he proceeded to lock the door behind them.

'Never knew you were a photographer, Chitterwick,' remarked Mouse, viewing the door locking with some surprise.

'I'm not,' said Mr Chitterwick. 'But I can press a bulb, I hope, as well as another man. I bought this camera yesterday, for the express purpose of taking those photographs. Your sister very kindly undertook to help me obtain them. At least,' said Mr Chitterwick with some misgiving, 'I hope I have obtained them; but a camera is really rather more complicated than I expected. However, your sister said she understood the things, so no doubt it will be all right.'

'I noticed she changed the films for you,' said Mouse slowly.

'I found that most difficult to master,' deprecated Mr Chitterwick, 'although I practised in my bedroom last night.'

Mouse looked at him. 'Come on, Chitterwick. There's more in this than meets the eye. What is it?'

Mr Chitterwick did not reply immediately. He sat down, placed his hands on his knees, and looked extremely solemn. 'It was a subterfuge, of course. I wanted those photographs.'

'But why?'

'Mouse,' said Mr Chitterwick soberly, 'I'm of the opinion that I have found the man who impersonated Major Sinclair in the Piccadilly Palace.'

'You have?' said Mouse, rather stupidly.

'Well – there's only one possible one, isn't there? I've suspected so for some time. It all depended on his nose. As soon as I saw that I was certain.'

'Benson?' said Mouse incredulously. 'But his voice, man. He's obviously American, if ever anyone was. He couldn't have taken Miss Sinclair in for a minute.'

'He's an actor. But he's a bad actor. He exaggerated the Oxford accent of Eccles over the telephone; he exaggerated his American accent this morning; when he realized he was doing so, he toned it down.'

'But he was in America at the time!'

'Was he?' said Mr Chitterwick briskly. 'That's just what I propose to find out. And that's the reason why I wanted those photographs. If he was here at the time of the murder, he would naturally have gone back again immediately afterward. I am go'ng to show his photographs to the clerks in the various shipping offices and ask them if they can recognize him as a man who booked a passage at about that date.' If Mr Chitterwick had entered upon this case reluctantly and with diffidence concerning his own powers of real detection, that reluctance and that diffidence had left him now; he spoke with unusual determination, and it was evident that the excitement of the chase had gripped him.

'I'll come with you,' said Mouse promptly.

'I was hoping you would see your way to do so,' said Mr Chitterwick with gratitude. 'You know, we really ought to start almost at once.'

'The sooner the better. Five minutes, if you like. But we must tell Judy the good news first.'

'Do you think so?' Mr Chitterwick hesitated. 'We haven't proved our case yet, you see. Would it not be better to wait until we can tell it to her as a fact instead of just a theory?'

'She'd never forgive us if we did,' Mouse assured him.

'Oh, well, perhaps it can do no harm.' But Mr Chitterwick still seemed a little dubious. 'No doubt you would prefer to tell her yourself, while I am making my excuses to your sister for this very brief visit.'

Mouse generously suggested that, the inspiration having been Mr Chitterwick's, he should be the one to impart it; but that gentleman, twittering something about keeping an eye on the car till Mouse arrived, hurried off to look for Lady Milborne, clasping his precious films inside his pocket. Mouse had evidently not seen through his little stratagem.

Within ten minutes they were on the road once more.

Mouse reported that Judith had been intensely interested in Mr Chitterwick's solution, but slightly incredulous. However, she had offered to keep an eye on the suspect while they were away.

During the journey Mr Chitterwick seemed wrapped in his thoughts, which were apparently of a rather onerous nature, for he sighed more than once. Mouse, respecting his silence, was taciturn too, and for the first fifty miles Mr Chitterwick volunteered only two remarks; the first being that a second reason for obtaining the photographs was that they could make inquiries at the costumiers for anyone buying a red wig round about that date, and the second to suggest that it was not necessary perhaps to go *quite* so fast as they could hardly begin their inquiries that evening.

They arrived in London just before six, and Mr Chitterwick directed his chauffeur to the shop where he had bought the camera. While Mouse stayed outside in the car he hurried in and handed over his two rolls to be developed, stipulating that it must be done, and prints taken, that evening, no matter what it cost. 'And I want enlargements of the fourth film on *this* roll, and the third on that,' he added, consulting his notebook. 'Those must be done tonight too. Everything must be ready first thing tomorrow morning.'

'I'm afraid we can hardly get the enlargements done tonight sir,' objected the shopman.

'I can get you authority from Scotland Yard if you like,' retorted Mr Chitterwick truculently, and quite without truth.

The shopman looked at him. 'It's something really important, sir?'

Mr Chitterwick assured him with emphasis that it was. The shopman thought that in that case something might be done. Mr Chitterwick gave his name, and got out of the shop just as they were beginning to put up the shutters.

It being then too late to do anything further, Mouse took Mr Chitterwick to his club and bought him an astonishing number of drinks.

They dined at the club and, by way of relaxation, went to a revue afterward, Mr Chitterwick having telephoned through to Chiswick before dinner. It was not till nearly twelve o'clock that they reached his aunt's house. To their surprise they found Judith sitting up for them.

'I simply couldn't help it,' she said. 'I know I promised to stay and guard the suspect, I know I've deserted my post, I know I'm everything that I shouldn't be – but I simply had to take the first train I could catch and come up to see how you were getting on. Well, Mr Chitterwick, tell me all about it. It's all over bar the shouting, is it?'

Mr Chitterwick smiled at her a little nervously. A very different Judith this from the desperate, half-hysterical woman of the evening before. 'I hope so, Mrs Sinclair, I hope so.'

'Oh, call me Judith,' she smiled. 'Really, Mr Chitterwick, I don't think I've ever known anyone so long (What is it? Nearly a whole fortnight!) without being called by my Christian name. It simply isn't done nowadays, you know.'

Mr Chitterwick murmured something which he hoped was suitable.

'What about the photographs? Have you developed them yet? I'm dying to see them.'

'We dropped them on our way,' put in Mouse, munching a sandwich.

'Dropped them?'

'To be developed.'

'Oh! You quite alarmed me for the moment. Well, have you discovered anything else?'

'Only that Celia Perry's legs are getting fatter. We've been to *Knees Up,* and the Princess'.'

'I don't care a bit about Celia Perry's legs. I want to know why Mr Chitterwick thinks our simple cowboy cousin poisoned an aunt he'd never heard of. At least, he says he never had. Tell me, Mr Chitterwick.'

Mr Chitterwick told her. Judith did not think Mr Benson had so much ingenuity. Mouse was inclined to agree with her. They argued for nearly an hour. Then Mr Chitterwick went to bed. As Judith assured him that she was far too excited to go to bed at all that night, and Mouse seemed quite ready to sit up till morning with her, he left them sitting.

But Mr Chitterwick did not sleep very much that night.

Nevertheless, he was down the next morning punctually for an eight-thirty breakfast, and so was Mouse. Judith, it seemed, having gone to bed the previous night after all, now found it a good deal more difficult to get up again.

Leisurely Mr Chitterwick helped his guest to porridge and sat down with his own. Murmuring an excuse, he began to open his post. Suddenly there burst an exclamation from him. His chair, abruptly pushed back, squealed on the boards. Mr Chitterwick half rose, sat down again, half rose once more, and then thrust a letter in front of Mouse. 'God bless my soul, this is dreadful,' he murmured quite distractedly. 'Read that.'

The letter which had so perturbed Mr Chitterwick ran as follows:

DEAR MR CHITTERWICK:

Of course I realized that you suspected me when you made that very thin excuse to see me without my spectacles. I was afraid then that you had recognized me from the Piccadilly Palace. But having been interviewed this afternoon by a policeman I see your suspicion has turned into certainty. Well, you are perfectly right; but naturally I am not going to sit here and wait to be arrested as an accessory in a murder charge. By the time you get this I shall be safe enough.

At least, I shall if you will let me, and the reason I am writing is to ask you to do so. It is perfectly true, as I said, that I helped Lynn get rid of the old lady, but he really forced me to it, in a way. He had got hold of some information about my past, which isn't quite so blameless as it might be, and held it over my head to make me help him. He had to get Miss Sinclair out of the way, because she was going to disinherit him, but he couldn't do it alone. He worked out the plan, and all I had to do was to dress up as a waitress and put that phial in her hand after she was unconscious to make it look like suicide, which was easy enough, but the silly fool went and left his fingerprints on it. But for that, and the rotten luck of you having been watching him, there would never have been the faintest chance of his being found out or even suspected.

Well, what I mean is, can't you let me off? I don't know what you've told the police, or whether you've told them anything beyond my being a suspicious character, but is there any need to tell them about my share in this job? I can assure you, I've been punished enough already. It's been hell. And they've got the real murderer, Lynn Sinclair. I should never have had a hand in it if he hadn't threatened me. Be a sportsman, Mr Chitterwick. Tear this letter up and forget you ever suspected me. It isn't much to ask, is it?

MARY GOOLE

PS In any case, I'm going to disappear, so catch me who can.

'My God!' said Mouse soberly as he put it down. 'So Lynn – This'll be rotten for Judy.'

'It's very – unexpected,' said Mr Chitterwick slowly.

'And all those cunning ideas of yours. All baseless!'

'The tendency is always to overelaborate,' said Mr Chitterwick in a mechanical voice, staring at his plate. 'It is so difficult to remember that the probable is always the simple.'

There was a silence. Mouse took up his spoon and began automatically to eat his porridge. 'Who's going to break it to Judy?' he mumbled. 'That's what I want to know.'

Mr Chitterwick seemed to come to a sudden decision. He jumped to his feet. 'I will.'

'Not this minute?' said Mouse, looking up in surprise.

'Why not?' asked Mr Chitterwick. 'She's got to be told some time. And procrastination can be just as dangerous as overelaboration.' But he hesitated.

'She may be asleep. Surely it isn't necessary to wake her up.'

'I won't wake her,' promised Mr Chitterwick, seeming to accept this as a compromise. 'If she doesn't answer my tap I will come down again.'

In two minutes he was back, and in answer to Mouse's raised eyebrows shook his head. 'She must be asleep,' he said.

Breakfast proceeded in gloomy silence. Mouse was evidently quite overwhelmed by the shock, and Mr Chitterwick wore the preoccupied air of one whose prophecies have come to disaster. Hardly a word was spoken.

In the middle of the toast-and-marmalade stage Mr Chitterwick came to sudden and most unexpected life. He astonished his companions by smiting the table with his clenched fist and speaking loudly and clearly. 'I *don't* believe it!' vociferated Mr Chitterwick.

'What?' asked Mouse in wonder.

'That letter.'

'What!'

'It's too elaborate. It's quite unnecessarily elaborate. It contains a detailed confession – incredible elaboration! Mouse, I – I believe this may be very serious.'

'What may?'

'That letter,' said Mr Chitterwick, rather incoherently. 'Miss Goole... Things – '

'Do you mean – you don't mean the letter may be a fake?'

'We must go at once,' said Mr Chitterwick, jumping up once more. 'At once. What is the postmark, I wonder?' he added, scrabbling among the envelopes on the table. 'Ah! London, SW4. Yes, we must go this minute. Are you ready?'

'Absolutely. But where are we going?'

'Why,' said Mr Chitterwick, in surprise, 'to Dorsetshire.'

'Right-o,' said Mouse. 'Lead on.' He had not the faintest idea why they were going or what it was that seemed to be so perturbing Mr Chitterwick, but that gentleman was clearly in no fit state to be questioned, and what he said was good enough for Mouse.

'Telling Judy nothing?' was all he ventured on the way to the garage.

Mr Chitterwick appeared to jerk himself out of a trance, and it was a second or two before he answered. 'Telling Mrs Sinclair nothing,' he said then with decision, and added, 'but calling for those photographs on the way.'

Once again the nose of the patient Bentley was headed for Dorsetshire.

At the photographic shop, however, a surprise awaited Mr Chitterwick. 'The photographs, sir?' said the shopman in surprise. 'But I gave them to your messenger not above ten minutes ago; almost directly after we opened.'

'My messenger?' repeated Mr Chitterwick. He did not seem very surprised. Mouse, on the other hand, listened with open mouth.

'He asked for them in your name,' said the shopman defensively, scenting trouble.

'Can you describe him?' asked Mr Chitterwick.

'Well,' said the shopman vaguely, 'he seemed quite a respectable man. I hope I've done nothing wrong, sir?'

'Did he remind you of anyone?'

'Remind me? No, sir. You don't mean – ?'

'He was no messenger of mine,' said Mr Chitterwick ruefully. 'I suppose you gave him everything? The films as well as the prints and the enlargements?'

'I'm afraid I did, sir. I'm very sorry, I'm sure, but I had no reason to doubt he was from you. "The photographs for Mr Chitterwick," he said; so, of course, I handed them over.'

'Of course,' said Mr Chitterwick, turning away. 'I quite see it wasn't your fault. I should have warned you. But I never... It was careless of me. Good morning.'

'Wait a minute, though, sir,' exclaimed the shopman excitedly. 'Seeing how important you said it was last night, I did duplicates of those two enlargements on spec. I thought they might come in handy for you some time.'

'And you didn't hand the duplicates over?' asked Mr Chitterwick, no less excitedly.

'They're in the next room, this very minute,' said the shopman.

Mr Chitterwick with difficulty refrained from falling on his neck.

While the shopman was getting them Mr Chitterwick turned to Mouse. 'Do you mind – er – starting up your engine? We mustn't waste a moment now.'

'She'll start the minute we're in the car,' said Mouse in some surprise.

Mr Chitterwick contrived to look both embarrassed and mysterious. Embarrassed because he was implying a lie, and mysterious because that is what he wanted to look. 'Still, I'd prefer to have the engine running as I come out of the shop, and the car perhaps even on the move.'

'Good Lord! You don't mean there's likely to be any – violence?'

'One never knows,' said Mr Chitterwick darkly.

Mouse went.

Mr Chitterwick waited for the photographs, examined them carefully, paid for them, and hurried out of the shop. One half of a second after he crossed the threshold the car was in motion, with Mr Chitterwick scrambling in an undignified way onto the running board. Mouse might not have many powers in the way of constructive thought, but he could obey orders.

'Dorsetshire?' he asked laconically.

Mr Chitterwick nodded. 'And – er – step on the gas, Mouse – that is the right term, isn't it?'

'Something pretty serious?'

'Perhaps a life,' said Mr Chitterwick drily.

Mouse stepped.

It was not until they were clear of London traffic that Mr Chitterwick spoke again. 'Thank God I acted then and there on my suspicions about that letter.'

'You're sure it's a fake, then?' muttered Mouse, shaving past a lorry.

Mr Chitterwick gazed at the speedometer needle creeping up from sixty toward seventy, and never saw it at all. 'I'm convinced of it. That matter of the photographs quite settles it.'

'Nippy bit of work, that.'

'Very nippy,' agreed Mr Chitterwick ruefully. He had been caught napping by that very nippiness.

'But how the devil did he know where we'd left them?'

'We're dealing with brains,' Mr Chitterwick sighed. 'Remarkable brains.'

'Well, I wouldn't have given that cowboy credit for it all,' said Mouse, and there was a note of distinct admiration in his voice.

They drove another forty miles in silence. Mouse, who was on his mettle to break all previous records into fragments, had no time for talk; Mr Chitterwick no breath.

The latter took advantage of the town of Basingstoke to put a question. 'Mouse, think hard. I want you to give me a list of all the places near Riversmead where somebody could be concealed: empty houses, disused mines, caves, anything.'

'That's rather a large order. Do you mean, any place where someone could hide?'

'No! Any place where someone could be hidden.'

Mouse whistled. 'Phew! You mean, he's got hold of Miss Goole and forced her to write that letter?'

'Something like that. Think, please. It's deadly important.'

Mouse thought for a few moments, 'Well,' he said with a short laugh, 'I can name a couple of dozen on the spur of the moment. That part of the country's honeycombed with all kinds of caves and quarries and things. It'd take a week to search them all.'

'In that case,' said Mr Chitterwick, his good-humoured face setting in grim lines, 'in that case we must resort to direct methods. We must tackle Benson himself.'

'I'm game,' said Mouse with enthusiasm.

In the intervals when the needle slipped below the sixty mark they discussed details. As it was not a matter of a sporting contest all such hindrances as Queensberry rules were to be considered shelved. The object was to get the truth out of Benson, and get it quick. Both Mouse and Mr Chitterwick being small men, each of them scarcely a match for Benson, it was decided to call in the under keeper as well, a young man of sturdy physique and a favourite of Mouse's. Against the three of them Benson could hardly stand a chance.

Hardly another word was spoken before they reached Riversmead. Mouse glanced at his watch as they turned in at the gates. The hundred and thirty-three miles from London had been covered in exactly two hours and forty minutes.

Greggs, the under keeper, happened luckily to be exchanging a few words with the head keeper outside the lodge. Mouse stopped the car and picked him up, explaining the situation briefly as they proceeded up the drive. Greggs, an intelligent young fellow, seemed to understand what was required of him and grinned in anticipation.

The rest may be briefly told. Greggs was put out at a convenient spot near a clearing in the woods which lined the drive, and Mr Chitterwick with him; Mouse went on up to the house to collect Benson if he were there. In a surprisingly short space of time he returned with him. Benson seemed to scent something amiss as he saw the other two grimly waiting for him under the trees, hesitated a moment, and turned tail. Mouse, however, who had kept well behind him, produced a cudgel which he flourished threateningly. Benson hesitated again, and Greggs had time to get up to him and deal him a tremendous buffet on the ear. Benson was lifted clean off his feet.

He lay where he had fallen, crying out indignantly and asking what they thought they were doing.

'Where is Miss Goole, you scoundrel?' demanded Mr Chitterwick, glistening with fury.

'Miss Goole?' snarled the other. 'Never heard of her. You three get to hell out of this, will you?'

'Hit him, Greggs,' cried Mr Chitterwick, almost beside himself. 'Have no mercy on him.'

But Mr Benson, it appeared, preferred to lie down.

'Hit him, Greggs, hit him,' implored Mr Chitterwick. 'This is no time for the niceties.'

Greggs paused for a moment, then darted to the side of the clearing and with a mighty wrench tore off a thick hazel shoot. 'I'll make the swine talk,' he muttered between his teeth, and began to lay on with all his strength.

'Where is Miss Goole?' Mr Chitterwick repeated shrilly.

Half a dozen strokes on the scrambling body was enough.

'Stop! I'll tell you.' Greggs stood by watchfully. 'In the ice house,' said Benson sullenly.

'Is she alive?'

'Course she is.'

'The ice house?' queried Mouse.

'I think I know what he means, Your Grace,' said Greggs. 'It's an underground room where they used to keep the ice in summer, I've heard say, though it's not been used now for years. But there's a good door on it yet. It's near here. Shall we go and see, Your Grace?'

'Yes, and bring that fellow along with us. If she's not there we'll borrow an idea from his own country and have a little private lynching party. I'd just love to string him up.'

But such extreme measures proved to be unnecessary. Miss Goole was in the ice house. Moreover, she was not at all pleased to be rescued. Her manner was ungrateful in the extreme. As for Mr Chitterwick, she characterized him without hesitation as a Nosy Parker.

A few questions, however, brought about a change of attitude. Miss Goole had been under the impression that a warrant was out for her arrest and that kind Mr Benson was thoughtfully rescuing her from that indignity; though she admitted that Jimmy, as she called him, was not generally noted for such altruism.

'Then you knew each other before?' asked Mr Chitterwick mildly.

'Know Jimmy the Rube? I should say I did. Why, we've worked together over there.' In the reaction of the moment Miss Goole was evidently disposed to be communicative.

'I see,' said Mr Chitterwick, as though the news were hardly a surprise to him.

'But I've not been in with him on this lay,' said Miss Goole, suddenly recollecting herself.

'You dam' little liar!' remarked Mr Benson discourteously. 'You know perfectly well you – '

'Put him in there, Greggs, and lock him in,' said Mr Chitterwick suddenly. 'I'll see him later.' With a neatly directed kick Greggs propelled Mr Benson in the required direction and slammed the door on him.

'Jimmy always had a white liver,' observed Miss Goole with disdain. She looked curiously at Mr Chitterwick. 'Has he squealed?'

'Not yet, but he's going to,' said Mr Chitterwick grimly. 'And so,' he added, 'are you.'

'Me?' said Miss Goole in high surprise. 'Whatcha mean? I know nothing about this business. I was after the old lady's diamonds, that's all. You can't mix me up with anything else.'

'What about that letter of yours this morning?' frowned Mouse.

'Letter?' echoed Miss Goole, this time in real surprise. 'What letter? I don't know anything about a letter.'

'Perhaps you'd leave this to me, Mouse,' suggested Mr Chitterwick, with such diffidence that Mouse looked thoroughly abashed. He turned to Miss Goole and spoke very mildly. 'You've been doing a little blackmail recently, haven't you?'

A look of distinct alarm passed swiftly across Miss Goole's face. 'What are you getting at?' she asked, a shade too shrilly. 'This is Greek to me.'

'I thought you had,' observed Mr Chitterwick with gentle satisfaction, as if she had answered with a simple affirmative. 'I thought so. Now, listen to me, young woman. That man Benson, of course, I have no option but to hand straight over to the police. With you I think I have an option.

At any rate, if you'll undertake to tell me the exact truth as you know it and answer any questions I put to you, I'll undertake that your name shall not figure in *my* report to Scotland Yard. It may be wrong of me, but I'll promise that.'

Miss Goole looked at him curiously. 'What are you? You don't look like a busy to me.'

'Never mind what I am,' returned Mr Chitterwick with dignity. 'I'll give you five minutes to decide on your answer. Greggs, please see that she does not run away.' He drew Mouse a little aside, while Miss Goole gazed after them with calculating eyes.

'Well, we've got 'em,' observed Mouse with much satisfaction, as soon as they were out of earshot. 'So friend Benson's a professional criminal, is he? A jolly sort of relation for the Sinclairs.'

'I rather fancied that might turn out to be the case,' murmured Mr Chitterwick, who seemed to have become somewhat distrait again now that the excitement was over.

'"Jimmy the Rube,"' meditated Mouse. 'Rather suits him, doesn't it? That's the line he was playing when he arrived yesterday, of course. But he overdid it.'

'Yes,' agreed Mr Chitterwick absently. 'Overelaboration, as I said, has been the mistake in this crime all the time.'

'And yet it seemed simple enough till you began to look into it. By the way, Chitterwick, I know it isn't my affair, but surely we must hand the Goole over to the police too. Accessory, you know, and all that.'

'Well, she *has* been an accessory after the fact,' admitted Mr Chitterwick. 'But only fortuitously. I mean, so far as guilty knowledge is concerned.'

Mouse looked puzzled. 'After the fact? And before it.'

'Oh, no,' Mr Chitterwick said, shaking his head with decision. 'No, no. Not before it.'

'But if she was the accomplice, and – '

'She wasn't the accomplice!'

Mouse stared at him. 'She wasn't? But – '

'There was no accomplice.'

For a moment Mouse looked completely bewildered. Then his face cleared. 'Oh, I see. There never was an accomplice. All those cunning theories of yours about the waitress crash, do they? Well, that simplifies matters. We've got the murderer, anyhow.'

'You mean Benson?' said Mr Chitterwick, looking rather uncomfortable.

'Well, of course.'

Mr Chitterwick cleared his throat. 'He isn't the murderer,' he said huskily.

'Hi, you two,' came Miss Goole's voice. 'I've made up my mind. I'll come across with what I know.' Neither of them took any notice of her.

'Not – the murderer?' stammered Mouse.

'No.' Mr Chitterwick seemed to be speaking with the greatest reluctance, as if he had to drag the words out of himself. 'He was just the unconscious tool of the real criminal. Though afterward, of course, he must have known that murder had been committed.'

'Then who – who is the real criminal? Not – Lynn?'

Mr Chitterwick shook his head, his eyes on the ground. 'No, not Lynn.' He fidgeted miserably with his foot against a root. 'Mouse, I fear this is going to be a great shock for you. A terrible shock. But I think you had better know at once.'

Mouse had gone dead white. 'My God,' he whispered, 'you don't mean – you *can't* mean – '

'Yes,' said Mr Chitterwick in a low voice, looking the other way. 'Yes. Judith Sinclair.'

chapter fifteen

Envoy

Lady Milborne pushed the olives toward Mr Chitterwick and consulted with the waiter about the wine. Mr Chitterwick ate an olive with an attempt at nonchalance and sipped his cocktail. He felt like a man who has wandered by mistake into the feminine portion of a Turkish bath and is hoping desperately that nobody will notice him before he can escape.

'You haven't had dinner in a women's club before, Mr Chitterwick?' Lady Milborne smiled, the matter of the wine satisfactorily settled.

'Er – no,' Mr Chitterwick confessed. 'No, I haven't.' From his expression one gathered that he hoped never to do so again.

'They don't do one so badly here really, considering,' said Lady Milborne. 'You'll have another cocktail?'

'No, thank you,' said Mr Chitterwick. 'No, really, thank you.'

Lady Milborne beckoned to the waiter. 'Two more side cars, please. I want another,' she added to Mr Chitterwick with her most dazzling smile, 'and I hate drinking alone. You don't really mind, do you?' If a combination of cocktails and

251

her own smile could put Mr Chitterwick at ease, then Lady Milborne was going to put him.

'Oh, well,' said Mr Chitterwick, melting already.

Lady Milborne waited until the second cocktail should have done its work. 'And now,' she said, 'I want to hear all about it. Everything!'

'Yes,' said Mr Chitterwick vaguely. 'Yes, of course. Er – Mouse is quite all right you said?'

'Yes, I think so, now. Judy's death was a terrible shock to him, of course, but he realizes that it was much better than – well, arrest and all that. I suppose she would certainly have been convicted?'

'With Benson's evidence, inevitably.'

'And what will happen to him?'

'A severe sentence, undoubtedly. He was an accessory after the fact, you see.'

Lady Milborne sighed. 'I can hardly realize it even now, Mr Chitterwick!'

'Yes?'

'I'm quite sure you had something to do with Judy poisoning herself and leaving that confession. Didn't you?'

Mr Chitterwick looked highly uncomfortable. 'Really, Lady Milborne – '

'If it's confidential I won't tell anyone. What did you do, Mr Chitterwick?'

'I... H'm! Well, it is confidential, but perhaps... After I had spoken with Benson, you see, and made sure (as I imagined would be the case) that he was only anxious to save his own skin at the expense of Mrs Sinclair's, I got rid of Mouse on some pretext and went up to the house, where I telephoned through to Chiswick. Mrs Sinclair was still there, and I told her quite bluntly what had happened, that I had no alternative but to put the matter in the hands of the police, but that I proposed to delay doing so until I had returned to London, which would not be for at least three hours. And I must admit,' said Mr Chitterwick with conscious guilt, 'that I hinted very plainly that, as conviction would be inevitable and escape was impossible, she might care to consider some easier way out. She was a good gambler and accepted defeat.' Mr Chitterwick sighed, remembering that terrible conversation and the jaunty courage with which the woman at the other end of the line received what had amounted to her own death sentence. Judith Sinclair may have been a callous woman, but she was certainly a brave one.

'As for the confession, I hinted also that she might care to leave that behind her in return for the quite illegal concession I was making her, and she agreed at once. She seemed to bear no animosity against anyone, certainly not against her husband, and not even against Benson. I remember she remarked that it was a mistake to rely on a broken reed, but the trouble was that one never knew that the reed was broken until one had leaned. She must have gone straight back to Queen Anne's Gate, written out the confession taking all responsibility for the murder, and swallowed the prussic acid.'

'The remainder of the same lot that she'd got for Miss Sinclair,' said Lady Milborne solemnly. 'That's tragic irony, if you like. And then you went to Scotland Yard. What did they say to you?'

'Not much, at first.' Mr Chitterwick was unable to repress a smile at the memory of Moresby's bantering incredulity as he had begun to unfold his tale, turning to open-mouthed amazement as Mr Chitterwick produced proofs of his case, and culminating in stern officialism when Greggs and Mouse brought in their prisoner to tell his own version. 'But afterward they were very kind,' added

Mr Chitterwick, remembering further first Moresby's ungrudging commendation afterward, and then the warm words of the assistant commissioner himself.

'And they let Lynn go at once?'

'As soon as the formalities could be pushed through. Er – I've hardly seen him since. How is he?' Major Sinclair had thanked Mr Chitterwick with stiff correctness for the efforts he had made on his behalf and at the same time contrived to intimate that he would have been a good deal more grateful if the Chitterwick nose had never been pushed into the affair at all.

'Oh, he'll get over it in time, no doubt. One always does. But naturally he's still terribly cut up. He adored Judy, you know. If it wasn't for the confession he'd refuse to believe in her guilt for a moment. But I'm not at all sure,' added Lady Milborne thoughtfully, 'that he didn't suspect the truth all the time, you know.'

'And kept silent for his wife's sake,' meditated Mr Chitterwick. 'He must be a noble fellow.'

'Yes, Lynn's a very good sort.'

The hors d'oeuvres disappeared, and a sole meunière took their place. The waiter poured out the Liebfraumilch.

'But what I can't understand,' Lady Milborne resumed, 'is Judy herself. We were all so fond of her, and yet she must have been a devil really. How did she take us all in?'

'She was a born actress,' replied Mr Chitterwick promptly. 'She didn't need a stage to display her talents, though she did use one at one time. Her whole life must have been spent in acting a part – the character in which she wished her friends to see her. In reality she was a hard, ruthless woman, with an ingrained dread of poverty, extravagant tastes, complete self-confidence, and great ambition.'

'Now, how on earth do you know all that?' asked Lady Milborne, with proper admiration.

Mr Chitterwick considered for a moment. 'I think it began in her childhood. The experience of poverty she had had then was enough to make her dread it for the rest of her life. Similarly the luxury she saw surrounding her when staying with you was enough to make her crave similar conditions for herself. No doubt she thought she had secured them when Major Sinclair, not too well off himself, but the heir of a wealthy old woman, asked her to marry him, though she kept even him waiting a year in case anything better turned up. But the wealthy old woman didn't die, and the Major's income only just sufficed to keep two; if anything, I daresay, she found herself even more hard put to it to keep up appearances in that position than when she was single. And, moreover, there was always the fear in the background that Miss Sinclair would disapprove of her nephew's marriage to the extent of altering her will.'

'And that brought her to murder, to make sure of it once and for all?'

'Not that alone. There was another motive, I think.'

'What?'

Mr Chitterwick looked a little embarrassed. 'You really wish me to tell you? It affects you personally, in a way, and you may find it rather unpleasant.'

'Still, tell me.'

'Well, I think the mainspring of the whole plot undoubtedly must have been the fact that your brother certainly was very deeply in love with her. I think he always has been, but when she married he was too young to be taken seriously.'

'Oh!' Lady Milborne paled a little. 'That's rather – beastly. You mean, if she could eliminate not only Miss Sinclair, but

Lynn as well, she had a good chance of becoming a duchess?'

'The practical certainty of becoming a duchess,' amended Mr Chitterwick. 'She was playing for high stakes.'

'How – foul.'

They sat in silence while the waiter changed the plates, and it was not till some minutes after the next course had been brought that Lady Milborne spoke again. Then she picked up the conversation at the exact point at which it had been left. 'So that's why there had to be that impersonation of Lynn by that Benson man?'

'Yes, from her point of view. He, of course, imagined he was doing it for quite a different reason.'

'I never have quite understood that. Tell me the whole plot, Mr Chitterwick, from the very beginning.'

'Well!' Mr Chitterwick inserted a mouthful of roast duck and began thoughtfully to chase some peas round his plate. The precautions of his hostess had met with their reward; he was no longer self-conscious and was quite ready to talk. 'Well, the whole thing seems to have begun with Mary Goole, as she calls herself (and I understand it is probably her real name). She, as you know, is a professional criminal. A clever one, because she knows exactly how much use to make of the truth. The story she told Chief Inspector Moresby and myself at our first interview with her was perfectly true, so far as it went; the result being that she was never under suspicion at all. They even corroborated it in America, and she had always covered up her traces so well that no question was raised.

'She took her post with Miss Sinclair in accordance with her usual method, which was to employ her position as companion to a wealthy old lady to rob that lady's wealthy friends. The character she adopted for these occasions, by the way, of an efficient machine with none of the ordinary feminine weaknesses for dress and so on, was an excellent one; and part of it no doubt came naturally to her, because she *is* an extremely efficient person.

'In the course of her duties with Miss Sinclair she heard frequently of an unknown cousin in America, to whom at first she attached no importance; gradually, however, what with the name and the nose and other indications, it dawned upon her that this cousin must be a man whom she herself had known there, with whom indeed she had actually engaged once upon a criminal enterprise – a hanger-on of the criminal fraternity, without enough courage or enterprise to strike out in big crime for himself, and yet constitutionally unable to lead an honest life. She, a highly efficient criminal, despised this man very thoroughly, but she now saw an excellent way of making use of him to their common advantage. She wrote to him, therefore, told him of the circumstances, and suggested that should he come over at once she had a plan all ready by which he could obtain possession of most of the old lady's fortune. Benson promptly came over.

'This plan of Miss Goole's was based on two facts. The first was that Miss Sinclair was very much more serious about her threats of altering her will than Major Sinclair ever imagined, and that given enough provocation, such as the fact of her nephew's marriage being broken to her in a sufficiently defiant way by the Major himself, she could undoubtedly be induced by Miss Goole to do so. The second fact was that Miss Sinclair was suffering from disease of the heart and did not herself expect to live more than a few months, though she insisted on this being concealed from Major Sinclair, saying that she hated a fuss being made over her and there was time enough for that when she really was dead. But the point that Miss Goole had seized on, of course, was that if Miss Sinclair did alter her will the chances were almost certainties that she would die before any reconciliation with the Major could take place and the will be altered again.

'The whole plan of the impersonation then was entirely Miss Goole's. Her idea was that Benson, who was known to her as a clever mimic, should meet Miss Sinclair, representing himself as the Major, in such circumstances that the chances of Miss Sinclair's detecting the fraud would be reduced to a minimum, and then tell her brutally of the marriage with such defiance and in such terms that she would never forgive him. That was the sum of Miss Goole's plan. The embroideries on it came from Mrs Sinclair.'

'It was a clever scheme of the Goole's,' commented Lady Milborne judicially.

'Exceedingly clever. And so was her way of carrying it out. The meeting place she decided on was the Piccadilly Palace lounge. There is always a good deal of noise going on there. Miss Sinclair would be out of her element and confused. Without her spectacles (an easy matter for Miss Goole to mislay) she would not only be unable to see clearly, but she would feel still more at a loss. As for arranging that Miss Sinclair should accept the Piccadilly Palace as a meeting place, that was simplicity itself. All she had to do was to substitute that place in the letter she wrote for Miss Sinclair to the Major making the appointment, change the latter from two-thirty to three-thirty, and tell her afterward that the Piccadilly Palace was the Major's own choice. Mouse saw that, and it is quite correct. And that is really all Miss Goole had to do with the affair.'

Mr Chitterwick leaned back and toyed with the glass, swishing the wine absently round inside. The duck had disappeared, a savoury had followed it. With a basket of fruit on the table and a glass of port expected at any moment, less interruptions would follow.

Lady Milborne waited until the port had been served and the waiter was out of the way. 'And then Judy came into it because – Oh, you go on, Mr Chitterwick. You're telling it beautifully. It's so much clearer, hearing it all like this instead of in snippets, which I've had simply to drag out of people.'

'Yes,' continued Mr Chitterwick, thus bidden, 'Mrs Sinclair came into it because Benson, not satisfied with the share of the spoils that Miss Goole had allotted him, thought he would try running with the hare instead of hunting with the hounds. Both he and Miss Goole are somewhat reticent on this point, but I gather that the discussions as to the sharing of the reward had been quite acrimonious. As the originator of the plan Miss Goole was sure that she ought to get the lion's portion, Benson himself being rewarded with not much more than a pittance. Benson didn't see that at all, especially as Miss Goole's ideas included, by way of making quite certain of things, no less than marriage, with a settlement conferring on her not much short of everything the two hoped to get from Miss Sinclair. So Benson, having thought things well over, decided that he couldn't be much worse off in any case and that he would double-cross (I understand that is the term) Miss Goole by making overtures to the other side with a view to finding out what they would pay to buy him off. By a fatal chance he tackled on the subject not Major Sinclair, who would have promptly kicked him downstairs, but Mrs Sinclair, who did nothing of the sort. Benson's sort, of course, always prefers to carry through shady transactions with women rather than men.

'Whether Mrs Sinclair had been already meditating some drastic method of obtaining for her husband possession of Miss Sinclair's wealth I cannot say, but judging by the alacrity with which she was able to see the advantages to herself of Miss Goole's plan I should think it most probable. It was she, I understand now, who had always insisted on keeping the marriage secret; she took Miss Sinclair's threats seriously, if the Major did not. In any case she embraced the opportunity without hesitation and, so far as Benson was concerned, immediately took the affair completely in hand. Miss Goole, of course, was ignorant that Benson had approached Mrs Sinclair, and she was kept in that ignorance all the time.

'Benson had not the faintest idea that murder was meditated. He was nothing but a pliant tool in Mrs Sinclair's capable hands. And I think he must have fallen under Mrs Sinclair's spell, for he seems to have carried out without question what must have appeared to him some quite remarkable manoeuvres. Mrs Sinclair told him, you see, to go ahead with Miss Goole's plan, but to adopt it for himself; if he took a strong line there would be no need to share the proceeds with her at all. Moreover, if he would carry out a few small suggestions of her own, Mrs Sinclair would back him up afterward in the exclusion of Miss Goole.

'Of course Mrs Sinclair was somewhat hard put to it to find a plausible reason why she should wish Miss Sinclair's money left away from her own husband; and plausible or not, what she told Benson was that the Major was a spendthrift and had treated her abominably, that she was on the point of leaving him, and that she would very much like to ensure his being left penniless in the future by way of some revenge for all she had suffered from him. That sounds thin to us now, but no doubt Mrs Sinclair was able with her histrionic powers to make a singularly convincing and moving story of it, adding hypothetical details of the Major's ill-treatment and so working on Benson's emotions that he was ready to do anything she wanted. What he was required to do first of all was to go, wearing the wig Miss Goole had procured him for his impersonation of Major Sinclair (and which, I understand, renders him quite surprisingly like the Major), and ask, not too ostentatiously but nevertheless in a way which would not be forgotten afterward, at three or four chemists' shops for prussic acid.

'Here again Mrs Sinclair must have had difficulty in finding a reasonable excuse, and what she told him was that it would be a good thing to endeavour to establish an indication that Major Sinclair was contemplating poisoning his aunt; this, she pointed out, would make it impossible that the breach between them could ever be healed. And to further this idea she induced him to undertake, in the Piccadilly Palace interview, to pour a few drops into Miss Sinclair's coffee from a phial with which she would provide him. This liquid, she said, would be nothing really but a violent aperient, but Miss Sinclair would be taken mildly ill, imagine she had been poisoned, and at once the story of the attempts to buy prussic acid would come out. In the same way, she added, it would be advisable if possible to engage the attention of someone sitting near who would be a witness to the fact that the Major had dropped something into Miss Sinclair's coffee. And that is how I came into the affair.

'Well, Benson, seeing that all these elaborations only strengthened his own interests, and not suspecting for a moment that Mrs Sinclair had other interests of her own behind them, agreed without hesitation to everything, and in due course the plan was put into effect. Every detail had been worked out in advance by Mrs Sinclair, even to Benson calling the waitress over and giving her his own empty cup. Mrs Sinclair, under pretext of keeping a supervisory eye on things, was to dress up as a waitress, as you no doubt know, and visit the table in that capacity, when Benson was to order a glass of kirsch for Miss Sinclair with her coffee, a liqueur of which she knew Miss Sinclair to be particularly fond.'

'She took an enormous risk there,' remarked Lady Milborne thoughtfully. 'Those girls all know each other. A strange face would be observed at once.'

'It was a risk, of course, but not such a very large one. And one of the other waitresses actually did speak to her, but she had her story pat. She said without hesitation that she was a new waitress and employed in the grillroom, but had been sent upstairs with an order for a client who had just gone up to the lounge. The police have found that out since, but at the time the girl's suspicions were not roused in the least. Mrs Sinclair carried off what might have been an awkward moment perfectly naturally; she really was a magnificent actress.

'And the rest followed almost exactly on the lines that I ventured to suggest to your brother,' continued Mr Chitterwick, not without pride, and recounted again his theory of how the poison had been administered, the traces removed, prussic acid left in the empty coffee cup, and the incriminatingly marked phial inserted in Miss Sinclair's hand.

'And you really guessed all that?' exclaimed Lady Milborne with proper admiration.

It was the only theory I could find to explain the facts,' said Mr Chitterwick modestly. 'I had to employ inductive methods, of course,' he added in a deprecatory tone, as if anybody could have done *that*.

'And you knew it was Judith all the time?'

'Oh no. Dear me, no. I must admit that at one time I very strongly suspected Miss Goole. Very strongly indeed. But the question of motive bothered me considerably. I could see no possible reason for Miss Goole wishing Miss Sinclair dead and plenty for wishing her alive. Similarly with Benson. I suspected him quite early as being the man in the case, but I could not believe that he was the murderer; it would of course have been sheer madness for him to kill Miss Sinclair before she had made a will in his favour. I was really led to Mrs Sinclair by a combination of elimination and motive, but even then I was not quite certain until we came to the fact of those photographs having been removed from the shop in my name. She was the only possible person who could have effected that. But with her usual prudence she sent a messenger, a chance loiterer glad to earn an easy shilling, instead of going herself. When I got no answer to my knock on her door I was almost sure she had gone out to do that.'

'You wanted the photographs for identification?'

'Yes, there was one enlargement of Benson, and one of Mrs Sinclair herself. But matters reached such a swift climax that all that part of the work passed into the hands of the police.'

'Who were able to have Judy identified as a woman who had hired a room at the Piccadilly Palace the day before the murder?'

'Where she changed into her waitress's clothes, as I had surmised – exactly.'

'But they haven't been able to find out where she got the poison, have they?'

'No. We think that very probably she had it by her for years, having secured it when she did so in order to make use of the opportunity, when it should arise, without fear of detection but with no definite object in view at the time. Indeed, it may very well be that the chance possession of prussic acid suggested to her the whole crime.'

Lady Milborne uttered a mirthless laugh. 'It's still almost incredible to me. I'd always looked on Judy as – Oh, well. And now you think she'd probably have killed Miss Goole as well?'

'I think it very probable,' said Mr Chitterwick gravely. 'You see, Miss Goole had committed not only the indiscretion of visiting the Piccadilly Palace to see her own plan in operation, whereby she became, unknown to Mrs Sinclair, a witness of its unexpected sequel, but the further indiscretion, too, of trying to blackmail Mrs Sinclair on the strength of what she had seen. Mrs Sinclair, not knowing that Miss Goole had actually been present, considered that she was drawing on her imagination and refused to be intimidated. Unfortunately, however, I let slip my belief that I had seen Miss Goole in the Piccadilly Palace, and that was quit enough to sign her death warrant; Mrs Sinclair would never feel safe so long as an actual witness of her actions was alive. But with her usual ability to take advantage of any circumstances she combined the elimination of Miss Goole with a detailed and singularly convincing attempt to throw the blame on her too, as she saw my own suspicions getting nearer and nearer the truth. She wrote the letter herself, came up to London, posted it, and then came on to Chiswick to keep an eye on me. I must admit that forged letter took me in completely for a few minutes, but thank heaven I had my doubts raised in time. I am quite convinced that we only saved Miss Goole in the nick of time. And so, now, is she.'

'But the man, Benson. He must have known that Judy had murdered Miss Sinclair?'

'He did. His trouble was that he thought (this, of course, was what she told him subsequently) she had done so through his agency. In other words, that the liquid he poured into Miss Sinclair's coffee was the prussic acid (in reality, of course, it was pure water). Naturally, after that, he could not give her away, but had to shield her as much as himself; their interests, indeed, were identical. Besides, my own evidence against Major Sinclair was equally strong against himself. Mrs Sinclair had cleverly put him in the position of having, if he wished to save his own skin, to stand by and connive at, even assist her in, the judicial murder of her husband. He is a scoundrel and a base fellow,' said Mr Chitterwick with indignation, 'but I could well believe him when he told me that those two months were just hell on earth for him.'

'But why didn't Judy do that, Mr Chitterwick? Put the prussic acid in the phial she gave Benson, I mean. That would have saved all the trouble and risk of dressing up as a waitress, and so on.'

'It would have been too unsafe. Prussic acid is the quickest poison and therefore the best for her purpose, but it has a very strong and characteristic smell. If Benson had only sniffed at the phial she gave him he would have recognized it at once and refused to administer it. As a matter of fact, he didn't, and that is how she was able to bamboozle him into thinking he had administered it.'

'And then he went back to America, didn't he?'

'Yes. She had him in a cleft stick, of course, and simply issued her orders. According to his own account he tried his best to get her to let him at least exonerate Major Sinclair anonymously, which she completely refused, but I doubt very much whether he made anything of a fight; she was by far the stronger character. Anyhow, what was arranged was simply that he was to behave in future exactly as he would have done had he been quite innocent and never left America. It was foreseen that the lawyers would have difficulty in tracing him and, of course, he would not answer any of their advertisements, but once he was definitely found he was to behave just as would be expected of him – in other words, come over here and, if Major Sinclair was dead by then, take possession of the estate; if he were not, pretend to be desperately anxious to help him. That, of course, is what he did. But he overdid it, just as he overdid Eccles' voice on the telephone, mimicking on that occasion the Oxford accent into something amounting almost to a caricature of the real thing.'

'Oh, yes, that was him, of course, on Mrs Sinclair's instructions.'

Mr Chitterwick meditated a moment. 'I always thought that incident a valuable clue, though its significance did not seem quite to have been appreciated. It showed, you see, that the person or persons behind the crime were very intimately connected with Major Sinclair, a conclusion which was, of course, corroborated by the fact that they had been able to obtain his fingerprints on the phial without suspicion. That was another thing which, to my mind, definitely ruled the unknown cousin out as the murderer, even before I realized that the man in the Piccadilly Palace could not have placed the phial in Miss Sinclair's hand.'

'I don't know how you ever found out what you did,' sighed Lady Milborne.

'Oh, but I made a great number of mistakes,' Mr Chitterwick hastened to assure her. 'A very great number. For a long time I was under the impression that the crime had been arranged by the man in such a way that he could clear himself if suspicion ever did fall on him. I was wrong there. Quite wrong. Though, curiously enough, this very mistake of mine led me on to further conclusions which were perfectly correct.

'I think that is all there is to tell you. Oh, the phial. It would have been quite easy for Mrs Sinclair to get the Major to handle it when his hands were in a state to leave good impressions. He might have washed them, for instance, and rubbed a little glycerine on them, as some people do, and then she would ask him to hand it to her. After the crime, with her usual attention to detail, she would replace it in the bathroom with another.

'I think that's all, isn't it?'

Lady Milborne did not answer immediately. She peeled a peach slowly and absently. Perhaps some memory was recurring to her of a solemn-faced little girl nearly all of whose games began by the prefix, 'Let's pretend'; and however the others might manage it, in the case of the little girl, at any rate, the pretending had always been consummately done. But for all that one hardly expects people to go on pretending all their lives, thought Lady Milborne.

'And she was so sure Lynn must be innocent,' she said aloud. 'Just as sure as all the rest of us. Surer. And seemed so dreadfully cut up. We almost feared a breakdown at first.'

Mr Chitterwick nodded. 'That was all in the character, you see. The loving, trusting wife. Dear me, dear me.'

'But what I can't understand is why she seemed so taken with the idea of getting you down to Riversmead and trying to make you realize that Lynn wasn't guilty.'

'Whose plan was that, by the way?' asked Mr Chitterwick.
Lady Milborne looked guilty. 'I'm afraid it was mine.'

'Well, what else could Mrs Sinclair do but fall in with it?
And enthusiastically. The character she was playing
demanded it. She must keep in character at all costs.'

'I understood from her,' said Lady Milborne rather
mischievously, 'that she was prepared to pay *quite*
substantial costs. Is that true, Mr Chitterwick?'

'Er – well, I believe there was… Er – yes,' mumbled Mr
Chitterwick, looking supremely uncomfortable.

'It was quite in character, of course,' said Lady Milborne
gravely, though there was a twinkle in her blue eyes. 'In
fact, judging by fiction and the drama one might almost call
the situation stereotyped and the offer conventional,
mightn't one?'

'She was a good judge of her fellow creatures,'
pronounced Mr Chitterwick, with an effort of scientific
treatment of the theme that was slightly marred by his
lingering blush. 'Of course, she knew perfectly well that I
should refuse her – h'm! – her offer. Otherwise… Besides, I
have no doubt she thoroughly enjoyed the situation. The
perfect wife, as one might say. It gave admirable scope to
her histrionic powers (and I must say she acted the scene
magnificently), and at the same time it must have appealed
immensely to her sense of humour. Yes, I have no doubt that
she quite enjoyed that – er – episode.'

'In fact, she acted it so magnificently that she succeeded
in persuading you to do what you had quite made up your
mind not to?' said Lady Milborne, with interest but not much
grammar.

'That is so. It was, in short, another instance of
overelaboration. A tendency toward that has been the only
flaw in the execution of her scheme, but that has occurred all

through; and I think I may even say that it has been that which really helped me to reach the truth. Mrs Sinclair was an artist in crime, but not a great enough artist to know just when to stop or to appreciate the value of simplicity. She thought she was on quite safe ground. She knew she could not make me doubt what I had actually seen with my own eyes, and it is quite possible that she wished to test me out under cross-examination. And if she had cut short her appeal that night at the right moment instead of adding an unnecessary breakdown, she would have achieved her effect and her object (which must have been that I should not reconsider my decision) as well.'

'Perhaps she was carried away by her own acting,' suggested Lady Milborne.

'That may be so; but in the end that lack of artistry cost her her life. A solemn thought.' Mr Chitterwick sighed. 'What must have been her feelings as she had to sit by and watch detail after detail that she had imagined would be hidden forever dragged out into the light! Terrible! And yet she scarcely ever showed them. Only once, I think, when I let fall the fact of Miss Goole's presence in the Piccadilly Palace, did she really forget herself.'

'It must have been an appalling strain. And all to be a duchess! Good heavens, what's a duchess?' demanded Lady Milborne indignantly.

Mr Chitterwick, not knowing, did not answer.

ANTHONY BERKELEY

DEATH IN THE HOUSE

When Lord Wellacombe, the Secretary of State for India, collapses in the House of Commons and dies, everyone suspects a stroke. His death causes political waves as a successor is sought and there is the question of a bill to be put through. But then tests show Wellacombe to have been poisoned and not by any conventional method – a thorn covered in South American poison is discovered under the dead man's coat collar. Is this the work of an international terrorist or someone closer to home?

'Anthony Berkeley is the supreme master not of the "twist" but of the "double-twist"!' – *The Sunday Times*

JUMPING JENNY

A Roger Sheringham case.

Gentleman sleuth Roger Sheringham is at a fancy-dress party where the theme is murderers and victims. The fun takes a sinister turn however when a real victim is discovered hanging on the roof. Is it suicide – or a perfect murder?

ANTHONY BERKELEY

THE LAYTON COURT MYSTERY

A Roger Sheringham case.

Mr Victor Stanworth, an apparently carefree sixty-year-old, is entertaining a party of friends at his summer residence, Layton Court. When one morning he is found shot dead in the library it is hard to believe it is either suicide or murder. As one of the country-house guests, gentleman sleuth Roger Sheringham resolves to solve the murder. As he pursues the truth he does not conceal any of the evidence, and the reader is able to follow his detection work to the conclusion of this original mystery story.

MURDER IN THE BASEMENT

A Roger Sheringham case.

'Don't come down, Molly. There – there's something pretty beastly here. I must get a policeman.'

When Reginald and Molly Dane return from their honeymoon to a new house, they are curious to explore the cellar. Reginald notices a corner where the bricks have been inexpertly put back to cover a hole dug in the floor. Convinced he will find treasure he takes a pickaxe to it – but discovers a body of a woman in a shallow grave, not treasure in a chest. Chief Inspector Moresby and gentleman sleuth Roger Sheringham are soon on the case. What was the vicitm's identity? Why was she shot through the back of the head and why was she buried naked except for a pair of gloves?

ANTHONY BERKELEY

THE POISONED CHOCOLATES CASE

Roger Sheringham's most famous case.

In this, the best-known of Anthony Berkeley's novels, amateur detective Roger Sheringham investigates his most famous case. When Joan Bendix makes a bet with her husband for a box of chocolates, no one imagines that winning will cost her her life. The seven she eats poison her, and the two her husband eats nearly kill him. The Sheringham Crime Circle find the unusual case baffling, but eventually come up with some very interesting theories – which they then proceed to disprove one by one. Due to a series of false clues the identity – and motive – of the killer appears to be out of reach...

THE SILK STOCKING MURDERS

A Roger Sheringham case.

Gentleman sleuth and novelist Roger Sheringham would not have ordinarily been curious about the suicide of chorus girl Miss Unity Ransome. However when he receives a cry for help from a country parson attempting to trace his missing daughter Janet in London he finds himself involved. And when three other young women are found hanged dead by silk stockings, Sheringham realises that what he is investigating is actually murder.

OTHER TITLES BY ANTHONY BERKELEY AVAILABLE DIRECT FROM HOUSE OF STRATUS

Quantity		£	$(US)	$(CAN)	€
☐	DEATH IN THE HOUSE	6.99	12.95	19.95	13.50
☐	JUMPING JENNY	6.99	12.95	19.95	13.50
☐	THE LAYTON COURT MYSTERY	6.99	12.95	19.95	13.50
☐	MURDER IN THE BASEMENT	6.99	12.95	19.95	13.50
☐	NOT TO BE TAKEN	6.99	12.95	19.95	13.50
☐	PANIC PARTY	6.99	12.95	19.95	13.50
☐	THE POISONED CHOCOLATES CASE	6.99	12.95	19.95	13.50
☐	THE SECOND SHOT	6.99	12.95	19.95	13.50
☐	THE SILK STOCKING MURDERS	6.99	12.95	19.95	13.50
☐	TOP STOREY MURDER	6.99	12.95	19.95	13.50
☐	TRIAL AND ERROR	6.99	12.95	19.95	13.50

ALL HOUSE OF STRATUS BOOKS ARE AVAILABLE FROM GOOD BOOKSHOPS OR DIRECT FROM THE PUBLISHER:

Internet:	www.houseofstratus.com including synopses and features.
Email:	sales@houseofstratus.com
	info@houseofstratus.com
	(please quote author, title and credit card details.)
Tel:	Order Line
	0800 169 1780 (UK)
	800 724 1100 (USA)
	International
	+44 (0) 1845 527700 (UK)
	+01 845 463 1100 (USA)
Fax:	+44 (0) 1845 527711 (UK)
	+01 845 463 0018 (USA)
	(please quote author, title and credit card details.)
Send to:	House of Stratus Sales Department
	Thirsk Industrial Park
	York Road, Thirsk
	North Yorkshire, YO7 3BX
	UK

House of Stratus Inc.
2 Neptune Road
Poughkeepsie
NY 12601
USA

PAYMENT

Please tick currency you wish to use:

☐ £ (Sterling)   ☐ $ (US)   ☐ $ (CAN)   ☐ € (Euros)

Allow for shipping costs charged per order plus an amount per book as set out in the tables below:

CURRENCY/DESTINATION

	£(Sterling)	$(US)	$(CAN)	€(Euros)
Cost per order				
UK	1.50	2.25	3.50	2.50
Europe	3.00	4.50	6.75	5.00
North America	3.00	3.50	5.25	5.00
Rest of World	3.00	4.50	6.75	5.00
Additional cost per book				
UK	0.50	0.75	1.15	0.85
Europe	1.00	1.50	2.25	1.70
North America	1.00	1.00	1.50	1.70
Rest of World	1.50	2.25	3.50	3.00

PLEASE SEND CHEQUE OR INTERNATIONAL MONEY ORDER
payable to: HOUSE OF STRATUS LTD or HOUSE OF STRATUS INC. or card payment as indicated

STERLING EXAMPLE

Cost of book(s):...................... Example: 3 x books at £6.99 each: £20.97

Cost of order: .... Example: £1.50 (Delivery to UK address)

Additional cost per book:.............. Example: 3 x £0.50: £1.50

Order total including shipping:.......... Example: £23.97

VISA, MASTERCARD, SWITCH, AMEX:

☐ ☐ ☐ ☐ ☐ ☐ ☐ ☐ ☐ ☐ ☐ ☐ ☐ ☐ ☐ ☐ ☐ ☐ ☐ ☐

Issue number (Switch only):

☐ ☐ ☐

Start Date: **Expiry Date:**

☐☐/ ☐☐   ☐☐/ ☐☐

Signature: _____

NAME: _____

ADDRESS: _____

COUNTRY: _____

ZIP/POSTCODE: _____

Please allow 28 days for delivery. Despatch normally within 48 hours.

Prices subject to change without notice.
Please tick box if you do not wish to receive any additional information. ☐

House of Stratus publishes many other titles in this genre; please check our website (**www.houseofstratus.com**) for more details.